Dark Gambit

THE PLAY

THE CHILDREN OF THE GODS

BOOK SIXTY-SIX

I. T. LUCAS

Dark Gambit The Play is a work of fiction! Names, characters, places and incidents are products of the author's imagination or are used fictitiously and are not to be construed as real. Any similarity to actual persons, organizations and/or events is purely coincidental.

Published by Evening Star Press

EveningStarPress.com

ISBN-13: 978-1-957139-39-5

"It's never boring in the immortals' village." Turner strode into Kian's office. "Not a week goes by without some emergency popping up."

It certainly felt like it, but as Syssi kept reminding Kian, they'd had many weeks of relative calm. Besides, compared to what Turner was dealing with day in and day out, the clan lived in a utopia.

Rescuing hostages from drug cartels and militias was one of the most adrenaline-inducing occupations Kian could imagine, especially since Turner was doing that as a private operator and didn't have an army at his disposal. His teams were comprised of former Special Forces personnel, but his incredible success rate was mainly attributable to his seemingly paranormal ability to execute Mission Impossible-style operations.

"Look who's talking." He chuckled. "I wouldn't trade jobs with you no matter what you paid me. I bet you don't get a single boring moment."

"You'd be surprised." Turner put his briefcase on the conference table. "Recon is seldom exciting. It's long days of sitting and watching mundane everyday activities for the chance of catching something useful. Then there is the planning stage, which I happen to enjoy. I'm in the zone when I visualize the operation unfolding. The mockups and the staging before the action are a little more exciting, and then there is the rescue mission itself, which is high-octane action. For me, however, the most exciting part is saving lives."

He was so full of shit.

Turner loved the impossible stunts only he could pull off, and the sense of satisfaction he got from that probably equaled the gratification he derived from saving the lives of the hostages his team retrieved.

"I assume that you being here means you are not currently in the midst of what you call high-octane activity, or you wouldn't be back home at such a reasonable hour."

He also wouldn't have time for this latest emergency. Turner usually tried to make himself available whenever Kian needed him, but there had been occasions when Turner had declined, and he hadn't pressed the issue.

Kian had managed the clan's defense long before Turner had joined it, and if need be, he could make do without his help.

"You assume correctly." Turner leaned back in his chair. "So, what do you need my advice on? Does it have to do with Jade?"

"It might. I'll give you a quick recap of the latest developments in Safe Haven." Kian pulled two beers out of the mini fridge and handed one to Turner. "As you know, the first paranormal retreat started this week, and one of its attendees befriended Marcel. He's the guy who figured out that the numbers in Jade's fable represent coordinates."

"I remember. He's William's replacement at the new lab, supervising the team of bioinformaticians who are working on deciphering Okidu's journals."

"Correct." Kian uncapped his beer. "The young lady's name is Sofia, and she's a linguist from Finland. As the two got closer, something about her bothered Marcel, and he asked Roni to investigate her past more thoroughly. When Roni didn't find any red flags, Marcel continued seeing her. She asked him to help her arrange a face-to-face meeting with Emmett, which wasn't suspicious either because many of the retreat attendees worship the guy like the guru he pretends to be. When she was alone with Emmett, Sofia made up a story of an argument she'd had with her father, and she beseeched Emmett for his help. Emmett agreed to talk with her father, and when she made the call, the guy on the other end of the line turned out to be a powerful compeller and nearly got Emmett to reveal his real name. Thankfully, Eleanor was monitoring the meeting from the adjacent room, and when she realized that something was wrong, she rushed in and disconnected the call."

Turner frowned. "How did she know that something was off? Did she sense the compulsion?"

"Eleanor is immune to compulsion, so she couldn't have felt anything even if she was with them in the room. As it happened, she was watching the interaction through a computer screen, but since Emmett is her mate, she realized that he was being coerced to reveal things he would have never admitted voluntarily. The compeller's first question had Emmett admit that he was a crook who had in the past manipulated his followers into giving him all of their possessions."

"The Fates must have been looking out for us." Turner lifted the bottle to his lips and took a long sip. "That was a very close call."

Turner was the most logic-driven person Kian knew, and to hear him invoke the Fates was like hearing an atheist thanking God.

"When did you become a believer in divine intervention?"

"It was just a figure of speech." Turner pushed the beer bottle away. "I assume that the compeller who tried to coerce Emmett was Jade's captor, and if Eleanor wasn't there to stop him, he would have discovered what Emmett knew about immortals, and that would have been the worst security breach in the clan's history. That being said, if the compeller had gotten ahold of Marcel or Leon, who know much more than Emmett, it would have been an even worse disaster. Thankfully, neither of them is a head Guardian, so they couldn't have revealed the location of the village, but they still know enough to cause irreparable damage to the clan."

The possible implications had occurred to Kian, but he was also aware of his paranoid tendencies to blow things out of proportion. Hearing the same sentiment voiced by someone as dispassionate and rational as Turner sent a chill coursing through his blood.

Suddenly, the security measures that had been implemented following the compeller's phone call didn't seem enough.

"All incoming landline communications are now rerouted through the voice changer, so that risk has been mitigated. I told Marcel to thrall the team of bioinformaticians to forget what they'd been working on and send them on a mandatory vacation. I also instructed him to cut the connection between the servers there and those in the village. The Guardian security force is on high alert, and I'm sending reinforcements tonight."

"What about the linguist?" Turner asked. "Did they interrogate her?"

"I was just getting to that part." Kian grimaced. "Turns out that Sofia has been compelled to keep quiet. She couldn't say anything about the compeller or even what she was supposed to find out. Eleanor tried to override the compulsion, but she was unsuccessful. Kalugal is going to try later tonight after the girl wakes up."

Turner frowned. "Did they knock her out or drug her?"

"There was no need. Sofia is human, and she was so distraught that when Eleanor took her to the bunker and locked her in one of the bedrooms, she fell asleep from exhaustion. The girl is clearly an amateur who has been forced to do something she has no training or aptitude for."

Turner looked doubtful. "She could also be a great actress."

"That's possible, but we won't know until we can use compulsion on her ourselves."

"What about thralling? It works differently than compulsion, so Marcel or one of the other immortals can peek into her recent memories, and if need be, the Clan Mother can look into her long-term memories."

"I wouldn't get the Clan Mother involved in something like this." Kian took a swig from his beer. "It's not worth risking her. Marcel tried to get a peek into Sofia's mind before contacting Roni, and he encountered a wall. The compeller had somehow created a barrier in there."

"Interesting. I didn't know that could be done with compulsion. Did you check with Kalugal or Toven if they can do it?"

Kian shook his head. "I didn't, but I will. There is more, though. Sofia had a pendant with a transmitter hidden in it, which was how she communicated with the compeller, and it was on when things were going down in Emmett's office. Fortunately, Marcel is a former Guardian and a smart guy, and he realized the opportunity for feeding the other side misinformation. He acted as if he didn't know that the locket had a transmitter, and he pretended to think that Sofia was a journalist looking to write an unflattering story about Emmett. He kept up that charade until the pendant was locked in the safe, and Leon ran a bug detector over the girl."

Turner's pale blue eyes started glowing. "Excellent. We can use that transmitter to our advantage. First, though, you need the girl's mind unlocked, and you shouldn't wait to see if Kalugal can do it. Send in the big guns from the get-go."

"You mean Toven?"

"I was thinking of Annani, but since you are so adamant about not getting her involved, Toven will do, and he might be even better. I don't know it for a fact, but given that all the males in his family are or were compellers, I suspect that he might be a stronger compeller than the Clan Mother. Have him meet Sofia face-to-face, just not at Safe Haven, and not until she has been checked for trackers. She might have a tracker that was surgically implanted, and when it's not active, the regular bug detector won't catch it. You need to send Julian with an MRI machine or use one that's available locally. The compeller who sent Sofia might activate the tracker when he doesn't hear from her." Turner reached for his beer. "It's possible that he sent an amateur on purpose, hoping that she would get caught."

"Why would he do that?"

Turner got that distant look on his face that told Kian he was organizing his thoughts.

"He must be very confident in his compulsion hold on the girl because he's not afraid that she'll disclose anything that can lead us to him. He also assumes that since Safe Haven is a resort run by humans and hosts humans on a regular basis, it's not the headquarters of whatever he suspects is going on here. When his spy gets caught, he activates the tracker, hoping that she will lead him to us."

"I have to admit that didn't occur to me. Someone who murdered the males of an entire tribe to get the females probably has no qualms about sacrificing a human pawn."

Turner nodded. "It's a possibility, but we shouldn't discount her culpability in it just yet. We need to proceed with caution as if she is an efficient spy, and also as if she's a sacrificial pawn."

"Of course. Could she have a communication device implanted in her body as well?"

Turner shrugged. "Everything is possible, but it's not likely. Two-way communication requires more power and a larger format. In either case, the MRI will find it, and Julian will remove it. We've been in this scenario before, and Julian knows what to do. After Sofia is certified clean of bugs and trackers, Toven can meet her somewhere outside of Safe Haven." Turner leaned down and pulled his laptop out of his satchel. "I'll get on finding a safe house for them right away. We can't waste any more time."

As Sofia nibbled at the food Marcel had brought, she was indifferent to the taste and texture of what was going into her mouth. Her stomach was too tense to feel hunger, but she knew that she needed to eat to keep up her strength, and she was anxious to be done so Marcel could call his compeller friend, a guy named Kalugal.

It wasn't a name she'd ever heard before, and she wondered what nationality Kalugal was. It wasn't one she'd encountered in all the languages she'd studied. Could it be Indian? She hadn't studied Hindi. Although she wanted to, it wasn't one of the languages that Igor was interested in, and now she might never get the chance to read the *Mahabharata*, the *Ramayana*, and the *Bhagavad Gita* in the language they'd been written in.

As if that was a big concern given the trouble she was in.

She should be more worried about what was happening to her family and whether Igor had retaliated against them after her failure to deliver worthwhile information to him.

Whatever that might be.

The only thing he might find interesting was that he had a lot of competition he wasn't aware of. Who knew that humans could be compellers?

Eleanor and Emmett weren't strong enough to offer Igor a run for his money, but maybe Kalugal was?

Other pureblooded Kra-ell could compel as well, but comparing their abilities to Igor's was like comparing an ant to a rhino. Could a human like Kalugal or someone else be stronger than Igor?

Could he or she free the compound from Igor's oppressive rule?

But who was to say that the new compeller would be any better?

They could be worse. Much worse.

Igor mostly ignored the humans in his compound. As long as they did what they were told and didn't make trouble, they could live reasonably well. They had their own quarters, and no one bothered them there. Well, except for the breeding of hybrids that the young human females were subjected to.

Rape wasn't officially sanctioned, but no woman in her right mind dared to refuse an invitation to a pureblooded male's bed. The consequences of that would be dire for her and for her family.

In that, Sofia had an advantage. As Valstar's granddaughter, she'd been given more leeway, and if she'd stayed in the compound, in a few years she would have been considered too old for breeding hybrids and free to choose a human husband. But her relation to Igor's second-in-command had come with a price—a mission she'd been ill-equipped to fulfill, and she was never going back.

She would have preferred to be a nobody like her cousin Helmi. No one expected anything from her. She had a hybrid boyfriend, who was actually a nice guy, and she was short and pudgy, so she wasn't attractive to the pure-blooded Kra-ell and most of the hybrid males who preferred tall, slim females.

"What are you thinking about?" Marcel asked.

"The benefits of being a nobody." She smiled at her own clever reply. "Eleanor's method is very helpful. As long as I talk in generalities, I can actually say something that's close to what I was thinking about."

"So what are the benefits of being a nobody?"

"When no one notices you, and no one expects anything from you, you are not asked to do things that you are not comfortable with. It's safer to be a nobody."

"I actually agree with you. I don't like attracting attention to myself either. That's why I chose a career in computer engineering. Most of the time, it's a solitary occupation. And when I do have to work with others, they are just as awkward around people as I am."

"You're not awkward." He was a little, but it wasn't enough to detract from his attractiveness.

In fact, it made Marcel even more attractive to her. She didn't want a guy who was perfect in every way and made her feel inferior. The Mother knew she was as flawed as the next human.

He chuckled. "Are you being polite or trying to butter me up?"

She was doing neither. She was being honest, and he was making her angry.

"You're annoying. You should learn how to take a compliment. Happy now? I can hurl more insults at you if that tickles your fancy."

Marcel gave her the first genuine smile since the shit show had started. "That's the Sofia I know. Prickly and adorable at the same time."

"Adorable? More like despicable." She pushed her plate away. "Can you call Kalugal now? I'm anxious to talk to him."

"Yeah. I should." Marcel put both plates in one of the boxes and put the boxes on the floor. "If he agrees, I'm going to use a video chat." He pulled out his phone and motioned for her to get closer to him.

When she scooted over, he placed the call.

The phone kept ringing for a long time before the call was answered, and when it was, Sofia heard a baby crying in the background.

"Is it a bad time?" Marcel asked.

"It's fine. Give me a moment. I need to move to some-place less noisy."

The man had a cultured voice, if somewhat haughty and impatient. He sounded as if he was trying his best to be friendly, though, which was nice of him, especially given the crying baby in the background.

Was it his child?

"Do you prefer to do it voice only or video?" Marcel asked.

"Let's do video. I'd like to see the lady who's responsible for all the brouhaha."

Sofia winced. "I'm sorry."

As Marcel switched to video and held the phone to her face, she was taken aback by the breathtakingly beautiful man on the screen. With his dark coloring, he could be a hybrid Kra-ell, but he had blue eyes, so that wasn't likely.

Was he human? Or was he like Marcel?

Different.

"Hello, Sofia." He gave her a charming smile that prob-ably had women falling all over him. "My name is Kalugal, and I will try to override the other compeller's hold on your mind. Look into my eyes and focus on the sound of my voice."

"Thank you for doing this for me." She looked into his blue eyes.

"I'm happy to help if I can." He focused those intense eyes on her. "I want you to feel free to say whatever you want to anyone you want."

She nodded, hoping it would work but suspecting it wouldn't.

"Tell me the name of the compeller who did this to you."

She opened her mouth, but nothing came out, and when she tried to force the words out, she was assailed by an excruciating headache. "I can't." She rubbed her temples.

"Write your compeller's name."

Marcel pulled a pen out of his pocket and lifted one of the cardboard boxes off the floor. "You can write his name here."

She took the pen, clicked it open, and that was as far as she got. Her hand refused to write the letters comprising Igor's name.

Maybe she could write it like an anagram? Like Gori? They could figure it out.

That didn't work either. As long as she consciously knew what she was trying to communicate, the compulsion prevented her from doing it. For some reason, making up stories was easier. Perhaps because she had to concentrate on making the analogies, or maybe because they could apply to many different things and not just what she needed to say.

"Type his name," Kalugal ordered.

"It's no use. I can't."

"What if I guessed his name? Could you nod?"

"I think so. But it would be useless. There are many people who have the same name, and I won't be able to tell you anything about him."

She could probably find a book that had a protagonist named Igor, but that would be just as useless for them.

Kalugal let out a breath. "I did my best. You will need someone stronger than me. Good luck, Sofia."

Her heart sank. Igor was probably the most powerful compeller on the planet, and no one could free her mind from his compulsion.

"Thank you." She forced a smile.

When Marcel ended the call, she sighed. "What if there is no one stronger? There is a reason that he..." She couldn't say more.

"Try to tell a story," Marcel suggested.

"My head hurts too much to come up with one." She rubbed her temples. "Do you have something you can give me for the headache?"

"I'll look in the kitchen, and if there is nothing there, I'll ask Eleanor to get the medication from the nurse."

"Thank you."

Marcel

Marcel left the room without locking it. The truth was that confining Sofia inside the bedroom made little sense. To enter or leave the hidden basement dwelling under the cottage, one needed to know the code to the door at the top of the stairs, and she wasn't a mind reader.

When he found no medication in the kitchen nor in the other bathrooms, he called Eleanor.

"Did you talk to Kalugal?" she asked.

"We did, and it didn't work. The compulsion was too strong even for him, and when Sofia tried to break through it, she got a headache. Can you get some painkillers from the clinic and bring them to her?"

He was too ashamed to admit that he wasn't familiar with the name of common drugs used by humans for aches and pains.

"Of course. I'll get her Motrin. Other than the headache, how is she doing?"

So that was the name of the medication. He should memorize it for future reference. What for, though? Yesterday, he would have thought that he needed it if he were to have a relationship with Sofia, but that was a foolish thought given what he now knew about her.

"Before the call, she seemed hopeful, but when Kalugal failed to override the compulsion, her mood took a nosedive."

"That's a good sign, right? She wants to cooperate with us."

"I think so. But she might also be a good actress."

"What do you mean? Was she pretending that it wasn't working?"

"She couldn't do that. Kalugal used compulsion when he asked her the compeller's name, and she still couldn't answer him. However, she could have been pretending to be frustrated by his failure to release her mind."

"Yeah. That's possible." Eleanor didn't sound like she shared his opinion, which made him hopeful. The woman was a big-time skeptic, and her default position was mistrust. If she didn't think that Sofia was acting, then maybe she wasn't.

"Thanks for getting the medication."

"You're welcome." Eleanor ended the call.

As he headed back to the bedroom, Marcel was glad Eleanor hadn't put Sofia in the one they'd used the night before. It would have been too painful to be back there with her and look at the bed they'd shared.

It was just his rotten luck that the best night of his life had been followed by such a miserable day, but despite the lingering bitter sense of betrayal that filled his gut with acid, it still couldn't compete with the worst day of his life.

Not by a long shot.

In comparison to what he'd been through, it was just an unpleasant bump in the road.

So why did it hurt so damn bad?

Perhaps the saying that time healed all wounds was true, and that's why what should have felt no worse than a paper cut felt like he was once again being torn apart.

He was about to open the door when his phone rang, and as he pulled it out of his pocket, he expected it to be Eleanor, but it was Kian.

"Hello, boss."

"I spoke to Kalugal," Kian said. "He told me that it didn't work."

"It didn't. What do we do now?"

"I have Turner here with me, and we have a plan ready to deploy."

Frowning, Marcel turned around and walked back to the living room. "What's the plan?" He sat down on the couch.

"I'm sending Julian over with an MRI machine and a team of Guardians. After they collect the MRI from the old clinic, they will head straight to the airstrip. They should land in Eugene Airport in three and a half hours. From there it will take them another hour and a half to get to Safe Haven. Julian is going to run Sofia through the machine to make sure that she doesn't have location trackers implanted in her body. If she does, he will remove them. Once she's clean, the Guardians will take her to a safe location to meet Toven. Hopefully, he will be able to unlock her mind."

Marcel tensed. Kian was going all out on the case, and he was deploying the big guns, which meant that Turner foresaw even more troubling outcomes.

"If Toven can't do that, we are in deep trouble, aren't we?"

"We are taking precautions to minimize the risk. I'm just glad that the compeller chose Emmett as his target and not you or Leon, and that Eleanor stopped him in time. The Fates were looking out for us."

The Fates, or Sofia?

It would have been much easier for her to convince the guy she'd just seduced and who she must have realized was falling for her to call the compeller than to have Emmett do that. She knew that Marcel was working on a secret project, and if she'd asked him to call her father, he would have done it for her without giving it a second thought.

Had she been protecting him by diverting the compeller's attention to Emmett? Or had it been the compeller's choice to speak with the head of Safe Haven?

Hopefully, Toven would be able to get all those answers from her.

"Can I go with Sofia to see Toven?" Marcel asked.

"Of course. Make sure that she rests and is ready when Julian arrives with the machine. I don't want to waste any time."

"I will. Why the urgency, though?"

"The sooner we get Sofia free of the compulsion, the sooner we can utilize your idea of feeding her boss misinformation. The last thing we need is for the compeller to send a rescue team to retrieve her. Not that I think he would. Turner suspects that she was set up to be found out, and that she has a tracker embedded in her body so she could lead him to our main base of operations."

A chill ran down Marcel's spine.

So that was what Turner had deduced, and he might be right. It was such a cold and heartless move, but then what else should he expect from a man who slaughtered his own people to get his hands on a few females?

"That kind of move puts even Navuh to shame."

Kian chuckled. "Don't underestimate Navuh. He has no problem sacrificing his warriors if he can gain anything by doing so, and he has no qualms whatsoever about sacrificing the human residents of his island. He and Jade's captor would get along splendidly. Anyway, once Sofia's mind is under our control, we will do our best to make the compeller think that things are back to normal and that she got only a slap on the wrist for her part in the attempted journalistic sting operation. It will buy us time."

"Time to do what?"

"We need to clear Safe Haven of anything that can point to us. It's unfortunate given the enormous investment we've committed to the place, but the location is compromised. Even if the compeller never comes or sends anyone else to investigate, I will not feel safe having our people there."

Unless they found him and eliminated him, but that wasn't likely.

Kian wouldn't want to open an all-out war with the Kra-ell and make them aware of immortals' existence. That being said, though, it might be wise to eliminate a future threat to the clan.

Provided that it was doable.

They needed to find out the kind of force the compeller commanded, which was probably why Turner wanted it done as soon as possible.

"What about Eleanor and Emmett and the paranormal program?"

"Regrettably, Emmett will have to step down and transfer leadership to someone else. The paranormal program will have to be moved as well."

What a major headache. "It almost sounds as if eliminating the compeller would be less of a hassle."

Kian huffed. "Sure. We can eliminate him and his followers, free Jade and the other females, and everyone will live happily ever after. That's not a realistic objective, but Turner says that we will re-evaluate the pros and cons after we learn more about the threat we are dealing with."

"Meaning getting Sofia to tell us all she knows."

"Correct."

Kian

Kian ended the call and put the phone down. "I'd better go talk to Toven before the Guardians load the MRI on the truck. We are basing this entire operation on the assumption that he will agree to go on a moment's notice."

Turner shifted his gaze away from his laptop screen. "Do you think he might refuse?"

"I don't think that he will say no, but he might need more time. He's not as much of a prima donna as my mother, but he is still a god, and he needs to be handled with caution and the proper respect." Kian got to his feet. "That's why I'm going to ask him in person."

Turner frowned. "You can't just show up on his doorstep either. You should call ahead. As you've pointed out, he's not your mother."

"Right." Kian raked his fingers through his hair. "He might not even be home. I'll call to say that I'm stopping by." He pushed to his feet. "I'm no good at this diplomatic crap. I would have asked my mother to call him for me, but then she'd be upset that I'm not taking her to talk to Sofia."

Palming his phone, Kian headed toward the door but stopped with his hand on the handle. "Do you need help in here? I can ask Shai to come in. He could take care of some of the arrangements."

"I don't need help." Turner continued typing on his laptop. "I've mobilized my team to make the arrangements for the safe house on the Oregon Coast, and Bridget is taking care of arranging the MRI transport. We are lucky that she had already been planning to send the rest of the medical equipment from the clinic at the keep to the one in Safe Haven and she had ordered the special case to transport the MRI. The thing needs to be steel lined to prevent its magnetic pull from affecting anything in proximity. The crate alone cost ten grand."

Kian released a whistle. "It's a damn shame that's money down the drain."

"It doesn't have to be, but that's a discussion for when we are not pressed for time. You should go talk to Toven."

"Right."

As he walked out the door, Kian placed the call.

The phone rang for quite a while before the god answered. "Good afternoon. I hope you're calling to tell me that the parts for the Perfect Match machines have finally arrived."

"I wish, but no. Nothing's changed in regard to that. I'm calling because I need to discuss an urgent matter with you. Is it okay if I come over?"

"Of course."

"I'm on my way. I'll be there in five minutes."

"Can you fill me in while you walk?"

He could give Toven the rundown and keep the asking for when he got there. "We have a situation at Safe Haven."

By the time Kian had finished telling Toven the high points, he was at the god's front door.

"Come in." Toven motioned for him to follow.

"Hello, Kian," Mia said. "I hope you don't mind me eavesdropping on your conversation with Toven." She wheeled herself to the dining table.

"Not at all."

He'd expected that and hadn't thought it was a problem. Toven would have told Mia everything anyway.

"Can I get you something to drink?" Toven asked.

"Thank you, but I've already downed a bottle of Snake's Venom, and I still have a long night ahead of me."

"I guess that you want me to override the compulsion." Toven motioned for him to take a seat and pulled out a chair for himself.

Kian nodded. "Kalugal tried to do it via a video call, and it didn't work. You can attempt to do the same, but Turner thinks that you need to be face-to-face with Sofia to be able to do it. Since the guy is holding Jade captive, and Emmett claims that she's a very strong compeller in her own right, we must assume that her captor is incredibly powerful."

"Are you flying her over here?" Mia asked.

"I don't want to risk it. I'm flying Julian there with a full-scale MRI machine to check her for implanted trackers. He'll do that at Safe Haven, and if she has any, he'll remove them. After that, he and a couple of Guardians will drive her to a safe house that Turner is arranging. And that's why I'm here. I came to ask you to fly out there with the team and meet her at the safe house."

"When?" Toven asked.

"Tonight. Julian and the Guardians are packing up the MRI as we speak, and once they have it loaded on the truck, they are heading to the airstrip. If you can be ready to leave in an hour or so, you can join them there and fly with them. If you need more time, I can fly you out there separately on the small jet."

Instead of answering him, Toven turned to Mia. "How quickly can you get ready?"

"If you help me pack, I can be ready in ten minutes."

That was a development that Kian hadn't expected. He could understand Toven not wanting to be separated from his mate, but her safety should come first. Toven was proposing to take her with him to a situation that might be a little dangerous.

Seeing his puzzled expression, Toven smiled and took Mia's hand. "You should never play poker, Kian. Your face is too expressive."

"Well, in that case, I was wondering why you want to take Mia with you. You're only going to be gone for one night, and although I'm doing everything I can to mitigate any risks, this trip is not entirely risk-free."

Smiling, Toven lifted Mia's hand to his lips and brushed them over her knuckles. "I'm a god, and as long as I'm awake, no one can get to Mia with me shielding her. I can freeze the minds of any would-be attackers. Still, I wouldn't have inconvenienced my mate with an overnight rush trip if I didn't think that I would need her help. Mia is an enhancer, and I might need the boosting of power she can provide me with."

Kian doubted that Toven needed the boost, and given the grin on Mia's face, he'd said that to make her happy.

So far, no one had asked Mia to boost their power for anything other than testing, and she was probably anxious to try her enhancing powers in a real-life situation.

"It's up to you both." He looked at Mia. "You might have to pull an all-nighter. Are you up to it?"

She squared her shoulders. "I'm an immortal now, and I can survive just fine with four hours of sleep. I'll nap on the way."

"Then welcome aboard." Kian rose to his feet and offered her his hand. "Thank you."

She beamed up at him. "Thank you for welcoming me to the team. I'm so happy to finally be able to utilize my gift for something useful."

Nodding, he let go of her hand and offered it to Toven. "Thank you. You're doing a great service to the clan."

"That remains to be seen." Toven shook his hand. "If I fail to remove the compulsion, you'll have to ask Annani to give it a try."

Had he said that to inquire whether Kian had asked Annani already? Or was it his way of politely expressing his displeasure about being asked to do something that Annani was capable of, but Kian wasn't willing to risk her?

"I doubt that will be needed. Turner thinks that you are a stronger compeller than my mother. I don't know if that's true, but in any case, I view you as a warrior while I can't see my mother in that role."

That should be enough to stroke the god's ego.

"I'm not a warrior. I'm an explorer, or was one a long time ago, and now I'm a creator of stories that lift people's spirits. I don't know whether I'm a stronger compeller than Annani, but it is true that I have more experience. If I fail, though, you might have to employ your mother's help, and you should be prepared to do that. Annani can do everything I can. We are both powerful gods, and in some ways she's more powerful than I am. Do you really think that the only way to keep Annani safe is by hiding her inside your village?"

Kian shrugged. "I do the best I can, and so far, I've managed to keep her out of trouble. I hope to keep it that way. Annani is extremely powerful, but she thinks with her heart, she is impulsive, and she's not as diligent with her safety as I would like her to be."

Toven smiled indulgently. "She's humoring you. You have no idea what she does when she's not here."

Kian winced. "Tell me something that I don't know."

As the door closed behind Kian, Mia let out a breath. "Are you sure that you want me to come with you?"

"I might need you." Toven sat back down and leaned toward her. "Besides, you were complaining about being bored. It's an opportunity for a little adventure. Something exciting."

She smiled. "When did I complain about being bored?"

The truth was that Mia hadn't complained about anything, but she'd seemed restless lately, and Toven assumed that the cause was boredom.

"So, you're not?" He took her hands in his.

"How can I be bored when I'm living with a god? If I seem restless, it's because I want Margo and Frankie to move into the village already, and those damn parts are still missing, so William's team can't finish building the Perfect Match machines, and until they get that done,

Margo and Frankie can't be the testers for new adventures."

"You are the one who insisted on waiting until they are ready so your friends will have jobs. For all I care, they can move into the village tomorrow, and if you are worried about them being bored with nothing to do, the café can always use more hands."

"I know, but I don't want them to start as waitresses. Their current jobs might not be a huge step up from that, but I want them to begin their lives in the village on the right foot. Besides, my grandmother has a long list of eligible bachelors she plans on inviting to her house to meet the girls on the weekends when we are back in Arcadia. They might find their one and only even before they get here."

Provided that they were indeed Dormants.

Neither girl had a paranormal talent, and the only indicators that they might be Dormants was the affinity he and the immortals who'd met them reported feeling and Lisa's hunch, which was just as unproven and subjective as Margo and Frankie's likability.

Mia pulled her hands out of his. "We'd better start packing if we want to be out of here in time to catch the plane." She put her chair in reverse. "We can keep talking while we pack, and you can tell me the real reason for wanting me to come with you. I know that it can't be my enhancing powers because I've never attempted to enhance your compulsion ability before."

He followed her to the bedroom. "There was no need, so we couldn't test it. This is a golden opportunity to do so. But I'm also thinking about Sofia. The girl is probably terrified, and being surrounded by a bunch of imposing males is going to make her even more so. Your presence will ease her mind and make her more receptive to my compulsion."

She cast him a sly smile. "You're good, and I appreciate you trying to make me feel needed, but I doubt Sofia will have a problem being surrounded by a bunch of hunky Guardians. No one needs me there."

Toven put a hand over his chest. "First of all, I always need you with me. And secondly, I meant every word. I want to test your enhancing ability on my compulsion, and I'm sure that Sofia will appreciate you being there. If she comes from a Kra-ell compound, she's used to females being in charge. She'll assume that you are running the show and will be relieved that our leader is such a sweet-natured female."

"Right." She cast him a doubtful look. "From what I overheard, Sofia is fully human, and she might have been picked at random from the university and compelled to do their bidding. She might not know a thing about the Kra-ell."

The possibility that the girl didn't know who'd sent her hadn't occurred to him, but it was possible.

"In either case, she will love having another female there."

"I'm just thinking about the logistics." Mia opened one of her drawers and started pulling out sets of sexy underwear. "I'm in a wheelchair, and if Turner's rented a house with stairs, you would have to carry me and the chair up. It's a drag."

"Not for me." He took a pair of lacy panties from her hand. "As long as I get to see you in these, I don't care if I need to carry a car up the stairs."

She laughed. "I can actually imagine you doing that. Should I take my motorized chair or the one that folds for travel?'"

"Whatever makes you more comfortable, love. You know that I have no problem lifting this chair with you in it."

Mia loved when he flaunted his physical strength and was turned on by it, but this time, she hadn't reacted as he'd hoped.

"I don't want to be a burden." She opened another drawer and pulled out two long skirts and two T-shirts. "Do you think that's enough? Or do I need to take more clothes?"

"We are only going to spend one night there and fly back tomorrow. I'm taking just one change of clothes and no pajamas." He wagged his brows.

Mia laughed. "You never wear pajamas. I thought that you left your only pair in Switzerland."

He'd had to wear pajamas when staying with Mia's grandparents in the rented apartment in Zurich while she'd been undergoing treatments for her heart condition, but he'd left them there because there had been no room left in his carry-on. He'd never bothered to replace them with a new pair.

"That's why I'm not taking any."

Kian hated asking anyone for favors, whether it was Kalugal or Toven, but at least with Kalugal he had an official treaty, and his cousin owed him a favor or two. Besides, under his bluster the guy was a decent fellow, and he also loved to flaunt his compulsion ability.

Toven was a different story.

Kian didn't know the god well, and just the fact that Toven was a god was enough to make him less approachable. Not only that, but Toven had also already paid his dues by helping Eric pull through his transition and by promising to help the rest of Kaia's family.

Never mind that Darlene was Toven's granddaughter, and if she knew that Toven's assistance was more than spiritual, she would have expected him to help her mate survive. But she didn't know, and therefore couldn't ask for it.

Kian had to do that.

Perhaps the thing that bothered him most, though, was not knowing what the god's limit was. Had he already depleted his quota of good will?

Toven was an incredible asset, and Kian hated wasting his favors for things that were perhaps not critical. Turner had convinced him that getting the information out of Sofia qualified as such, but he wasn't sure that it did.

With the god's compulsion power, the clan could possibly take on Navuh and his island, Jade's captor and his compound, or both. It depended on whether Toven was more powerful than Navuh and the Kra-ell leader, and whether he could wrestle control over their people from the two despots.

Turner was right that they couldn't move against the Kra-ell without getting more information on their leader. Come to think of it, the guy might not even be a pure-blood. Navuh was just an immortal, the son of a god and a human, but he was a more powerful compeller than most of the gods of old. The same might be true of Jade's captor.

Not that it made any difference to Kian. The hybrid Kra-ell were formidable enough.

The clan's small Guardian force didn't stand a chance against the Kra-ell unless there were only a handful of them, which was unlikely, given that they had slaughtered Jade's tribesmen and then kidnapped her and the other females.

The other option for the clan possibly coming out victorious in a face-to-face confrontation with the Kra-ell was that the Kra-ell relied on their brute strength and didn't own modern weaponry. That would give the Guardians the edge they needed.

The best option, the one that would result in the least casualties, was Toven taking over their minds in one fell swoop.

Was it fair to ask him to go to battle for the clan, though?

Annani was just as powerful if not more so, and yet Kian would never even consider risking her like that.

Kri accused Kian of being a chauvinist, and maybe she was right. Despite her training, and despite her being a damn good Guardian, he still couldn't bring himself to risk her in a battle with the Doomers or with the Kra-ell because she was a female.

Annani was a force to be reckoned with, and she could be a great asset in battle, but all he could think of was how small she was, how delicate, and how soft-hearted.

He was well aware that aside from the soft heart all the rest was an illusion, and that there was nothing fragile about his mother, but she was the clan's heart, and if anything happened to her, it would be the end of them.

Toven was cold, and he looked the part of a warrior.

Kian had no problem seeing him going into battle with his mind or with his bare hands.

When he got back to his office, he found that Bridget and Onegus had joined Turner.

"How did it go?" Bridget asked.

"Toven is coming, and he's bringing Mia along. His excuse is that he might need her enhancing powers, but I think he just wants her to feel as if she's contributing to the war effort."

Bridget lifted a brow. "Are we at war?"

"Not yet, but we might be." Kian pulled out a chair at the conference table. "Toven and Mia will head out to the airstrip as soon as they are done packing. What's the progress with the MRI machine?"

Bridget grimaced. "The guys thought that they were strong enough to lift it and carry it out, but they realized that they overestimated their muscle power. Turner arranged to have a power lift delivered, and it's going to delay them by forty-five minutes."

Kian shook his head. "Julian can just take Sofia to a human hospital, thrall the staff, do what he needs with her, and be done with it. Why bother with transferring that enormous machine?" He pinned her with a hard look. "Why didn't you tell me that the shipping crate would cost ten grand? I might have scrapped the whole idea."

She snorted. "Do you know how much a new MRI machine costs? We've already decided that we are transferring all the equipment from the keep to Safe Haven and getting new equipment for the keep, sans the MRI machine. We don't need two of them, and the model we have in the village is newer than the one in the keep."

"I know, but that was before we decided to evacuate Safe Haven. If we are not using the facility, why do we need a fully equipped clinic there?"

"You might be able to lease the place for more," Turner said. "We could turn the paranormal area into a medical facility of some sort. A recovery area after plastic surgery or something of that nature."

"It's premature to talk about evacuation," Onegus said. "Let's first hear what Sofia has to say, and what we are dealing with. Maybe the Kra-ell are not a threat after all."

"I wish." Kian crossed his arms over his chest.

Bridget put a hand on his shoulder. "In the same way that we don't want to poke the hornets' nest, they might want to avoid us as well. Maybe we can just coexist with them."

"Given what they did to their own people, I don't think so. We might be able to keep hiding and avoid discovery by them, but I'm afraid that ship has sailed."

"Not if we erase all traces of our existence from Safe Haven," Turner said. "And if we decide to leave Jade in captivity."

It was tempting, but Kian's gut was not comfortable with that plan, and experience had taught him to trust his intuition.

Sofia lay awake in bed, waiting for the headache medicine to start working.

Marcel had told her to get some sleep because a doctor was coming later tonight to check her for implanted trackers, but how was she supposed to fall asleep after he'd told her that?

Was it possible that Igor had done that without her knowledge?

What if he'd compelled her to forget it?

Was it even possible to make someone forget things with compulsion?

Compulsion was like hypnosis on steroids, and if hypnotists could make people forget things, it made sense that Igor could have had a chip implanted in her body and then compelled her to forget it.

What else had been done to her that she couldn't remember?

The problem was that the more she tried to remember the worse the pounding in her head became, and she couldn't think at all past the pain. Perhaps she should turn her thoughts to something else, like how she was going to get out of this mess.

Marcel had left her alone in the bedroom without locking the door, but he was in the living room, so if she tried to leave, he would stop her.

Besides, where would she go?

Safe Haven was isolated, with nothing for miles around, so unless she managed to steal a car, which she had no clue how to do, she wasn't going anywhere on foot.

Why the hell had Igor and Valstar sent her on a spying mission without giving her any training? They could have at least taught her how to steal cars. Were they going to send people to retrieve her or just leave her there?

Would Valstar even care that she wasn't coming back?

Would her mother?

Not likely.

The only ones who would miss her were her father, her aunts, her cousins, and her friends.

As tears leaked out of her eyes, Sofia swiped at them angrily.

How often had she dreamt about escaping the compound and life under Igor's thumb? But now that she was free, she was crying over the people she loved and was never going to see again.

She just hadn't expected for it to ever happen. Besides, she wasn't free. What were Marcel and his people going to do with her?

Her fantasies about having a life with Marcel had certainly gone down the drain. He hadn't been cruel to her and he didn't even look angry. He just seemed indifferent, treating her with remote politeness as if she was a stranger, a ward to take care of until he could hand her off to someone else.

She was so freaking alone.

As the tears started flowing again, Sofia had no more strength left to fight them. Grabbing a pillow, she covered her face to muffle the pitiful sobs and just let it all out. When she heard the door open, she turned on her side with the pillow still firmly pressed against her face, and when the mattress sank on that side, she turned to the other.

"Sofia." Marcel put a hand on her shoulder. "Is your headache that bad?"

She could've lied and said yes, but the truth was that sometime during her self-pity fest, the Motrin had kicked in and the headache had abated.

"I'm fine," she mumbled under the pillow. "Please, go away."

"You are obviously not fine." He caressed her back. "Are you scared?"

"Should I be?"

"If the doctor finds a tracker, he will surgically remove it, but he will anesthetize the area first, and you won't feel a thing."

Was that what he thought? That she was crying because she was scared of a little physical pain?

"I'm not afraid of the doctor."

"So what are you afraid of?"

Tossing the pillow aside, she turned to face him. "What are your people going to do with me? Are you ever going to let me go?"

His expression was pained as he shook his head. "You will not be physically harmed. I can promise you that. Beyond that, I don't know. I'm not in charge."

"Give it your best guess."

"I don't think you are ever going back."

"That's what I thought." She grabbed the pillow and covered her face with it.

"Why would you want to go back? If the male who sent you is who we think he is, he's a ruthless murderer."

How could they possibly know anything about Igor?

Had Jade managed to overcome his compulsion and tell someone about him? What did she expect to gain by that?

These people weren't Kra-ell, and they couldn't help her. They were probably more dangerous to her than Igor.

Maybe Marcel was just shooting in the dark.

Lifting the pillow off her face, Sofia wiped her tear-stained cheeks with the blanket. "I have a life back in Finland. I want to go back to the university and resume my studies. I have family and friends whom I miss."

Marcel arched a brow. "Are they in Finland? Or are they a little farther to the east?"

He knew about the compound, and the only way he could was if Jade had told them about it.

"I can't say."

She wouldn't even if she could. She didn't know these people and what they wanted with Igor. They could have him, but they couldn't have all the innocent people living under his rule.

"Try to get some sleep." He patted her shoulder and got up. "I'll wake you up when it's time."

Marcel

Once Sofia had finally fallen asleep, Marcel left the bunker and headed to the clinic.

Her tears had sliced at his heart, and yet he couldn't bring himself to comfort her above promising her that she wouldn't be physically harmed.

Even though he believed that she'd been forced into the situation, he couldn't overcome the disappointment he felt and be there for her.

When he got to the new clinic in the clan's enclave, the Guardians were muscling a huge crate through the doorway. The door had been removed and was propped against the wall, but the opening was so tight that the crate scraped the jambs on both sides.

Marcel had never seen an MRI machine before, and he had never had a reason to go over its specs either, so he'd assumed that it was a reasonably sized medical device, but given the Guardians' sweaty foreheads and their grunts, the thing was not only large but also heavy. It was on a wheeled platform, and yet the men were working hard to push it through the doorway.

Standing next to the orphaned door, Julian observed the operation with a frown.

Marcel stopped next to him. "I didn't know the device was so large."

"It's a monster. My mother must have forgotten how heavy this thing was when she decided to move it here."

"How heavy is it?"

"About six thousand pounds."

"What's in it, lead?"

"Close. It's a magnet. Magnetic resonance imaging uses the body's magnetic properties to produce images. I won't bore you with the details of how it works. If you are interested, you can look it up."

"I might do that. Can it harm Sofia?"

Julian shook his head. "An MRI doesn't use radiation, so it's much safer than X-rays. It won't harm her in any way. Some studies have reported an increase in DNA damage due to cardiac MRI scans, but I wouldn't worry too much about it. These devices are routinely used as a diagnostic tool in hospitals and are considered very safe."

"I'm surprised that Bridget sent the big machine here after Kian decided to close operations in Safe Haven."

Julian shrugged. "I wasn't told anything about plans to shut the place down. Is it because of your spy?"

"She's not my spy or my anything." The lie tasted sour on his tongue. He cared about Sofia whether he was willing to admit it or not. "And not because of her. If you want to blame anyone, blame Jade. This whole mess started because of her."

Julian lifted his hands. "I'm not blaming anyone. I'm just stating cause and effect. She came, and we need to leave."

"I'm not sure that's a certain outcome. We need to interrogate her first and find out what force we are dealing with."

As the doctor nodded, the Guardians managed to push the crate through by dislodging the doorjambs.

"It will take me about half an hour to set it up, and then I'm ready for your girl. Is she asleep?"

"She's cried herself to sleep." Marcel sighed. "It's not her fault, you know. She was compelled to do this." He lifted his eyes to Julian's. "Am I a fool to feel sorry for her?"

"You're not." Julian clapped him on the back. "I would be too if she was my potential mate."

Marcel's back stiffened. "She's not my mate. She's human."

"A human with a paranormal ability. I'm sure the thought that she's a Dormant has crossed your mind."

It had, but he hadn't allowed himself to hope, and in retrospect, it had been a wise decision. An even wiser decision would have been to stay away from her when he'd encountered the block in her mind.

"It would be too much of a coincidence for the human spy sent by a Kra-ell leader to be a descendant of the gods."

Julian smiled. "On the contrary. First of all, that's the Fates' mode of operation. They like to orchestrate those seemingly random encounters. And secondly, there are Mey and Jin, who have Kra-ell genetics. We postulate that the Kra-ell and the gods came from the same stock, so we might feel toward the Kra-ell the same affinity we feel for Dormants and other immortals."

"Sofia is not a hybrid. She's fully human."

"Right." Julian frowned. "Still, she might be the daughter of a hybrid. Maybe Jade's captor doesn't prohibit his hybrid males from impregnating humans like she did. Although, from what we know about the Kra-ell, their second generation cannot be activated. Emmett bit Margaret while having sex with her, but he failed to induce her transition."

"Maybe the Kra-ell and the gods are not compatible that way. Perhaps if he'd bitten a Kra-ell Dormant, he would have induced her transition."

Julian pursed his lips. "There is also another option, the one that Emmett kidnapped Peter for. Maybe only immortal males' venom has what it takes to induce transition, and we can do that for our Dormants and for theirs."

Marcel snorted. "I hope that's not the case, and if it is, that Jade's captor never finds out about it."

"Are you sure? What if you could induce Sofia? Wouldn't you want that?"

Marcel swallowed. "I don't know how I feel about her right now."

"I think you do." Julian regarded him with a smirk lifting one side of his mouth. "I'll text you when the machine is ready."

"Time to wake up." Marcel's warm hand rested on Sofia's shoulder. "The doctor is waiting for you."

It felt as if she'd fallen asleep only minutes ago, drifting off into blissful oblivion, and she didn't enjoy the glum reality rushing into her mind.

"I'm awake." She pushed the blanket off. Except for shoes, she was still fully dressed, but she urgently needed to visit the bathroom. "Give me a couple of moments to freshen up."

"No problem." He took a step back. "I'll wait for you in the living room."

After taking care of her bladder, Sofia stood in front of the vanity mirror and winced at what was reflected in it. It wasn't just the messy hair, the red-rimmed eyes, and the dark circles under them. It was the other image that was superimposed over her face, an ugly evildoer with twisted features.

She knew that it was just her imagination and not some strange paranormal talent. That had been a lie, her ticket to get into the retreat. She wasn't a bad person. She'd just been used to do a bad thing, and it made her feel bad about herself.

The worst part was hurting Marcel's feelings.

He'd admitted to having trust issues, especially with women, and she'd proven him right.

Splashing cold water on her face helped with the eyes, and brushing a comb through her hair helped tame it into a presentable updo, but there was nothing she could do about the second image other than get rid of the guilt.

Not as easy as it sounded.

When she was ready, Sofia walked into the living room. "Do I need to bring anything with me? A change of clothes, maybe?"

Marcel shook his head. "If Julian finds a tracker and needs to operate, you might need a nightdress, but I can come back here and get it for you."

That was an odd answer. Unless the implant was in her brain, its removal wouldn't require an overnight stay in the hospital. What the heck were they planning to do to her?

She'd expected him to take her to the nurse's office in the lodge, but when they'd passed through the lodge without stopping at the nurse's office, she frowned. "Where are you taking me?"

"The new clinic in the secluded part of Safe Haven."

She tensed. "Do you mean the one the government is using for its secret projects?"

"Yes and no. It's in that general area."

"Tell me the truth, Marcel. Are they going to do anything to me other than remove the tracker?"

"To find the device, the doctor needs to scan your body using an MRI machine. That's why we need to use the other clinic."

"Do you swear that's all the doctor will do to me?"

"I swear it."

It was so dark that she couldn't see his expression, but he'd sounded sincere, and her anxiety level subsided.

As they kept walking, passing through three different gates that Marcel opened with his phone, she wondered how he could see where they were going. There were no lights, and the moon was shadowed by clouds. She could barely see one step in front of her and had to hold on to his arm.

Wondering whether his eyes were glowing, she cast him a sidelong glance, but since she couldn't see them, the answer was that they weren't.

"Why is it so dark here? Couldn't they put up at least one streetlamp?"

Marcel chuckled. "I'll mention it to the boss when I talk to him again."

Who was the mysterious boss he kept bringing up? Was he the equivalent of Igor? Maybe he was also a powerful compeller, and that was why Igor was interested in the place. What if he was another Kra-ell?

"That's the clinic," Marcel said.

He led her up to a door she couldn't see, and when he pulled it open, the light spilling from the inside blinded her until her pupils adjusted to the brightness.

Taking her by the elbow, he led her into a room with a big scanner.

"This is our doctor, Julian," he introduced a guy who wasn't wearing a white coat and didn't look like any doctor she'd ever seen.

He was gorgeous, with shoulder-length light brown hair, blue eyes, and full lips that were curved in a friendly smile.

"Hello, Sofia." He offered her his hand. "I'm Doctor Julian, but everyone calls me Julian."

"Hi." She shook his hand. "Nice to meet you." She glanced at the padded bench that was partially inside a bagel-shaped device. "Do I need to take off my shoes before lying down on that?"

"Yes, please. We want to keep things as clean as possible. Also, if you have any jewelry on you or anything made of metal, you should take it off. The MRI is a powerful magnet."

She had leggings and a T-shirt on, so that wasn't a problem, and her pushup bra was the kind that didn't use wires and had memory foam padding instead. Her pendant was still locked in the safe, so the only things remaining were her hairpins.

"Are these a problem?" She took one of them out and handed it to Julian.

His eyes widened. "Were they checked?"

Marcel nodded. "Leon ran a scanner on her."

"I bought them in a supermarket in Helsinki." Sofia took the rest out. "There is nothing special about them."

Naturally, they had no reason to believe her, and when all the pins were out, Julian handed them to Marcel. "Give them to Leon. He's out in the front room."

"I will. How long is it going to take?"

"About half an hour. I need to scan Sofia's entire body."

"Can I be here while you do that?"

The young doctor shook his head. "It's not mandatory for you to leave, but it's preferable. It's very difficult to lie perfectly still inside the device while it's doing its thing, and the less distraction Sofia has to filter out, the better."

"Then I shall wait out in the hallway." Looking reluctant to leave her side, Marcel cast her an encouraging glance and a smile before heading out the door.

"Okay, young lady." Julian offered her his hand again. "Hop on the bench."

She used his hand as a lever to hoist herself up, and when she was sprawled on the platform, Julian arranged her arms and legs the way he wanted them.

"You're not claustrophobic, right?"

"Not as far as I know."

"Good. If you were, I would have to give you sedatives. Try to relax and think of your happy place. If you can doze off, it would be even better."

"I'll try." Sofia closed her eyes and imagined her room in the university's dorms, and when that didn't do the trick, she imagined her room back in the compound with her cousin sitting on her bed and telling her about everything that had happened while she was gone. That brought a smile to her lips, and she tried to keep thinking happy thoughts as the machine started buzzing and the platform started moving.

Marcel

"These are just plain hairpins." Leon handed them back to Marcel after crushing a couple to make sure they were not hiding anything inside their tiny plastic bubbles. "But I want you to take a look at that locket of hers. Can you tell where it was made without taking it apart?"

Marcel smiled. "I'm way ahead of you on that. The thing was so cheaply made that I figured it wasn't a high-end piece of equipment. I've looked it up, and it turns out that you can order them on the internet. Like everything else, they are made in China."

"Bummer." Eleanor leaned against the desk and crossed her arms over her chest. "I was hoping it was a piece of alien technology and that we could learn something from it."

"We did learn something from it." Marcel put the pins in his pocket. "That particular group of Kra-ell doesn't have advanced technology and they use commercially available things. We have a clear advantage over them in that."

Leon looked doubtful. "Jade had access to advanced technology. She launched a telecommunications company with what she knew."

Eleanor huffed out a breath. "She must have had an engineer and a scientist in her group, and that's how she had access to advanced technology. Her captor's group was probably comprised of meatheads, the types who don't know how to build anything and only know how to take it from others. They must have emptied her tribe's bank accounts. Emmett says that the tribe was wealthy thanks to its many enterprises, but when Vrog came back from Singapore and found the compound burned to the ground, all he found was the cash that Jade had kept in the safes. The money in the banks was gone. The compeller must have forced her to surrender that money to him."

Leon still looked doubtful. "The Chinese government could have confiscated the funds. Having money in the bank in China is a risky proposition."

"Maybe it wasn't in a Chinese bank," Eleanor countered. "Jade was a smart lady." She shook her head. "Correction. She is a smart lady."

The discussion about Jade and the possible fate of her money turned into a discussion about international banking, which Eleanor knew a lot about, and then moved to the subject of precious metals and where best to store them.

Marcel wasn't overly interested in the topic, but it provided a good distraction while they waited.

An hour or so later, when the door finally opened and Julian stepped out, the grim expression on the doctor's face told Marcel all he needed to know.

"I found a tracker on her," Julian said. "It's so small that I missed it the first time around, but I had a hunch and repeated the scan. It's in her thigh, and it's the size of a grain of rice."

Eleanor cast Marcel a mocking glance. "Can that be ordered on the internet as well?"

"No."

"I didn't think so." She turned to Julian. "Did you take it out?"

"Not yet. She wants Marcel to be with her when I do."

Why the hell did that make his heart swell?

"Are you going to use a local anesthetic?" he asked the doctor.

"Of course. Thankfully, it's close to the surface, so the incision will be minimal."

Eleanor snorted. "I had a plastic surgeon take out the tracker in my arm without an anesthetic, and I only took Motrin for the pain."

Leon arched a brow. "Why did you have a tracker?"

"Everyone working for Simmons had one. Heck, I think that everyone in that damn underground city was implanted with trackers. The only difference was that I knew I had it. The others didn't." She rubbed her arm. "Lucky for me, I turned immortal, so there is no sign of it left. Sofia is not that lucky."

Maybe she was.

Julian's words from before still reverberated through Marcel's cerebrum. What if Sofia was a second-generation hybrid that was fully human? What if he could activate her?

It didn't seem likely, but on the other hand, the Fates were known to weave a complicated tapestry and steer events toward the outcome they were after.

What if this entire brouhaha was about him and Sofia meeting and falling in love?

Marcel stifled a bitter chuckle.

If that was so, the Fates had a twisted sense of humor. They made Sofia both attractive and repulsive to him at the same time. She'd manipulated him, used him, and he'd sworn never to fall victim to those exact two things ever again.

Couldn't they have given her a different character flaw?

Except, unlike the one who had scared him off love for centuries, Sophia hadn't acted in self-interest. She'd been coerced, and she was probably protecting loved ones as well.

Leon got to his feet and walked up to Julian. "Are you sure that's the only tracker on the girl? What if there are more? A tracker the size of a grain of rice can be easily missed."

"I'm sure. After I found it, I double-checked, but I'll look at the slides again if you want."

"Please do. Toven did us a great favor by coming out here to release Sofia's mind, and my job is to make sure that no harm comes to him. We don't want to lead the compeller straight to him."

As Sofia rubbed over the spot where Julian had found the tracker, the feeling of violation was even worse than what she'd routinely experienced in Igor's office. At least there she'd been aware of what was being done to her, and even though she would have never agreed to it voluntarily, she kind of understood the need for the compulsion, and if that was the price she had to pay to be allowed out of the compound, she was willing to pay it.

Igor was protecting his people, and he had to make sure that she couldn't reveal the Kra-ell's existence and the location of the compound.

But implanting her with a location device without her knowledge was a different story. It had nothing to do with keeping his people safe, but it had everything to do with his need for control. He had tried to make sure that she could never escape.

The question was how and when he'd gotten the device implanted. He could have made her forget, but there would have been a mark, and the area would have been tender for a while. She would have noticed it.

When the door opened, and Julian walked in with Marcel, Sofia forced her hand away from her thigh. "I don't remember this being done to me. How could that be?"

"The tracker is very small." Julian turned the screen toward her so she could see it. "It could have been injected. Did you receive vaccinations or antibiotic shots?"

"Not in my thigh. They were always done in the arm."

"You might have been compelled to forget," Marcel said. "Usually, that's not how compulsion works, but some compellers have an extra ability that enables them to do that."

"Can Emmett or Eleanor compel memories to be forgotten?"

Marcel shook his head.

"What about Kalugal?"

He nodded. "Kalugal can do that, but he has an extra talent that enables it."

"Then that's how it must have happened to me."

Julian snapped on a pair of gloves and motioned for her to lie down. "I need you to take off your leggings."

"Are you going to give me a shot?"

"Yes."

She turned to Marcel. "Can you hold my hand? I hate needles."

"Of course." He took her hand. "Don't look at what Julian is doing. Look at me."

That wasn't a difficult command to follow. Julian was gorgeous, but he was like a beautiful sculpture to her. His perfect features and his pleasant nature didn't affect her.

Marcel was the one who made her heart somersault every time he got near her. Everything about him appealed to her, from his ruggedly handsome physique to his serious, nearly somber attitude. Every time she'd managed to make him smile or laugh, it had felt like an accomplishment.

Would she ever get to see those glimpses of levity again?

The prick of the needle made her cringe, and when the burning started, she squeezed Marcel's hand.

He winced. "I don't like seeing you in pain."

The emotional pain he was causing by withdrawing from her was much worse than the physical one the doctor had inflicted, but to admit it was to give him even more power over her and to lose the little pride she still retained.

"The pain is due to the perforation of the skin," Julian explained. "The liquid activates stretch receptors in the deeper tissues. It will subside in a moment." He pulled out the needle and swiped something cool over it.

She let out a breath. "It doesn't hurt anymore."

"Good," the doctor said. "I'm going to poke you with the needle again in a couple of minutes."

Sofia closed her eyes and concentrated on the feel of Marcel's large hand enveloping hers.

"Can you feel this?" Julian asked.

"No."

"Good. Let's do it."

As the doctor cut into her skin, she felt pressure but no pain.

"It's out," Julian pronounced. "Easy peasy." He wiped the incision and then put something sticky over it. "I didn't even have to suture it."

Sofia braved a look at her thigh, but there was nothing to see. Julian had covered it with surgical tape.

"Where is the tracking device?" she asked.

He used a pair of tweezers to lift the blood-covered tiny pebble off his surgical tray. "Here is the little devil. I wonder if it was made in China."

"I don't think so." Marcel leaned over her to take a closer look. "That's a sophisticated little sucker."

A knock sounded on the door, and a moment later Eleanor poked her head in. "Can we come in now?"

"Give us a moment," Julian told her and then waved at Sofia. "You can put your pants back on."

"That was easier than I expected." She pulled her leggings on, taking care with the incision area. "Will I feel pain later?"

"I'll give you something for it."

As Julian put the tracker down on the tray, the door opened again, and Eleanor walked in with Leon.

"How did it go?" Eleanor asked.

"Easier than I expected." Sofia sat up slowly. "I feel a little woozy, though."

"You should lie down for a little bit." Julian pulled out a pillow from under the platform and handed it to her.

"Thank you." She tucked it under her head and brought her knees up.

It was probably the stress, or maybe the combined effect of the headache and the anesthetic, or maybe it was the fear of putting weight on the leg where Julian had dug the tracker out, but whatever the reason was, she was glad to stay horizontal.

Hopefully, her nausea wouldn't get worse and force her to get up and rush to the bathroom to puke.

"Is that it?" Eleanor leaned over the tray. "It's tiny. Mine was so much bigger. No wonder it hurt like a son of a bitch to take it out, and the area was still painful to touch for a couple of days later. I winced every time I moved my arm."

"What do you want me to do with it?" Julian asked. "Should we send it to William to take apart?"

"No!" Leon and Marcel said at the same time.

"We need to retain the illusion that she still has it on her." Leon pulled out his bug checker and waved it over the pebble. "It's not transmitting. How is it activated? Can it be done remotely?"

Marcel nodded. "I'm not familiar with the technology, but I know that it can be done. The thing needs to be inside a body, though. It's powered by the body's electrical signals. To keep the illusion going, we need to put it inside a dog or a cat, preferably one that doesn't move much. It will look suspicious if they activate the tracker and see it bouncing all over the resort."

"I know the perfect cat," Eleanor said. "Cecilia is the laziest cat ever. She sits on the windowsill in Anastasia's office all day long, and she only comes down to feed or to pee and poop."

"Poor cat," Sofia said. "I feel bad about hurting an innocent animal."

Julian gave her a smile. "My mate and I have two small dogs, and we put chips in both of them in case they ever get lost. It's not a big deal, and I'll make sure it's painless."

Marcel

"I need to call the boss," Julian said. "Do you want to talk with him?"

Marcel looked at Sofia. "Are you okay staying here alone for a few minutes?"

She nodded. "What's next? Are you taking me back to the bunker? I could use a few hours of sleep."

That wasn't going to happen. Marcel was taking her to see Toven, but first, he needed to confer with Kian.

"I will tell you the plan after I talk to the boss."

She sighed and closed her eyes. "I'll probably be asleep when you get back."

"Then I'll carry you wherever you need to be." He leaned down and planted a soft kiss on her forehead. "Rest."

The smile she gave him could melt an iceberg. "I will."

When they were out of the room, Julian regarded him with a raised brow. "You didn't tell her about Toven?"

"Not yet. She's scared and overwhelmed. I figured that it would be easier for her to deal with one thing at a time."

"True. We also need to figure out what to tell her about Toven. The guy is not easy to explain."

Marcel shrugged. "After dealing with the compeller who imprisoned her mind, Sofia shouldn't be surprised to meet another compeller who is just as powerful or more so."

"Let's hope that he's more." Julian pulled out his phone and dialed Kian's number.

"What's the status?" the boss's gruff voice thundered through the microphone.

"She had a tracker in her. It was tiny, and I almost missed it. But it's out now, and Marcel says that we should implant it in a cat so it will seem as if she's still wearing it."

"That's an excellent idea. I wish we could examine the device, but for now, it's more important to keep the illusion going. Is Marcel next to you?"

"He's right here, and so are Leon and Eleanor."

"Good. What's your take on that tracker?"

"It's a very sophisticated piece of equipment that is not easy to come by. In contrast, the pendant she was using to communicate with the compeller is readily available on the internet. It's not cheap, but it's not difficult to obtain."

"That reinforces Turner's theory. He suspects that the compeller wanted Sofia to get caught so she could lead him to our headquarters or center of operations. That's why he sent an amateur. She was a pawn."

Eleanor bared her teeth. "What a bastard."

"That's a gross understatement," Marcel said. "He's a murderer."

Leon cleared his throat. "We are judging him by our modern moral standards, but what he did might be acceptable by Kra-ell tradition. We know that they are warlike people and that they scoff at soft emotions. Furthermore, if we look back at human history, it was common practice for one tribe to attack another, slaughter the males and take the females. Sacrificing a pawn for the greater good of the community is also a common tactic."

Eleanor huffed. "It was also common practice to sacrifice children to idols, tie child virgin brides to the bed and rape them, and a thousand and one other evil customs, some of which are still practiced to this day. That doesn't make any of them okay, and I have no tolerance for that. I say let's kill the evildoer and free his people."

"I like the way you think." Marcel clapped her on the back.

"Thank you." She grinned at him. "Most people think that I'm a bloodthirsty bitch."

"That's because you are bloodthirsty." Leon smiled at her. "But I like that about you."

"People," Kian groaned. "We are pressed for time. Can we schedule the mutual admiration club meeting for later?"

"Indeed." Marcel rubbed a hand over the back of his neck. "I didn't tell Sofia that we want her to feed the compeller false information yet. What should I tell her about Toven?"

"Only that he's a powerful compeller and that he might be able to free her. He calls himself Tom when he deals with humans, so you can use that name."

"She's smart, and she suspects that we are not regular humans. I don't know how to answer her questions."

"Since we need her to feed the compeller false information about us, you should start giving her that information first. We are a group of paranormally talented people, and we gather others like us to create a community. That's why we have several compellers among us as well as people with other abilities. I'll instruct Toven and Mia to tell her the same story."

Eleanor frowned. "Why did Mia come with Toven?"

"He thinks that he might need her enhancing abilities."

It was a good idea, but Marcel hoped Mia's talent wouldn't be needed. If Sofia's compeller was more powerful than Toven, they were in big trouble. "I assume that you want me to take Sofia to him. Should I take Guardians with us?"

"Naturally. Julian is coming with you too. Once the compulsion is taken care of, and the interrogation is done, he goes back to the village with Toven and Mia. After that, you will take Sofia back to Safe Haven, and the charade will start tomorrow. Turner and I will attend via a video call, and we will work out a narrative to feed the compeller according to what she tells us about him."

It was on the tip of Marcel's tongue to say that it might take longer than a few hours to get Sofia to confess everything she knew, but then he realized that they wouldn't need to employ regular interrogation tactics that took a long time to establish rapport and weaken her resistance. Once Toven overrode the other compeller, he could compel Sofia to tell him everything.

Sofia

Sofia was about to have another compeller take a crack at her, and this time, it would happen in person.

Given that she was being escorted by Marcel, Julian, and two guards, and with Marcel carrying a concealed weapon, she suspected that the compeller was the leader of their organization, and that they were taking precautions in case they were attacked.

By whom? Did they expect Igor or Valstar to come to her rescue?

Fat chance of that.

"Who are you people?" she asked Julian because Marcel had deflected all of her questions so far.

She was seated between the two of them in the back of the minivan, with the two guards sitting up front. It should have been enough space for three average-sized people, but she would have preferred not to be in the middle. The minivan had a third row, but it had been folded down to make room for boxes that the doctor had brought with him.

"What do you mean?" Julian smiled with fake innocence.

She rolled her eyes. "I might be just a linguist, but I'm not stupid. You are well organized and well-funded, and you have more compellers than I ever thought could exist."

The doctor gave her a condescending look. "You shouldn't be surprised to find paranormally talented people in a place that runs specially curated retreats for them."

"So that's it? You are an organization of paranormals?"

Julian nodded. "It's difficult to be a paranormal among normals. The founders of our organization decided to create a community for us."

"Do you have a paranormal talent?"

Julian nodded. "I'm an empath. I feel what others around me feel, which can be very useful for a doctor, but it's also a curse. That's why I can't work in a hospital. The anguish is too much for me to bear."

"I can imagine. So where do you work?"

He smiled, this time genuinely. "I work in a halfway house for semi-rehabilitated victims of trafficking. When they are well enough to venture into the outside world, we provide a safe place for them while they get acclimated, and once they are ready to fly, we help them live independently. But they are always welcome to return and enjoy the cocoon of safety again."

"Aren't you affected by their misery? They probably carry horrible emotional and physical scars."

"They do, but they are happy about having a new lease on life, they form friendships with each other that help them heal, and they are full of optimism for the future. We try to make it a wonderful experience for them, a real safe house, and they pay us back with love and appreciation. It's very fulfilling."

"I bet. What about them?" She pointed at the two guards. "What are their talents? Or are they just hired muscle?"

Next to her, Marcel shook his head, but he didn't say a thing.

Had she insulted his buddies? He'd said that he was friends with the people in security.

"What's your talent, Eigen?" Julian asked.

"I can turn into a meat popsicle." The guy snorted a laugh.

"Seriously, dude."

"Seriously. I can lower the temperature of my body so I appear to be dead."

That was a useful talent for a soldier, but she still wasn't sure that he wasn't pulling her leg. "What about the other one?"

"I can sing you to sleep."

She crossed her arms over her chest. "Prove it."

"I can't. If I start singing, Eigen is going to fall asleep at the wheel, and we will crash."

"You are both full of shit. No one at the retreat mentioned talents like that." She turned to Marcel. "What about you? Do you have a talent?"

His lips twitched with a suppressed smile. "I can also put you to sleep by telling you about my workday."

"Very funny. What if I find computer engineering fascinating?"

His eyes sparkled. "I would be delighted to tell you about the latest program I wrote."

She slapped his arm. "I'm not in the mood for jokes. If you don't want to tell me, just say so."

"I'll tell you later."

"So you really do have a paranormal talent?"

"I do." He turned to the window. "Just look at this house. It's spectacular."

Was he deflecting her question?

Sofia tried to see what he was looking at, but all she could discern was a dark, rectangular shape on top of a cliff. Whoever was inside either hadn't turned any lights on, or the windows were shuttered.

Still, it wasn't the first time that she'd noticed Marcel could see better than she could in the dark.

"I know what your talent is. You have paranormal night vision."

"That's part of it." He put his arm around her shoulders. "When we get to the house, I want you to be respectful toward Tom. He came all the way out here to help you. It would be rude of you to give him a hard time."

So she'd been right, and they were going to see the boss of their organization.

Was he as bad as Igor?

Worse?

Better?

"Are you implying that I'm rude?"

He chuckled. "Fates forbid. But you get prickly when annoyed."

That was true. "Tell me a little bit about him. Should I be scared of him?"

"Not at all. Tom is a novelist who comes from a very old and wealthy family. He's old school, and modern vernacular might sound offensive to him. Act as if you are meeting a prince, and you should be fine."

"What if I say something that he finds offensive? Would he compel me to stand on one leg and crow?"

Julian chuckled. "The worst he would do to you is look down his nose at you and make you feel like a bug. Tom is a good guy, but he's condescending without meaning to be. It's just his natural sense of superiority."

She hadn't detected any resentment, and there was real fondness in the doctor's tone, so maybe their leader wasn't as bad as Igor; but he was still a compeller, he was still a man who imposed his will on others, and that couldn't be good even if he was human.

In her experience people seldom, if ever, chose to use their talents and other advantages to help others. Mostly, they used them to get a leg up and step over those who were less gifted.

Marcel

As they neared the structure, Marcel let out a relieved breath. The ride had taken less than an hour, but it had been difficult sitting next to Sofia and pretending that her closeness didn't affect him.

He was still waging a battle with his determination to never fall victim to a woman's wiles again. His heart was demanding that he stop resisting the pull and embrace the rose that Sofia was, with all of her soft petals and prickly thorns, but his mind knew better than to listen to that squishy organ that had led him astray before.

But even his mind wasn't as steadfast as he would have liked it to be.

So Sofia wasn't perfect. So she'd been sent as a spy and used him to get close to Emmett. So what?

None of it had been her choice.

But had her feelings for him been real? Or had it been a superb act, and he'd fallen for it like he had done in the past because he was putty in an attractive woman's hands?

If it had been an act, Sofia must have studied method acting under a masterful teacher because her performance had been flawless. Her anger after he hadn't shown up as she'd expected, her refusal to let him explain, had all of that been for show?

It very well might have been.

After all, they'd ended up in bed together the same night, and she had rocked his world, demolishing the last of his resistance.

Fates, he was such a fool.

Summoning the vestiges of his resolve, he forced himself to enter the familiar state of indifference and looked at the house Turner had chosen for their rendezvous with Toven.

What had the guy been thinking?

The structure was a glass and concrete rectangle that was supported by big pillars and perched over a cliff overlooking the ocean. It was beautiful, and the view must be spectacular, but the large expanse of glass made its occupants an easy target for snipers.

Marcel doubted that the windows were bulletproof.

Other than Sofia, they were all immortal, so bullets and even shards of glass wouldn't necessarily kill them, but they could knock them out long enough for the attackers to finish the job.

Perhaps Turner was using the compeller's tactic and luring him or his warriors by dangling their own pawn as bait?

Given that they had just removed the tracker from her, it didn't make much sense. If Turner wanted to flush out the enemy, he should have told them to leave the tracker in and surrounded the place with Guardians.

Perhaps he'd employed a bait-and-switch tactic?

Make the enemy think that they were complacent because the tracker had been removed, but surround the property with Guardians?

"How many Guardians did Kian send?" he asked the driver as the guy drove the minivan into a parking spot under the structure.

"Eight. Two are in the house, we are with you, and the other four stayed in Safe Haven. Why?"

"I was wondering about Turner's location choice. A house of glass is not easily defended."

The Guardian shrugged. "I trust Turner. He knows what he's doing."

"I hope you are right because all those windows are a sniper's wet dream." Marcel opened the door and offered Sofia his hand.

She looked up. "It's a beautiful house, and the curtains hide what's going on inside. Besides, who are you expecting to attack us?"

Was that her way of telling him that she wasn't expecting a rescue?

As if he believed anything that came out of her pretty mouth. He wasn't straight out accusing her of lying, though. Not yet.

Until Toven got a hold of her mind and forced her to tell the truth, Marcel was going to give Sofia the benefit of the doubt. But if she was lying, and she was expecting a rescue, then he could keep the pretense the same way he had done with her pendant.

"Yeah, you are right." He took her hand and led her up the stairs to the front door. "With the tracker gone, no one could have followed you here."

The Guardian who opened the door gave Sofia an appraising look before offering her his hand. "Hi, I'm Malcolm."

"I'm Sofia." She shook it. "Are you the boss?"

He laughed. "I'm not. Please, come in."

Sofia

When the guy who had opened the door stepped aside and motioned for her to come in, the most beautiful man Sofia had ever seen rose to his feet and walked toward her.

This man wasn't human, she was willing to bet on it, but he wasn't Kra-ell despite his nearly black hair. He was too perfect, too cultured, and too refined. He lacked the savagery lurking beneath the surface of all the purebloods and most of the hybrids, males and females alike. There was an animalistic quality to them that was totally absent from this gorgeous man.

"Hello, Sofia." He offered her his hand. "My name is Tom."

It took her a moment to find her voice. "Hi," she croaked. "You must be the compeller."

He smiled. "I am many things, but I am not a compeller. Compulsion is an ability I was born with, but it doesn't define me, and I don't enjoy using it."

With that one sentence, he'd won her over.

"I'm glad. It's not right to take people's will away from them."

He chuckled. "Unless it's to prevent them from doing harm to another, right?" He offered her his arm and walked her to the dining table. "If you had the ability to stop a murderer from firing a gun at an innocent person, wouldn't you do it?"

"Of course."

He pulled out a chair for her. "Nearly every ability and technology is not intrinsically good or evil. It's how it is used that's either beneficial or harmful. And quite often, the boundaries are not clear. And if that's not bad enough, sometimes what is beneficial in one way is harmful in another, and you have to weigh the good versus the bad and make a judgment call about the winner." He smiled a sad smile. "So, as you can see, God's job is not easy."

While Tom was delivering his speech, Marcel and Julian sat across the table from them. She'd been so mesmerized by him, that she'd forgotten that she hadn't arrived alone.

"I'm glad that I'm not a goddess." She huffed out a breath. "I would have gotten one hell of a headache if I had to make those judgment calls."

"Ah, but you make those calls every moment of every day," Tom said in his velvety smooth voice. "It's just that the consequences of your decisions are usually not of life and death caliber."

As Sofia searched her mind for a clever response, a young woman drove her wheelchair into the living room.

"Hi." She waved a hand at Sofia while navigating her motorized chair with the other right into the empty spot next to the dining room table. "I'm Mia, Tom's fiancée."

Tom had just won another point in his favor.

Mia looked like a really nice and friendly person, and that reflected well on Tom.

Still, she had to wonder what their reflection in the mirror looked like. Were they as beautiful on the inside as they were on the outside?

She smiled and waved back. "I'm Sofia."

It was on the tip of her tongue to add that she was Marcel's girlfriend, but right now she was Marcel's suspect, not his love interest.

Throughout the drive, he had been physically close but emotionally distant.

As Mia reached for Tom's hand, he shook his head. "I want to try it first without your help."

“Right,” Mia said. “I forgot. I’ll move a few feet away. Usually, that’s enough.”

Was Mia a compeller as well?

She looked too gentle, too fragile, and Sofia would have never suspected her of possessing the ability. She looked so kind, and Sofia couldn't imagine her using compulsion to gain an unfair advantage over others.

In contrast, Eleanor looked the part and was quite intimidating. Still, she was nothing like Igor or even Jade. She just had an aura of someone who was used to getting her own way, but she loved Emmett, and she'd been kind to Sofia.

Emmett clearly loved Eleanor, and he put up a good act as the benevolent guru, but Sofia wouldn't trust him with a key to the bathroom.

Suddenly, it occurred to her that Emmett had swindled his followers by using compulsion to get them to surrender all of their possessions to him.

Bastard.

That must have been what had piqued Jade's curiosity. She must have read about that and realized that Emmett was a compeller. Maybe she'd thought that he was stronger than Igor and could free her.

Emmett wasn't in the same league as Igor, but Sofia had a feeling that Tom was in an even higher league.

He displayed a level of confidence that even Igor couldn't front.

It occurred to her that Igor strived to be perceived the way Tom was—a powerhouse that was nonetheless cultured and refined, but what he projected paled by comparison. Igor was cold and ruthless. He demanded respect and was afforded it out of fear.

Tom didn't demand anything. His personality just commanded respect.

Marcel

As Mia moved away from the table, Toven turned to Sofia. "Tell me your full real name."

"My name is Sofia Heikkinen."

Toven looked at Marcel. "Is that the name she's registered under?"

Marcel nodded.

Toven leveled his gaze at Sofia. "How old are you?"

"Twenty-seven."

Marcel nodded to confirm.

"Did you study at the University of Helsinki for the past seven years?"

"Almost eight. I study languages."

"That's nice. Did you go home often?"

She nodded. "Once a month."

"Was home far away from the university?"

"Yes."

"Did you fly home?"

"No."

"Did you take the bus?"

"No."

"Did you drive?"

"Yes."

"How long did it take you to drive?"

She opened her mouth, but nothing came out. "I can't say."

"Was it longer than two hours?"

"Yes."

"Longer than four?"

"Yes."

"Longer than eight?"

"No."

Toven smiled. "We are making progress, and I didn't even use compulsion yet. Tell me why you came to Safe Haven," he commanded.

This time, Marcel could feel the compulsion reverberating in his voice.

"I was sent to observe and report."

Marcel let out a relieved breath. She'd answered Toven's question, which meant that his compulsion could override her compeller's.

"What were you supposed to observe?"

"I wasn't given any details. I was told to get close to the management and report anything unusual that I noticed."

"Who did you report to?"

"Valstar."

"Is he the one who compelled you?"

Sofia shook her head.

"What's the name of the compeller?"

"Igor."

"Is Igor the leader?"

She nodded.

Finally, they had a name for Jade's captor.

Toven glanced at Marcel before turning back to Sofia. "Tell me about the people of your community. What makes them special?"

She shook her head. "I can't."

Toven narrowed his eyes at her. "Maybe that was too general. Is your community hidden?"

She nodded.

"Where is it located?"

"I can't say."

"How many people live in your hidden community?"

"I can't say." She rubbed her temples. "My head hurts."

Toven leaned closer to her. "Did you see anything suspicious in Safe Haven?"

Marcel figured out what the god was doing. It seemed that Sofia could answer questions about recent events, probably because the compulsion about those hadn't been reinforced countless times.

She nodded.

"What did you find suspicious?"

She turned to look at Marcel. "I saw your eyes glowing on occasion. You can also see in the dark. I don't think you are human." She turned to Toven. "You're not human either."

Toven smiled. "What am I?"

"I don't know." She lifted her hand to her temple and rubbed at it. "I think of Marcel, Eleanor, and Emmett as others, but now that I know your community is all about paranormal talents, maybe that's the otherness that I sense. The paranormal talents make you feel not fully human."

"That's a very particular observation. What other nonhumans do you know?"

"I can't." Tears started streaming down Sofia's cheeks. "Please. I can't take it anymore. My head is going to explode."

"She needs to rest." Julian turned to Marcel. "Take Sofia to the bedroom so she can lie down."

Mia drove her chair around the table. "I'll show you where it is and get you some Motrin. Luckily, they have a first aid kit in the bathroom that is nicely stocked." She smiled. "It's force of habit. I always check what's in the cabinets when I settle in a new place."

Marcel got up, walked over to Sofia, and offered her his hand.

When he pulled her to him, she swayed on her feet. "I'm so sorry. But every time Tom asks me questions that I'm not allowed to answer, and I attempt it anyway, it feels like I'm trying to pull my brain out through my skull."

Was it an act?

All it would achieve was to drag out the interrogation longer.

Maybe that was her objective?

Was she hoping for a rescue?

"You can rest for a few minutes, and then Tom will continue."

Mia glared at him. "Sofia needs more than a few minutes. It will take at least half an hour for the Motrin to kick in, and then she will need a few hours of shuteye in the dark."

"We don't have time for that," Marcel said as calmly as he could, not only because he didn't want to upset Sofia, but because he needed to be cordial to Mia.

She was only trying to help, but they didn't have the luxury of coddling Sofia. Kian and Turner were waiting for answers.

"We have plenty of time." Mia glared at him. "Tom and I don't plan on going to sleep tonight, and we can continue the interrogation early tomorrow morning."

It was already nearly morning, but one look at Toven made it clear that the god agreed with his mate.

"A couple of hours. That's the most we can afford." Holding on to Sofia's elbow to keep her steady, Marcel followed Mia to the bedroom.

As soon as they neared the bed, Sofia pulled out of his hold and dropped on the bed with a groan, and Mia drove the chair into the open layout bathroom.

She returned a moment later with a bottle of pills and a glass of water. "Here you go, sweetie. Take three at once." She opened the bottle and shook out three pills into Sofia's palm.

"Thank you." She popped the pills into her mouth and followed with the water.

"You're most welcome." Mia turned her chair around. "I'll turn the lights off on my way out."

As Mia turned the lights off, Marcel remained standing next to the bed and just looked at Sofia with a frown creasing his forehead.

Was he angry at her for getting a headache?

It wasn't her fault that Igor's compulsion stuck to her like glue. Tom hadn't removed it, he hadn't freed her mind, he'd overpowered it with his own compulsion and added an additional layer on top of the sludge that was already there.

His compulsion hadn't felt as slimy and as heavy-handed as Igor's, but it was still nasty.

"He didn't try to free my mind," she said quietly. "He overpowered the weaker components that were there before. Now I'm a slave to two masters."

Marcel sat on the bed next to her and took her hand. "I'll speak to Tom and ask him if he can change his tactic and free you, or at least get rid of some of it."

His voice was gentle, but it lacked the warmth and mirth that had been there before he'd discovered her duplicity. Did he still care for her?

Lifting her hand, she cupped his cheek. "Do you still want me?"

He let out a shuddering breath. "I never stopped wanting you." He took her hand and removed it from his cheek. "I hoped to learn more about your motives and that it would help me sort out my feelings for you. But getting you to talk is proving to be a more difficult task than we expected." He patted her shoulder awkwardly. "Get some rest."

Sofia caught his hand. "Don't go yet. You promised to tell me your paranormal talent."

He sighed. "It's not a very unique talent. I can make people forget things or remember things that didn't happen."

Her heart, which was already shriveled like a prune, constricted further. Had he manipulated her mind as well?

No wonder her head was hurting so badly. She'd had two compellers and one memory manipulator mess with her mind. She would be lucky if by the end of those terrible twenty-four hours she retained any cognitive function at all.

"What did you do to me?"

"It was a very small thing just to test whether you are susceptible to my talent. Do you remember the expensive gift I bought for my ex-girlfriend that you couldn't recall any particulars about?"

"You made me forget what it was."

"I did. I told you that it was a diamond necklace, but that wasn't it. I got her expensive jewelry, but she wanted more than shiny objects to prove my love for her."

The pain in his voice indicated that it was much worse. Had she made him betray his people? Forsake his family?

"What did she want?"

He shook his head. "That's a secret I'm going to take to my grave. I haven't told anyone, and I don't intend to."

Why did that hurt so much?

He hadn't told his family or his friends, and she was no one to him. Why should he tell her his deepest secret?

"You can keep your secrets." She let go of his hand. "Just promise me that you'll never make me forget anything again or remember a false memory."

"I'm sorry, but I can't promise that. I might have to make you forget about meeting Tom as well as other details about our organization. People with paranormal talents fear persecution and exploitation. We need to keep our existence a secret."

Sofia snorted. "Then running a paranormal retreat might not be the best strategy."

"How else are we going to find more of us? Besides, people on the outside think it's all fake. Sometimes ridicule is the best defense. It allows us to hide in plain sight."

She thought about the Kra-ell and how they'd gone undetected despite looking very alien.

"People think along the parameters they are familiar with. When something doesn't fit, they dismiss it as an aberration or a hoax."

"Precisely." Marcel pushed to his feet. "How is your head? Has the Motrin started to work?"

"It's a little better." She rubbed her temple. "But it still hurts."

"Get some rest. You didn't get enough sleep tonight, and all the excitement must have exhausted you."

"I barely slept at all." She grabbed a pillow and hugged it to her chest. "It's hard to fall asleep while my whole world is falling apart around me."

He grimaced. "I wasn't the one who caused it."

"No, you were not."

He was just the one who broke her heart.

Marcel

With a heavy heart, Marcel left the bedroom and closed the door behind him. He'd closed himself up emotionally as best he could, but Sofia's sadness had managed to penetrate the shields he'd built around his heart and poke a dagger right through it.

"Is she asleep?" Mia asked.

"Not yet." Marcel sat down next to Julian.

"That compeller is extremely dangerous," Toven said. "I'm afraid to use too much power on Sofia and fry her brain. The best approach would have been to chip away at the walls he's erected around her brain slowly, but we don't have the luxury of time. I understand that you want to use her to feed him false information, and to do that, we need to have her on our side. I need to break through his compulsion and use mine to get her to talk."

"I wonder if she knows the kind of monster he is," Mia said. "We know that the purebloods don't share information even with the hybrids, let alone the humans in their community, so Sofia might not be aware of what he did to Jade's tribe and possibly to others as well. Maybe if we tell her, she will be more inclined to talk."

Toven took his mate's hand. "It's not her reluctance that I'm worried about. What I'm worried about is that he might be a stronger compeller than I am, and that I will need your enhancing powers to break through his compulsion. I'm also worried about what it will do to Sofia's mind."

It was inconceivable that anyone could be stronger than a god. The Kra-ell were less evolved than the gods, and it didn't make sense that one of them was more powerful than Toven.

But then Navuh, who was the immortal equivalent of a hybrid, shouldn't be such a strong compeller, and yet he was.

"Is Navuh more powerful than you?" Julian asked, giving voice to Marcel's thoughts.

"He wasn't stronger than me back when I still knew him, but five thousand years later, he might be. Power grows with age."

"So yours grew as well," Mia said. "If you were stronger then, you should be stronger now."

"It isn't an exact progression, and Navuh has used his ability much more extensively than I have. I wouldn't be surprised if he grew stronger than me."

If that was true, it could partially explain why the Kra-ell leader was so powerful. He used his talent a lot. But on the other hand, he couldn't be as old as either Toven or Navuh.

Unless he was a god, and that was unlikely.

Or was it?

"Who did you inherit your compulsion ability from?" Mia asked. "No one ever mentioned Ekin being a compeller."

"He wasn't, but his brother Ahn was, and so was Mortdh. Since Ahn and Ekin only shared a father and so did Mortdh and I, the common compeller ancestor must have been our paternal grandfather."

"Who was he?" Julian asked.

"I never met him." Toven pushed to his feet. "Anyone want coffee?"

Marcel had a feeling that Toven knew very well who his grandfather was but didn't want to share the information with them, or even with his mate, which was odd.

What was he hiding?

"I'll make it." One of the Guardians got off the couch. "There is a pod machine in the kitchen. Who likes it strong?"

"I do." Marcel lifted his hand.

After the Guardian had collected everyone's preferences, Marcel decided to voice his improbable hypothesis. "Igor is supposedly a pureblooded Kra-ell, which means that he can't be more than a thousand years old. It doesn't make sense that he's more powerful than a god, unless he's a god himself, or maybe a hybrid of a pureblooded Kra-ell and a god. If we assume that the Kra-ell came from the same place, and that they are a more primitive version of the gods, it's not such a big leap to consider that as a possibility."

Toven's brows dipped low. "It actually makes sense. When I was trying to break through Igor's compulsion, and Sofia kept resisting mine, I wondered how it was possible for a Kra-ell to be a more powerful compeller than I am. I'm aware that they are physically very strong, but they shouldn't possess more powerful mind manipulation abilities than those of the gods. If they do, we are in even deeper trouble than Kian or I have ever considered."

"Why is that?" Mia asked. "What else can a god do?"

Toven smiled. "Do you want me to reveal all of my secrets?"

She laughed. "It was a rhetorical question. We all know that gods can manipulate minds, and the stronger the god, the more minds he or she can manipulate at once. But you can't conjure an explosion, manifest rain, cause a flood, or any such things. You can only cause people to think that those things are happening, and we know how to block compulsion with those special earpieces."

"Compulsion can be blocked, but thralling and shrouding cannot unless you are immune. If Igor can thrall as well as compel, our people will have no defense against him."

Mia frowned. "Can't you shield us? You and Annani combined should be able to do that, right?"

Toven shook his head. "It's not something that I've ever tried doing, and neither has Annani. I don't know how."

"Did it work?" Syssi turned on her side.

"I haven't heard from them yet."

"Then come to bed. They will call you if they have something to report."

Kian had come home less than half an hour ago to take a quick shower and change into a fresh set of clothes. Sleep was not part of the plan.

It was already five in the morning, and there was still a lot to be done, but he planned to do it from his home office. Once things were on track, he would catch a little nap before starting his day.

He walked over to the bed and wrapped his arms around Syssi's warm body. "Go back to sleep, my love." He kissed her lips. "I'll be in my office."

"You need to get some sleep."

"I'll catch a short nap on the couch later. I'm expecting a call from Toven or Marcel any minute now."

She yawned. "Wake me up when you hear from them."

"I will." He kissed her again.

Kian had no intention of waking her up. She had work tomorrow and a baby to take care of. She needed her sleep.

He made himself a cup of coffee, took the mug to his office, sat on the couch, and propped his feet on the coffee table.

It had been a long while since he'd pulled an all-nighter, but it wasn't a big deal. Back in his bachelor days, he'd done so many of them that it was like slipping back into an old pair of pants that were a little too tight but still familiar.

The call from Toven came at seven minutes after five.

"Hold on. I'll get Turner on the line with us."

"Isn't it too late?" Toven asked. "Or rather too early?"

"He didn't go to sleep either." Kian called Turner. "You are on the line with Toven."

"Good evening," Toven said. "Mia, Marcel, and Julian are here as well."

"Good evening to you all. Did it work?" Turner echoed Syssi's question.

"It did, and it didn't," Toven said. "The more recent compulsions were not difficult to override, but the old ones that have probably been routinely reinforced are very difficult to overpower. With Mia's help, I can probably break through, but I don't want to push too hard and fry Sofia's mind. She was exhausted and got a severe headache just from the little I managed to get out of her. We had to take a break and let her rest."

That wasn't good.

Kian had been sure that Mia's help wouldn't be needed, and it was very disturbing that it was.

"What did you learn so far?"

"We have a name for the compeller. It's Igor, which is obviously not his original Kra-ell name, and it makes me wonder why he chose to adopt a human one. Did he have a shameful name like Emmett's? Perhaps he's a hybrid, and his father or mother wasn't happy about his arrival. Marcel suspects that he's half Kra-ell and half god."

Kian's blood chilled in his veins. "Why does Marcel suspect that?"

"Igor's power level. The Kra-ell are not long-lived enough to have their power grow that much. But since we don't know much about them, they might be naturally more gifted that way. Still, Marcel's hypothesis is a possibility, and until we know more, we shouldn't dismiss it."

"When are you going to continue the interrogation?"

"I want Sofia to get some sleep, but Marcel is impatient, and he wants to wake her up in a couple of hours."

Kian wanted to be done with it as well, but not if it meant causing damage to the girl. "We can wait an hour or two longer. I bet everyone is tired and wouldn't mind some shut-eye."

Crawling into bed with Syssi could be so lovely for an hour or two.

"I need to take care of the bioinformaticians," Marcel said. "I planned to do it today, but if we let Sofia sleep more than two hours, I won't make it back in time to open up the lab for them, and they'll wonder what happened."

"You were supposed to thrall them to forget the project and send them home," Turner said.

"There was no time."

"It doesn't have to be you," Kian said. "Leon can do that. In fact, it would be easier to explain why they are suddenly being sent on a paid vacation. He can tell them that you had an emergency and there is no one available to take your place. Case closed."

"That could work." Marcel sounded relieved. "Nevertheless, if we want to keep up the charade and have Sofia contact Igor with false information, we can't wait too long to have her do that. He might send people to retrieve her, if he hasn't done it already."

"I doubt it," Turner said. "Given the sophistication of the tracker compared to the communication device she was given, Igor wanted Sofia to get caught. In my opinion, he has people on standby in one of the nearby towns, and he's waiting for her to get moved. He won't do anything until that tracker leaves Safe Haven."

"Then maybe we should move it," Toven said. "We can set a trap for Igor's people and catch them. I'll be much less reluctant to force my way into the minds of those murderers than I am with Sofia."

Turner chuckled. "Sounds tempting, but we shouldn't do that until we know what we are dealing with. If Igor's force is superior to ours, our best tactic is to evade him at all costs. We will need to abandon Safe Haven and do our best to hide from him the same way we do with Navuh."

Toven groaned. "I hate this. I'd rather fight than hide."

The god had been hiding for thousands of years. Was he suddenly eager to fight because he had the clan's backing?

Kian would have loved to fight as well, but his number one priority was to keep his people safe, and his own wishes and desires were a distant second.

"We would all prefer to fight rather than hide," Kian said. "I want to find the bastard, free Jade and the other females, and dispose of Igor and his cronies, but the safety of my people comes first."

"Of course," Toven capitulated. "I'll call you after I get more information out of Sofia."

"I'd rather be part of the interrogation," Turner said. "Kian and I can't be there in person, but we can be via a video call."

"Why video?" Kian asked. "I don't want her to see us. The less we need to erase from her memories later, the better."

"What do you plan to do with Sofia?" Marcel asked.

"I don't know yet. It depends on her part in this. If she's just someone random that the compeller found and forced to do his bidding, we might be able to erase her memories of us and let her loose somewhere with a new identity and enough money to start a new life."

"She is not," Toven said. "Sofia is part of Igor's community. She told us that she made a monthly trek back home that was a nearly eight-hour drive. I assume that it was a mandatory trip to get the compulsion reinforced."

"That's what Navuh does with his warriors," Kian said.

"I wouldn't risk releasing her even if she was randomly picked," Turner said. "Igor might have implanted a deep-seated compulsion in her to react to a certain trigger and find her way back to him or let him know where she is. We can't allow that. Like it or not, we are stuck with her. The best thing we can do is fake her death and keep her with us for the rest of her life."

Sofia

The smell of coffee woke Sofia up, or maybe it was the bed sinking under Marcel's weight.

She didn't need to open her eyes to know it was him.

His scent was so familiar by now that she couldn't mistake him for anyone else. Besides, she would have known it was him even if her nose was blocked up. Her body's reaction to his presence was predictable as well. She longed to reach for him, to pull him to her and press against him, but most of all, she wanted him to wrap his arms around her and tell her that everything would be okay, and that they belonged together.

But wishing wouldn't make it so, and it only made her feel sad for what could have been but probably would never be.

"Is it morning yet?" Reluctantly, she opened her eyes and pushed up against the pillows.

"It's after eight in the morning." He handed her the mug. "I wish we could let you sleep more, but we don't have time."

Why not?

What did they expect to learn from her?

If Tom compelled her to reveal the compound's location, she would have no choice but to tell them where it was, but she couldn't tell them anything useful about its defenses because she didn't know much about them.

Sofia was glad that she didn't have the information they needed, and that no matter what they did to her, she wouldn't help them launch an attack against the compound. She didn't give a damn about what happened to Igor and his inner circle, but she cared about everyone else that was in the same situation as she was, forced to live a life they hadn't chosen.

Did she care about her grandfather?

He'd been nice to her during the preparation period, and they had gotten a little closer, but he should have warned her that she might get caught. Stupidly, she hadn't considered the possibility that she wasn't coming back from the mission. If she had, she would have at least said goodbye to her father and her aunts and cousins and everyone else she was never going to see again.

Cradling the mug between her palms, Sofia looked down at the dark brew to hide her tears. "Did you get any sleep?"

"None of us did. We were waiting for you. How is the headache?"

"Better, but it's still there." She took a couple of sips. "I'd better freshen up." She handed it back to him.

Marcel nodded. "I'll wait for you in the living room. Do you want me to leave the mug here or take it?"

"You can take it. I will be out in a minute."

It ended up taking a little longer than that because the tears sprang out the moment she closed the bathroom door behind her, and she needed to calm down and wash her face before braving the group waiting for her in the living room, or more specifically, Tom and Marcel.

The others didn't seem like a threat.

"Good morning." Tom smiled in what was his version of a friendly manner. "How are you feeling?"

"A little better, thank you." She sat next to where Marcel had put her mug down.

Did Tom even deserve her politeness?

Marcel had warned her to be cordial to Tom and react to him as if he were a prince, but the good will she'd initially felt toward him had evaporated once she'd realized his agenda.

Tom wasn't there to help her. He was there to help his organization and pump her for information.

"Would you like something to eat?" Mia asked.

"No, thank you. I still feel a little nauseated. For now, I'll just stick with coffee."

"I'll get you a fresh cup." One of the guards pushed to his feet.

They were all pretending to be so nice, but Tom was about to barrel into her mind again and get her to tell him things she wouldn't even if she was free to.

"I thought of another approach," Tom said. "Instead of trying to override Igor's compulsion one item at a time, which will take forever, I will override his command to keep everything about him and his community a secret. Wouldn't you prefer that? Your mind will be your own."

Right. Up until she refused to answer a question or avoided direct answers, and he compelled her to talk.

"That would be nice."

"I thought so." He took his fiancée's hand. "Do your thing, love."

She chuckled. "I don't do anything consciously. I just need to be near you."

What were they talking about? Was Mia a compeller who needed to channel her power through Tom's?

He brought her hand to his lips. "That's what I meant."

Turning his eyes to Sofia, he said, "You are free to speak your mind. All your thoughts and memories belong to you, and you can do as you please with them."

Sofia waited for the headache to start, or for something inside of her to change, but she didn't feel any different than she felt a moment ago.

"I don't think it worked."

Toven smiled. "Let's try a question from yesterday. Tell me about your community. Is it big?"

Marcel

So far, Sofia hadn't noticed the tablet next to Julian. The camera was pointed at her, so Kian and Turner could see and hear the interrogation, but the screen was black, so she couldn't see them. Julian wore an earpiece, so if they had any questions, he could ask them.

"My community is not big." Sofia seemed to be surprised by her own answer.

"How many people live in your community?"

Was Toven using compulsion? Marcel could feel the compulsion before, but not now.

She seemed reluctant but answered anyway. "Several hundred."

"What else can you tell us about it?" Toven asked. When she didn't answer, he added, "Is it hidden?"

"Yes."

"How?"

She looked at him as if she didn't understand the question. "I don't know what you mean."

Toven leaned forward. "I mean, how can a community of several hundred people be hidden? Do you live underground? Is it camouflaged to look like something else? Maybe ruins? How is it possible for people living in the area not to know about it?"

"It's partially underground, but most of it is above ground. It's located in a densely wooded, remote area that is not accessible by vehicles and barely accessible on foot. No one has reason to pass through."

Toven leaned back and crossed his arms over his chest. "There must be a way to deliver supplies to a community that size, and I bet they don't do it on horseback."

"They don't." She lowered her eyes. "I guess there is a hidden tunnel somewhere."

Marcel was willing to bet that she knew where that tunnel was. She'd already told them that she'd had to come home once a month, and she'd said that she'd driven home. If the place was inaccessible, she must have used a tunnel or a bridge or some well-camouflaged road.

Then again, it was possible that she was picked up from a collection point and taken to the compound blindfolded or in a windowless vehicle.

"Is there a wall around it?" Toven asked.

She nodded.

At the rate they were going, the questioning would take forever. Sofia was reluctant to volunteer information even though it seemed she was now free to do so.

"Why are you resisting?" Toven asked. "I can force the answers out of you, but I'd rather you give them voluntarily."

"I have a family there, and most of the people there are not bad. I don't know what you want to do or why, and if I can help it, I won't endanger my people."

"We would never harm innocents."

She grimaced. "Unless they are collateral damage?"

"Not even one innocent life is collateral damage to us." Toven leveled her with such an intense gaze that she looked away.

"Is Igor a good guy?" Julian asked her.

"No."

"Is he terrible?"

She hesitated for a moment. "To some, but not to all. It could be worse."

Toven sighed. "I have a feeling that you don't know how your leader operates. Otherwise, you would be much more critical of him."

"I know that he keeps everyone under his control with heavy compulsion, and that's not right. But you could be even worse. I could be trading one ruthless dictator for another."

Toven turned to look at Julian's tablet. "Should I tell her what we know about Igor and his compound?"

Marcel was surprised that Toven was asking Kian's permission. The god didn't strike him as someone who bowed to anyone's authority.

Julian nodded. "Except for what we know about you know who."

Toven nodded and turned back to Sofia. "Perhaps once you realize how much we already know, it will make it easier for you. We are well familiar with the Kra-ell, and generally speaking, we don't mean them harm."

Sofia gasped. "How do you know about them?

"We have three hybrids living in our community."

She looked shocked. "How did you find them? And how did they end up in your community?"

"They were discovered through their paranormal abilities," Julian said, probably repeating what Kian or Turner told him in the earpiece. "The retreat is not the only way we find new people with paranormal talents."

Toven nodded. "The three people who joined us told us a very disturbing story about what happened to their tribe."

Sofia swallowed. "What happened to it?"

"You might not believe me if I just tell you, so I'll start with a few leading questions. You are probably aware that many more boys are born to the Kra-ell than girls."

She nodded.

"On average, for every four boys, only one girl is born, and yet I'm guessing that the ratio between adult pure-blooded Kra-ell males and females in your compound is not four or five to one. Am I right?"

"It's not. Their numbers are almost equal."

"Doesn't that strike you as odd?"

"It does." She swallowed again. "Do they get rid of the boys? There are more hybrid males than females, though. So maybe they only do that with the purebloods."

"They don't," Toven said. "They raid other Kra-ell tribes, slaughter the males, and capture the females. That's how Igor evens out the numbers."

Sofia

Were they telling her the truth?

Sofia couldn't deny that he'd been spot on. Then again, Tom had said that he was much more than a compeller, so maybe he was a mind reader as well?

But if he could read minds, why did he need to interrogate her? He could have bypassed Igor's compulsion by just reaching into her mind and plucking the thoughts out of there. She wasn't prohibited from thinking about all the things she was forbidden to reveal, but evidently Tom couldn't do that.

Jade's loathing of Igor made much more sense now. If he'd slaughtered the males of her tribe and kidnapped her and the other females, she was probably plotting his murder day in and day out.

Hell, if she were in Jade's position, Sofia would do that too, and she was not nearly as vicious as that pureblooded female. The only thing keeping Igor alive was his compulsion power.

Tom hadn't mentioned Jade by name, but Sofia was sure he'd been talking about her and her tribe.

Jade was a natural leader, and Sofia had noticed that she hung out with several of the pureblooded and hybrid females, especially with Kagra, whom she referred to as her second.

Now it finally made sense.

Kagra didn't have any special position in Igor's organization, but she must have been Jade's second-in-command before they'd been captured.

"Did Jade figure out that your paranormal retreat was somehow connected to the other Kra-ell? Was that why she was spending so much time on the Safe Haven website?"

Tom looked at the doctor, or rather the tablet propped on a stand in front of Julian. Someone was watching on the other side, which meant that Tom wasn't the boss. Someone else was, and he didn't want her to see him.

When no one answered her, she repeated the question. "Is that a yes or a no?"

"It's irrelevant to our discussion," Tom said. "I assume that there are many Kra-ell females in your community who are there against their will, and who are compelled to hold their grief inside them and not tell anyone how they got there. They deserve to be freed, and we need your help to do that. I assume that you are fully human. Is that correct?"

Sofia nodded.

"Were you born to a hybrid father and a human mother?"

"The other way around," Marcel said. "As unlikely as it is, her mother is the other."

Tom looked at her with a raised brow. "Is that true?"

Marcel had guessed it from what she'd stupidly told him about her parents, and they knew so much already that there was no reason to deny it. "My mother took a human lover to piss off my grandfather. She didn't expect to get pregnant, and she wasn't happy about it. But the Kra-ell don't believe in abortion, so here I am."

"That makes you very unique," Tom smiled as if she'd just told him some great news.

Sofia shrugged. "I'm still human, and other than my coloring and my body shape, I didn't inherit anything else from that side of my family, and I'm thankful for it. I like my human side much more. My father, the real one, is a great guy who loves me unconditionally, and I have two aunts who were much more like mothers to me than the female who gave birth to me. I also have cousins and friends, and some of those friends are hybrids. As I said, there are many good people in the compound, and if you try to free the pureblooded females, many of them will get hurt or killed." She sighed. "Frankly, as much as I feel bad about the terrible thing that was done to the pureblooded females, they are not worth the lives of the other people in our community."

"I have a question," Mia asked. "We know that a hybrid and a human produce a human child. How about two hybrids? Are their children human or hybrid as well?"

"As far as I know, the children born to hybrid females are fathered by pureblooded males. But the Kra-ell are not exclusive, so it's difficult to tell who has sex with whom and why. The Kra-ell females have an odd fertility cycle. Since they want to preserve their blood, I assume that they hook up with purebloods while they are fertile, and with hybrids when they are not. Or maybe they use protection when having sex with hybrids and humans. Though my mother obviously didn't use contraceptives." She let out a breath. "You might be surprised to know that, but most of what I know is based on rumors and guesses. Humans are not privy to the inner workings of the Kra-ell society, not even a human like me who has Kra-ell blood in her."

She'd almost blurted out 'a human whose grandfather is Igor's second-in-command,' but she had stopped herself at the last moment. It was better that they didn't know she was so-called connected, especially since that connection didn't make her any more knowledgeable or important than the other humans in their community.

"How many of each category of people are there?" Marcel asked. "Purebloods, hybrids, and humans. Adults, children, males, females. We need to know what we are up against."

She cast him a glare. "I hope that you are not thinking about attacking a community that has children and other innocents just to free some stuck-up Kra-ell females."

"We are not," Tom said. "But we need to ascertain the risk to us."

"What risk? And to whom? Igor wouldn't have sent me to snoop around if one of ours hadn't found the Safe Haven website so fascinating that she spent unreasonable amounts of time on it. Was she looking for compellers who could do for her what you did for me?"

Tom smiled. "I have no way of knowing what that person was looking for. I'm not a mind reader. I need those numbers, though."

Sofia shifted her gaze away from Toven. "I don't know the exact numbers."

"Ask Toven to make her tell us," Turner said.

The god didn't have to be told. "Give it your best guess. How many purebloods, hybrids, and humans are there in your compound?"

Sofia looked at him with hurt in her eyes. "There are over a hundred purebloods. Twenty or so of them are children and teenagers. More or less the same number of hybrids, and about a hundred and twenty humans, of whom about a quarter are children."

"What's the male-to-female ratio?" Marcel asked.

She gave him the same hurt look she'd given Toven. "The adult purebloods are divided almost equally, just a little tilted toward males, but together with the children, I think there are about sixty males and forty females. The hybrids have many more males, the ratio being closer to four to one. Humans, as you'd expect, are divided more or less equally."

"Igor must have an inner circle," Toven said. "How many are in it?"

"Sixteen males." Sofia let out a breath. "It's easy to figure out who they are. They don't have collars around their necks."

"Collars?" Marcel asked.

She nodded. "All the other purebloods and hybrids wear collars. No one knows what they are for. Some think that they denote rank, others think that they have location trackers in them." She rubbed a hand over her thigh. "But that's probably not true since he obviously implants them in us. But then the hybrids and purebloods hardly ever leave the compound other than to hunt, so maybe the collars are really trackers."

"Do the females get to leave the compound at all?" Toven asked.

"They have to. They need to go hunting."

That was a good morsel of information. Maybe they could save Jade by waiting for her to go on a hunt and pluck her from outside the compound.

Kian silenced the microphone. "That's how we will get her out. We just need a tech guy to remove the collar. It's probably booby-trapped."

Turner nodded. "I hope it's not some alien technology we can't handle. The compulsion is another issue. If we remove the collar, she will still resist us because of the compulsion. We will have to knock her out."

"I don't have a problem with that. Although given that it took three immortal males, two of them Guardians, to take one hybrid female down, we will need to tranq her." Kian reactivated the microphone. "Ask her if the females are escorted by guards when they go hunting."

"Are the females allowed to hunt without an escort?" Julian asked.

"They need to get a pass," Sofia said. "This informs security that they are out, and if they don't come back, I guess guards are sent after them. But I've never heard of something like that happening. They all come back." She rubbed a hand over the side of her neck. "Maybe there is something in those collars that forces them to return, or maybe Igor's compulsion is enough."

From what Kian had heard so far, he was convinced it was both. Igor didn't leave anything to chance.

"How come you got to leave and attend university?" Mia asked.

"For some reason, Igor is much laxer with the humans living in the compound. He either feels sorry for us because of our short lifespans, or because his control over us is even stronger than the control he has over the pure-bloods and hybrids. Some of the human descendants of the Kra-ell are sent to study all kinds of subjects. I thought that the compulsion was enough to keep track of us, but evidently I underestimated Igor's paranoia."

She huffed out a breath. "As if I would voluntarily endanger my family." She chuckled bitterly. "He obviously didn't expect me to encounter a compeller who was more powerful than him."

"What about the close-circle females?" Toven asked. "I'm sure his original cell had some females in it."

"I don't know. I wasn't told. All the females have collars."

Toven nodded. "The Kra-ell are a traditionally female-ruled society. The females in his cell were supposed to be the leaders. When he chose to make his community patriarchal, he subdued all the females."

"So the rumors were true," Sofia whispered.

"Where did you hear the rumors?" Marcel asked.

She shrugged. "Here and there."

Obviously, she was trying to protect whoever she'd heard it from, but she shouldn't worry about them using that information against her source. She was most likely protecting them from Igor.

"Is it against the rules to spread rumors like that?" Toven asked.

She snorted out a laugh. "What do you think? Igor is the undisputed ruler of the compound. Even to suggest that he's not supposed to be is considered treason."

"Makes sense." Toven crossed his arms over his chest. "That's why Navuh keeps his mate hidden. He doesn't want anyone to know that she outranks him."

"Is Navuh a Kra-ell?" Sofia asked.

"He's not, but he has a lot in common with your Igor."

"He's not mine," she hissed.

"Ask her about their training," Kian told Julian.

"How well are the purebloods and the hybrids trained?" The doctor repeated the question. "And do the females get training too?"

"The males train a lot, and the females train as well, but not officially. Igor allows it because they need an outlet for their natural aggression, but he never takes them out on missions."

"Finally, we are getting somewhere," Kian murmured. "Ask her about those missions."

"What missions do Igor and his males go on?" Julian asked.

"I don't know. I don't even know when they leave and when they return or what their objectives are. It's not like he makes it official."

Toven regarded her with a sad smile. "Does he come back with new females?"

She shook her head. "As far as I can tell, there haven't been any new adult females brought into the compound during my lifetime. I might not have been aware of what was going on when I was little, but I'm sure that none were brought in over the last two decades."

Turner closed the microphone before turning to Kian. "Jade's tribe must have been one of the last to get raided. He either didn't need more females or didn't know how to find more tribes."

"What I want to know is how he found the ones he had."

"Maybe they had trackers on them," Turner suggested.

"Then why did he wait so long to raid them? He could've done it decades ago."

"Maybe he was still getting organized and didn't have the means." Turner opened the mic. "Ask her about weapons."

When Julian repeated the question, Sofia shrugged.

"I don't have a clue. The guards at the gates have rifles, but no one carries weapons inside the compound. Their training is old-fashioned. It's hand-to-hand, swords, fangs and claws."

"What about aircraft?" Marcel asked.

"None that I know of. I've never seen one take off or land near or at the compound."

Marcel

It seemed that Turner and Kian had heard enough because Julian tapped the tablet, which was the signal that it was time for a break.

"I think we have all we need for now," the doctor said. "It's getting late, and Sofia needs to return to Safe Haven for the next part of our plan."

"What part?" Sofia asked.

"The part where you feed Igor false information. The first thing you need to do is convince him that you are fine and that you are continuing your investigation. That way, he will not send a rescue team for you, or if he has already done that, then he will call them back."

She snorted. "I very much doubt that. I'm the definition of collateral damage."

"Nonsense," Mia said. "He invested many years in your education. He will not want to lose you."

Sofia's expression brightened a little. "I would like to think that, but you are not going to let me be taken back, right?"

"Do you want to go back?" Mia asked, disbelief coloring her expression.

"If you're asking if I'm eager to live under Igor's rule, the answer is no. Most of my life, I've fantasized about a future where I was free to choose the man I wanted to spend my life with, and where I wanted to spend that life." She didn't look at Marcel, but her words cut at his heart nonetheless. "But I didn't even get to say a proper goodbye to my father and my aunts and cousins. I'm going to miss them."

"That's perfectly understandable," Mia said. "But I think they would want you to be free and live your life. They would be happy for you."

Sofia grimaced. "If I don't come back, they will assume that I'm dead."

"We might have to fake your death," Julian said. "We did that for my partner, her mother, and her brother. That was the only way to save them from a Russian oligarch who was after my mate."

Sofia looked at the doctor with a frown. "Did they have to leave family and friends behind?"

He nodded. "My mate had a very good friend who now thinks she's dead, and the same goes for her mother and brother, but they are glad to be free, and they made new friends in our community."

"Will I be welcomed in your community even though my paranormal talent is questionable?"

Toven nodded. "As long as you cooperate with us, you will be welcomed."

Marcel wanted to add that she would be welcomed regardless, but he wasn't sure what Kian's position was on that. She wasn't a random human that Igor had picked up for the job, so they couldn't thrall her to forget what she'd learned and help her settle somewhere else. They would have to invite her into the village, where she would basically live out her life as a prisoner.

That shouldn't make him happy, but on a selfish level, it did. If she was confined to the village, she couldn't betray him, and if her feelings for him were real, maybe they could resurrect their relationship.

Was he once again letting his dormant romantic hijack his reason?

Sofia huffed out a breath. "I doubt that I can convince Valstar, let alone Igor, that it was just a big misunderstanding, and that you just returned the pendant to me, asked my forgiveness for mishandling the situation, and invited me to stay for another retreat. Neither of them is that gullible."

Julian lifted a finger. "Hold on, I'm getting instructions." He pulled out a pen and a tiny notebook from his shirt pocket and started writing down bullet points.

After several minutes of scribbling, he lifted his eyes to Sofia and smiled. "Here is how you are going to play this.

We were afraid that you were a journalist snooping around the paranormal community we are building, but you managed to convince us that you weren't. We brought a truth-teller to test you, and you were sure that you were done for, but he couldn't tell when you were lying. He was probably a fake, or maybe he couldn't read you because your Kra-ell heritage protected you in some way. He verified that you were telling the truth."

"Is there someone like this in your community?" Sofia asked.

"There is," Marcel said.

"What do I tell him about handling the compulsion attempt on Emmett?"

"You told us that your father is a powerful compeller and your mother is a telepath, and that's the real reason you came to the retreat. You didn't understand why your parents had such incredible gifts, while you did not. You also told us that your father was against you coming because he read about Emmett's crookedness, and when you called him, he wanted to prove to you that he was right, but then Emmett's girlfriend intervened because she knew he would never admit that to anyone other than her. From what you have learned so far, we knew all about compulsion because we had several compellers in our community, including Emmett's girlfriend. The reason we were running the retreats was to collect more people with paranormal abilities and build a community of enhanced people. You suspect that we intend to cross-breed talents to produce an even stronger crop of paranormals, but you don't know that for a fact, and you want to stay on to investigate this for Igor, hoping that he can use the information to his advantage in some way."

Sofia pursed her lips. "It's a good story, but you're forgetting one thing. Igor can make me tell him the truth."

Julian cast her a blindingly bright smile. "Don't worry about that. We've developed an earpiece that will filter out the compulsion. He can't compel you while you are wearing it."

That was good to know, but given that Eleanor and Emmett were both compellers, and she had no defense against them now that her mind was free from Igor's compulsion, they could and would force her to do whatever they wanted.

"What are you going to do to the compound?" Sofia asked again.

It was probably futile, but maybe she would be able to chip away at them until they told her their intentions. Not that she could do anything to prevent them from doing it, but she might be able to warn Igor.

"For now, we are just collecting information," Toven said. "We already know the general area, but knowing the exact location will save us trouble." He pulled out his phone and typed in something. "That's the area we were searching. Please point with your finger to where the compound is."

His tone was laced with coercion, and she found herself pointing to the spot despite a tremendous effort to resist.

"I detest compellers," she murmured under her breath.

Tom chuckled. "I get it, I really do, but we all have a job to do here, and it's saving people from unnecessary suffering, current and future."

"Right." Sofia grimaced. "Igor probably tells his victims the same thing."

Ignoring her muttering, Tom handed the phone to the doctor. "Find the location on the tablet. We need a larger map for Sofia to tell us how to get there."

"I don't know how to get there," she said.

"Nice try." Tom patted her shoulder. "I know that you do."

"Don't worry," Mia said. "I promise you that we will not do anything that will result in harming innocents. If we can't find a way to save them without incurring casualties, we will not even attempt it. I guess Igor does not murder or torture any of the people living inside the compound, just those he steals the females from."

"I haven't heard of him killing anyone." The torturing was a different story. Except, he didn't call it torture. He called it punishment.

Julian rose to his feet and brought the tablet to her. "This is a screenshot of the area." He handed her a stylus. "Please mark the spot with an X and draw the road leading to it."

"Do as Julian says," Tom said with compulsion lacing every word.

Her hand moved on its own, marking the spot and a squiggly line leading from the closest paved road to the compound. Since no one asked, she didn't mark the hidden entrances to the underground tunnels. There were four of them, but even though each tunnel was no longer than a hundred feet across, there was no other way to cross the rivers with a vehicle. There were no bridges, and swimming across the freezing water was not something any humans would want to attempt.

Igor had chosen an excellent strategic location for his compound. The place was hidden from above by a dense wood, and to get to it on the ground required precise knowledge of where it was and the entrances to the four separate tunnels.

Julian looked at the map and frowned. "I don't see any bridges marked over these rivers."

Sofia shrugged. "Not everything is marked on maps."

Let them try to find the entrances to the tunnels. It would take them days even with the map.

When Julian's tablet made a whoosh sound, Sofia knew that he'd sent the picture to his boss, the one who had been listening and probably watching everything through the tablet's camera and microphone.

"We should head back," Julian said.

Toven rose to his feet, and the rest followed, except for Mia of course.

"How does it feel to be free of the compulsion?" He offered her his hand,

"Am I free?" Sofia took his hand reluctantly.

"You are freer than you were before. I apologize for having to compel you to tell us what we need to know, and I can add my promise to Mia's that we will not harm any innocents in your community."

"Why should I believe you?"

He shrugged. "You don't know us, so you have no reason to. But we have no reason to make promises to you either. We can force you to cooperate with us whether you want to or not."

That was true.

"Goodbye, Sofia." Mia extended her hand. "I hope to see you again when you join our community. I'm certain you will like it much more than your old one."

"I will just be exchanging one prison for another. At least in my old one, I was allowed to attend university and have the illusion of freedom."

Kian

When Sofia had left with Marcel and two of the Guardians, Julian turned the tablet's screen on.

"Good job, Toven," Kian said. "You managed to free Sofia's mind without turning it into mush."

Toven took Mia's hand. "I couldn't have done it without Mia's power. It was such a wonderful experience working with her. She somehow turned my power from a sledgehammer into a cozy blanket. From now on, I will only compel with her by my side."

A fetching blush crept up Mia's delicate face. "I didn't feel anything. I truly don't know what I am contributing, if anything."

"But you can observe the results," Toven said. "When I first compelled Sofia, I managed to penetrate only the most recent layer, and I caused her a bad headache. When you enhanced my power, I managed to free her from

Igor's compulsion, and she felt no discomfort whatsoever."

"Mia is a valuable addition to our arsenal," Turner said. "But the bottom line is that we can't take on Igor's compound with the force we have. If we want to strike a preemptive blow and eliminate the threat of him before it manifests, we need to think creatively."

"Turner summed it up succinctly." Kian uncapped his bottle of water and took a sip. "Igor has about a hundred trained male warriors, and we know that the Kra-ell females are formidable as well. We are talking about a hundred and fifty purebloods and hybrids, each of which is three or four times stronger than a Guardian. But even if we were equally matched in strength, we don't have that many Guardians. If I pull everyone who ever served on the force from all three of our locations, that's only ninety-four."

"They seem to have less advanced weaponry than we do, and they mainly train to fight hand-to-hand." Turner leaned back in his chair. "Also, they might be susceptible to Merlin's sleeping potion. The weak solution he prepared for the children in Vrog's school knocked Vrog out just enough for Richard to take him down. If he prepares a stronger solution, we can test it on Vrog and Emmett and dial it in for quick results. The problem is that we don't have a pureblood to test it on."

"What about attacking from the air?" Julian suggested. "We could use precisely calibrated missiles to target Igor's office and take him out. We can get Sofia to draw us a plan of the compound."

Turner shook his head. "Sofia doesn't know enough. We need to get our hands on one of the pureblooded males. We can do that by kidnapping one or two of them while they go on a hunt, or we can try to move Sofia out of Safe Haven along with the cat that has her implant and see if anyone follows her. I have a hunch that we will catch a pureblood, maybe even Valstar. If the communicator in the pendant is as basic as Marcel thinks, its range can't be too great, and someone needs to be nearby to forward the signal all the way to Karelia."

"We should plan on both," Kian said. "Whichever comes to fruition first will be the one we will execute."

Turner nodded. "Agreed."

"Can you get your local guy to snoop around over the next week?" Kian asked.

The contractor was supposed to end his operations on Friday, local time, which was two hours ago. He was probably still in the area.

"I can, but I don't think it's a good idea to send humans snooping around Kra-ell on a hunt. We don't want them finding out about aliens, and those Kra-ell are pretty obviously not human. Especially when they chase an animal down to drink its blood."

"There is another problem," Toven said. "Even if we send Guardians to do the recon, and they manage to catch a male, take off his collar, and bring him in for questioning, Igor would know that one of his was plucked off the hunt and he will lock down the compound. We don't want to give him advance warning. The only way I can see that working out is for me to be there and compel the information out of the male and then thrall him to forget what happened to him. One problem with that is that if Igor suspects anything, he can compel the guy to bring up the suppressed memories. The other problem is that Mia can't run around in the forest."

Kian shook his head. "I don't feel comfortable risking you like that. I don't want you or Mia anywhere near that compound."

Toven frowned. "What good is having a god on your side if you are not willing to use me? I'm the best weapon in your arsenal, and I'm willing to lend myself to the clan whenever you need me."

"I appreciate that, but let's keep that formidable weapon for Armageddon, shall we?"

Mia chuckled. "Don't forget that you have two of those. Put Toven and Annani together, and you can take down Navuh, Igor, and the gods' homeland."

"That's a bit of an exaggeration." Toven wrapped his arm around Mia's slim shoulders. "But thank you for the vote of confidence."

"What about the noise cannon?" Julian asked. "The Kraell have sensitive ears like we do, and the noise cannon could knock down the entire compound without causing any casualties. Just a lot of ear damage."

"I like the way you think," Turner said. "That might be an option if we decide to attack. The problem will be the humans in the compound. The damage to their ears might be irreparable. Not to mention what it can do to the children."

"Right." Julian rubbed his jaw. "So that's not a solution either."

"We can use the exoskeletons to even out the strength disparity," Kian said. "But that still leaves us with not enough warriors. I'm not willing to leave the village, the Scottish castle, and the sanctuary undefended to launch an attack on the Kra-ell."

Turner chuckled. "You might have enough warriors if you are willing to think outside the box. You have an entire army stored in your catacombs. You could wake them up, have Toven compel them to his will, and voilà, you have a formidable force to unleash on Igor. Not only that, you can turn some of them into gardeners, cleaners, builders, and whatever else you need workers for."

Kian grimaced. "I'm not a hopeless romantic like my mother, and I will never let those monsters loose on women and children who cannot defend themselves. They've been monsters for too long to change, not even with the help of Toven's compulsion."

Turner shrugged. "It could have been fun to watch the Kra-ell females tear them to shreds."

Kian shook his head. "You have a sick sense of humor."

Turner grinned. "Thank you."

"Have a great day at work." Eric pulled Darlene into his arms. "Are you coming back to have lunch with me?"

"I sure am." She wound her arms around his neck and kissed him softly. "Are you cooking again?"

Eric chuckled. "Are you sure you want me to?"

The pasta he'd made for lunch the day before had been barely edible. The noodles had come out soggy, and the ready-made sauce had been too salty. He'd grated a mountain of Parmesan cheese on it to give it some taste, but it wasn't enough to save the dish.

"You'll get better with practice." She cupped his cheek. "I promise to eat anything you cook."

"That's true love for you." He kissed the top of her nose. "Now I have proof."

She smiled. "I thought that I proved it to you last night."

"That was just you enjoying my body. There was no sacrifice involved."

"True, but love is what made it spectacular." She pulled out of his arms. "I have to go. I'm already late."

Yesterday he'd walked her to the lab, and he would've loved to do it again, but he had a few phone calls to make. After that, he was going to do a deep dive on YouTube, watching cooking videos.

"I hope to wow you with something special when you come home for lunch, but if I produce another culinary disaster, I'll compensate by wearing an apron with nothing underneath."

She laughed. "Now you've made sure that I won't be able to concentrate on work."

"That was the idea. When we are not together, I want you to be thinking about me."

"I do." She kissed his cheek before opening the door. "All the time."

Smiling, Eric closed it behind her and went to sit on the couch. Being with Darlene was pure joy. He couldn't help comparing this incredibly supporting and loving relationship with the mess that his marriage had been.

There had been tender moments, and he'd thought that he was in love, but the bad stuff outweighed the good, even without taking the infidelity into account. His ex's volatile temper, the anger tantrums that had come out of nowhere, the bruises she'd caused that he'd hidden with clothing to save himself the need to lie about how he'd gotten them. How had he endured that for so long?

Why had he?

He was a handsome fellow if he said so himself, pretty smart too, and a pilot. He could have found someone else easily. His damn stubbornness, his refusal to call it quits, that was what had kept him chained to a disaster.

Perhaps it had been the Fates' way of preparing him for Darlene. He might not have appreciated her gentle and giving nature if he hadn't gone through the ordeal with his ex.

Now, he couldn't imagine life without her, and the thought of losing her terrified him. The fear was like a hungry beast, gnawing at his insides and infusing him with an unbearable sense of urgency. That was why he was beating down his possessive instincts and orchestrating her transition with Max's help.

Hopefully, he was doing the right thing.

With a sigh, Eric picked up his phone and dialed Bridget's number.

She answered right away. "How are you doing?"

"I'm doing fine. My gums are a little swollen, but they don't hurt yet. I can't believe that I'm actually looking forward to the pain."

"It will come. What can I help you with?"

That was Doctor Bridget. No beating around the bush with her.

"I have a question. I know that it hasn't been done before, but I want your opinion. Can a female Dormant's transition be induced by two different male immortals? I won't have fangs for another six months, and I'm afraid that Darlene doesn't have the time. I ran the idea by Max, and he's willing to do the biting while I do the other part." He took a breath. "He says that I will need to be chained down so I don't attack him, but I don't think it will be necessary. I'm not a violent person by nature."

For a long moment, the doctor didn't reply, and he wondered whether he'd shocked her into silence. "What do you think?"

"Frankly, I don't know. We speculate that insemination is a catalyst, enhancing the venom's potency. Theoretically, it shouldn't make a difference whether both are produced by the same male or not, but since there is also a bond involved, I would be wary of introducing competing catalysts."

That was an angle he hadn't considered. "I think that Darlene and I have already bonded. I feel a connection with her that I've never felt before. That's why I'm willing to do this crazy thing. I can't bear the thought of losing her because we didn't do everything we could to induce her in time."

"Fear is a powerful motivator." Bridget sighed. "As a scientist, I should encourage this experiment, but as a friend, I'm conflicted. Darlene can probably wait the additional six months and still transition successfully. She's Toven's granddaughter, so her immortal genetics are strong. That being said, I don't want to recommend waiting and bear the responsibility for her not making it."

"That's precisely the position I am in. Bottom line, do you think it will work?"

"It should, but it's not guaranteed. On the other hand, nothing will happen if it doesn't work. Darlene just won't transition, but at least you will know that you've done everything you could."

"That's how I think about it too."

"Is Darlene willing, though?"

"She's not crazy about the idea, but Max and I figured out a way to do that with minimal involvement on his part, and she's semi-comfortable with that."

Bridget chuckled. "I don't need to hear the details. Good luck to you all. Let me know how it goes."

"I will. Thanks, doc."

Marcel sat next to Sofia in the backseat of the minivan, but without Julian, they had plenty of space. Not that it made a difference either way. He could have been on another continent as far as emotional closeness was concerned.

She hated it.

If he was being a dick, she could at least lash out at him, but he was polite and soft-spoken as always, just distant.

The two guards accompanying them weren't talking between themselves either, and the silence in the minivan was oppressive.

Shifting, she faced Marcel. "I know that Tom was talking about Jade when he told me about the slaughter of the males and the kidnapping of the females. I always wondered why she loathed Igor so much, and why she tolerated being his prime female despite that. Maybe she's looking for a way to avenge her people, and that's why she found Safe Haven's paranormal program so fascinating. A powerful compeller like Tom could release her from Igor's compulsion and then she could kill him, but to do that, she needs to have access to him."

"What about the other females?" Marcel asked. "Do they find him less loathsome?"

"They all want to be his prime, but Jade is the most powerful, and that's why he tolerates her. She gave him a daughter, which as you know is rare. Not that it matters. Igor prefers a son to be his successor."

She might be disclosing too much information, but at this stage, it wasn't important. The inner workings of the Kra-ell society wouldn't give them any military insight into the compound, so it wasn't relevant. It was just something she knew Marcel would find fascinating and it would encourage him to engage in conversation with her.

Maybe he would even reciprocate with information about his people. She still doubted that paranormal abilities were the only thing distinguishing them from regular humans. The story about finding the three hybrids while looking for people with paranormal talents also didn't make sense. If those hybrids could pass for humans, they wouldn't disclose their deepest secret willingly. Being the progeny of aliens and their inhuman longevity put them at tremendous risk.

Then again, Tom or another powerful compeller could have forced the information out of them, so there was that.

"He murdered Jade's sons," Marcel said quietly. "He most likely did the same to the other females that he brought to the compound. We know that Jade is a strong compeller in her own right, so she might have been able to retain more of her independent thinking. The others might not have been as strong, and he compelled them to forget their loss, or did something else to make them want him despite what he did to their males."

Sofia was grateful for the information Marcel had shared and horrified by the tragedy that had befallen Jade. She didn't know how old the female was, so when Tom had told her about what Igor had done to her people, she hadn't thought about Jade having male children that had been murdered along with the other males.

"Thank you for sharing this with me, but I wish I didn't know that. Poor Jade." She let out a breath. "I never thought I would say that about her. She's so strong and so condescending. She is not very likable."

"She's not." Marcel gave her a tight smile. "The three survivors from her clan don't like her, but they respect her, and two of them still feel loyal to her."

"What about the third?"

"They had a falling out, but he would still help her if he could."

Sofia nodded. "It demonstrates that he's a good person."

Marcel pursed his lips. "Most people have some good and some bad mixed in. You said that even Igor wasn't all bad."

She chuckled. "In his case, the scale tips heavily to the bad side."

What about her grandfather? Had Valstar been involved in the slaughter?

Probably.

He'd killed children.

The realization pulled a gasp out of Sofia. "Mother above, my grandfather is a monster."

Marcel tilted his head. "Does he belong to Igor's inner circle?"

She nodded. "He's under Igor's compulsion, though. Everyone is. But he doesn't have a collar around his neck."

"Does your mother?"

"Of course. Even Igor's daughter with Jade has one. Not that she would ever attempt to escape. Her life is charmed despite not having a chance to become his successor and having a bitchy, demanding mother. She's treated like a princess."

"In a traditional Kra-ell community, she would be the ruler. Not because she's Igor's daughter, but because she's Jade's. From what you told me, Jade is the most powerful female in the compound."

Sofia nodded. "So if your people ever get rid of Igor, Jade would become the next leader?"

That wouldn't be a great improvement.

Jade was ruthless, and she wasn't kind, and she didn't even try to hide her low opinion of humans. If it were up to her, they would all be just servants and farm workers. At least Igor accepted that humans were as intelligent as the Kra-ell and were useful for more than breeding and menial jobs.

"I don't know," Marcel said. "The people who were born into Igor's rule are used to his patriarchal regime. They might be resistant to things going traditional again. The best would be a new system that is not gender-based. A new democratic era for the Kra-ell, where those who are the most capable and willing to serve their community get elected with the help of a confidential voting system."

Sofia snorted. "That doesn't work all that well for humans, who are much less hotheaded than the Kra-ell. Democracy is not suitable for everyone." She leaned back. "Besides, Jade found a way to teach the children about the old ways of female rule with her stories, so the concept would not be completely foreign to people. I wonder if she did that to prepare the next generation for her own rule."

"How did she manage to do that under Igor's nose?"

"She used Eleanor's tactic to circumvent Igor's compulsion. She uses fables and fantasies to plant the seeds of ideas in the children's minds."

"That's gutsy of her. How come he didn't forbid it?"

"Most people think about those stories as just that. They don't think about the hidden meanings." She gave him a tentative smile. "It's like what Da Vinci did with his paintings. He couldn't speak out about the church's narrative, so he hid his message in his paintings." She chuckled. "I didn't notice anything unusual about The Last Supper until I read the *Da Vinci Code*. After that, it became glaringly obvious to me that the apostle on the right was a woman. There are only two people without beards in the picture, and the other one has really big hands. Her hands are small, and they are demurely clasped in front of her."

"I get what you're trying to say. We've all seen that picture countless times, but until someone pointed the anomaly out to us, our eyes glossed over it."

Vrog

Vrog's heart was pounding as he took the steps up to Kian's office two at a time, but it wasn't due to exertion. Emmett had only shared with him and Aliyah the bare minimum of details about Jade's situation, and he was eager to learn more.

"Good morning, Vrog." Kian motioned to the conference table. "Please, take a seat."

"Good morning." Vrog nodded his head in Turner's direction.

The guy's presence at the meeting meant that things were getting serious and that Kian was considering helping Jade, but Turner might not be the best person for the job. Vrog had heard about his hostage retrieval operations, and the guy was supposedly the best in his field, but he was used to rescuing humans from other humans.

The Kra-ell were a much more formidable adversary.

Kian put a bottle of water next to each of them and sat down. "You are probably wondering why I invited you to join us this morning."

"I assume that it has something to do with Jade. Did you find out anything more about where she's being held?"

"We know the exact location, but we don't know much about what we are dealing with. I hope that you can help us with that."

Vrog's heart sank. He wasn't a warrior, and he knew nothing about strategy. He'd hoped that Kian had a plan. "I only have experience with Jade's tribe and how she ran things. It was also a long time ago. I wouldn't know the first thing about the security measures her captors employ."

"Since we assume that they all came on the same ship, we can also assume that they received similar training, which they maintained after getting shipwrecked." Kian leaned back in his chair. "Let me bring you up to speed about what we've learned so far."

When he was done, Vrog's fangs were fully elongated, and he suspected that his eyes were glowing blood red. Nevertheless, he was a civilized male, and he kept his tone level when he was finally able to respond. "What do you need from me?"

"I need to know about the training regimen of pure-blooded and hybrid Kra-ell in Jade's tribe. Did all of them train? Just the warriors? What weapons did they train with?"

"All the pureblooded males trained. Their job was to protect the tribe. The females trained as well, but it was more of a sport than warrior training. Their job was to lead and produce the next generation. The hybrids were different. Jade chose only those who had the aptitude for combat to train as warriors. I was smart and good with numbers, so she put me in charge of supervising the tribe's investments in various businesses. Others had different jobs. The hybrid females were treated almost the same as the pureblooded ones, just with no authority. Nevertheless, all the hybrids were regarded as second-class tribe members, including the females."

"What about technology?" Turner asked. "How advanced were they?"

"Jade was very technologically savvy. She used what she knew to make money for the tribe."

Turner looked at Kian. "She or one of the others in her original group must have had engineering or scientific training. Using technology is simple. Building it requires learned skills."

"True." Kian took a sip from his bottle. "If I were stranded on an alien planet, and my ship was destroyed, I would become a caveman and a hunter. I wouldn't know how to build any technologically advanced things. The clan had knowledge thanks to Ekin's tablet that Annani appropriated, but we didn't know what to do with it until our people learned the basics of engineering from humans." He looked at Vrog. "Do you know who the tech person was?"

"I guess it was Voltav. Jade always took him with her on her business trips, and now that I think about it, I didn't see him training as often as the others. Jade herself was pretty knowledgeable, though. I don't know if she arrived with the knowledge or learned it from Voltav and human sources."

"What about weapons?" Kian asked.

"We had semi-automatic pistols and semi-automatic combat shotguns, but the purebloods preferred mode of fighting was hand-to-hand. They also trained with swords and other cold weapons, and they did some target practice with the guns, but not often."

"Sofia reported the same thing." Kian pushed the bottle away. "We have an advantage in that regard. The problem is that Igor's compound is full of innocents, including children, and we can't just bomb the place. So far, the noise cannon seems like the best option, but that's problematic as well because of the humans, and especially the children."

"A noise cannon?" Vrog asked.

"It's a device that can incapacitate humans and immortals by producing a loud noise," Turner said. "We would need to test it on a Kra-ell to see if it affects you the same way."

"I volunteer," Vrog immediately offered.

"Thank you," Turner said. "Testing it on you will be very helpful in gaining data on how it affects hybrids, but we need to catch a pureblooded male to see how it affects them. Also, we can't make any plans before we know more, and only a pureblooded warrior will have all the information we need."

"Right." Kian looked at Vrog. "How much stronger are the purebloods than the hybrids?"

"As you would expect, they are stronger. In a hand-to-hand fight between a similarly trained pureblood and a hybrid, the pureblood will win. If the hybrid was better trained, he might be able to hold up longer, but he will eventually lose."

"We might need your help to catch one. Can we count on it?"

"Of course. But just to remind you, I was never trained as a warrior, and I'm a hybrid. I don't know how helpful I would be."

"We are still figuring it out, and we might end up not needing you. I just want to know that I can count on you if needed."

"Of course. I'm sure Aliyah will gladly help as well." Vrog smiled. "You shouldn't discount her just because she's a female. She's very strong, and she's also resourceful."

Kian drummed his fingers on the table. "I don't like using females in combat, and I don't care if that makes me a relic or a chauvinist, but perhaps we can utilize Aliyah in some other way." He looked at Turner. "What do you think?"

"I'll put her name on my list of assets."

During the drive back to Safe Haven, Sofia had been making an effort to get back into Marcel's good graces, and despite his resolve to stay firm and not succumb to her charms, his resistance was slowly eroding.

The truth was that it was working both ways.

Sofia had been suspicious of their motives, and she'd resisted sharing information as best she could to protect her loved ones. But the more they'd talked, and the more she'd learned about Igor and what he had done to Jade, the more inclined she seemed to believe that their agenda wasn't conquest but liberation.

Perhaps if he told her about Turner's suspicions with regard to the tracker, she would be even more inclined to cooperate with them, provided that they didn't endanger her family.

And that was a problem he didn't have a solution for. If Kian chose to attack her compound, there would be casualties no matter how diligent they were to protect innocent lives.

Hell, even some of Igor's inner circle could be decent people who had been coerced into doing his bidding. With his compulsion power, he was like a god, or rather a devil.

At least the gods had done their best to appear benevolent. Igor had made no such effort.

They entered Safe Haven's outer security ring when Marcel finally decided to share it with Sofia. "I looked up the pendant you were given to communicate with Valstar and Igor. It's not very sophisticated, and it can be bought online. The design is also very tacky, and it looks cheap. In comparison, the tracker we removed from your body is state-of-the-art. I don't even know how he got a piece of such advanced technology. Maybe he brought it with him from the home planet."

Sofia frowned. "Is there a question in there somewhere? Because I don't know anything about alien technology or where he got it. I've never seen anything in the compound that looked like it wasn't human made, but that doesn't mean much. Igor might be hiding the good stuff."

Marcel had to smile. It didn't even occur to her to wonder about the discrepancy between the two pieces of equipment she'd been given, one knowingly and one unknowingly.

"We talked about it, and we have a hypothesis. We think that you were given a simple piece of technology for communication because you were supposed to get caught. The tracker would have led Igor, or whoever he sent to trail you, to our base or headquarters or wherever else he thought you would end up after getting caught. Somehow, you've outsmarted everyone, though. Our instruments didn't pick up on the transmission. I guess you used your daily runs to get a few miles away from Safe Haven and activated the communicator there."

"I did, but Valstar told me to find a secluded spot where no one could overhear me."

"Did he tell you to get far away from Safe Haven?"

She shook her head. "The first day, I went on a walk on the beach, looking for a good spot, but when I was stopped by one of your guards, I got scared and decided to walk much farther than I planned." She tilted her head. "Do you monitor transmissions to and from Safe Haven?"

He nodded. "We are conducting classified research here."

"Is it something that Igor might be interested in?"

"Not likely, and I doubt that he suspected what we're doing, but the fact remains that the device you were given was not very sophisticated while the tracker was. It might not mean anything, but it seems suspicious when combined with your lack of experience and that you haven't been told what you were supposed to look for."

Sofia let out a breath. "When Valstar trained me for the missions, we got a little closer, and in my naïveté, I thought that he finally approved of me, but I was so damn wrong. I was worthless to him. If he expected me to get caught, he should have at least warned me so I could say goodbye to my family, but he's just the cold-hearted bastard I've always known he was." She shook her head. "He's much worse than that. He's a cold-blooded murderer of children. How old were Jade's sons?"

"I think they were adults, but I'm sure there were male children among the slaughtered too."

Vrog had said that he found the rings that the adult males had worn, and he counted all of them. He hadn't mentioned children, who probably hadn't been given rings yet, but since the remains had been incinerated, there was no way to know.

"It makes me so angry." Sofia crossed her arms over her chest. "I wish I could see Valstar just one more time so I could spit in his face."

Marcel's suspicion made sense, and it had Sofia seething with anger. The nerve of her damn grandfather. If not for everyone else she cared about in the compound, she would have led the attack against it herself.

Yeah, right.

She was just a human, completely helpless even in comparison to a Kra-ell child. They were so damn strong.

As Marcel opened the door to Leon's office, the first thing she noticed was the cat perched on the windowsill. It was orange colored and fat. The new carrier of her tracker, no doubt.

As they joined Leon, Eleanor, and Emmett at the conference table, Leon got to his feet. "Say hello to Cecilia." He lifted the cat into his arms. "She likes to be petted." He handed her to Sofia.

The cat settled into her arms as if she'd known her forever and started purring.

"I think she likes me." Sofia smoothed her hand over the cat's soft fur. "We didn't have any pets in the compound, but my roommate at the university had a cat. Her name was Hydra, and she was black and white and kind of skinny." Thinking about the friend she was probably never going to see again, Sofia teared up. Stroking Cecilia helped hold the tears at bay. "Is the tracker already inside of her?"

Leon nodded. "Anastasia is really fond of Cecilia, and she warned me that if anything happened to her because of the tracker, she wouldn't let me in her bed for at least a year." He smiled. "But that's an empty threat because my Ana wouldn't last two days without me."

The love in Leon's tone tugged at Sofia's heartstrings. She wanted Marcel to talk about her like that, but those kinds of warm feelings were a thing of the past. He was nice to her, but he still felt cold.

How could he have just turned off his feelings like that? Was he a machine?

He sat next to her and gave the cat a perfunctory pat on the head. "Why did you choose this cat if she's so dear to Anastasia? I've seen a couple of others roaming the grounds."

"One belongs to Riley, and she would have thrown a fit if anyone had even suggested using hers. Cecilia and Albert don't belong to anyone specific, but Albert is much more active. The tracker would have moved too erratically throughout the resort to look as if it was inside a person."

Sofia chuckled. "I didn't know that I moved as much as a lazy cat."

"Do you have the pendant?" Marcel asked.

"It's here." Leon pulled it out of his desk drawer. "I suggest that we take the cat and the pendant to the spot that Sofia previously used to communicate with Valstar, but she should rehearse what she's going to say first."

Evidently, someone had given Leon a full update about what had been discussed in the glass house, and it hadn't been Marcel. It had to be Tom or the mysterious boss who'd been listening through the doctor's tablet.

"She also needs an earpiece," Marcel said.

"Right." Leon pulled a small case out of his pocket and handed it to Sofia. "It might be a little tricky to use the earpiece from the pendant on top of those. You will have to hold it really close."

She opened the case and looked at the two earpieces inside. They looked like a regular pair of earphones, just a little bulkier. "How do they work?"

"It's really quite simple. They are built on the same principle as translating earbuds, but instead of the machine voice talking in a different language, it just repeats the words spoken into it, and it filters the compulsion sound waves. For it to work, it needs to fit very snugly, so none of those waves enter your ear. That's why it is made from a material that molds to the ear canal."

He took the case from her and took out the earpieces. "You put it in like this." He demonstrated. "To activate, you tap on it once, and to deactivate, tap twice. Put them in, and let's practice it."

"I'll take the cat." Eleanor lifted Cecilia off Sofia's lap. "Make sure that you don't have any cat hairs on your hands when you handle the earpieces. You want the seal to be really tight."

Sofia examined her hands. "I don't see any hairs, but maybe I should wash them first."

"That's a good idea. After you get the hang of using them, we will start coaching you on what you're going to say to your contact."

Nodding, she rose to her feet. "Where is the washroom?"

"I'll show you." Eleanor handed the cat to Emmett, who immediately transferred it back to Leon.

"He's not a cat person, is he?"

Eleanor laughed. "He only likes animals he can drink from."

Marcel

Marcel was sure that Eleanor's comment would clue Sofia in to Emmett's real identity, but she just smiled and followed Eleanor out of the room.

She knew what hybrids looked like, and she should have figured it out by now. But the truth was that Emmett looked human, even more so than Vrog. Only Aliya looked alien. Perhaps the hybrids in Igor's compound looked more like Aliya than Vrog and Emmett.

"Should we tell her?" Marcel asked Leon.

"Tell her what?"

"That Emmett is a hybrid, and that he's the reason Jade has been spending time on the Safe Haven website."

"First, let's see how she does with the story we want her to tell and how well it is received. If all goes well, we can tell her, but I don't really see the need. It doesn't make a difference to her one way or another. She's human, and her affinity is with the other humans in the compound. She hates her hybrid mother."

That was true. During all of their conversations and the many times she'd mentioned all the people she would miss, Sofia hadn't said a thing about her mother. The female was like a stranger to her.

When Sofia and Eleanor returned, Sofia put in the earpieces with Eleanor's help and tapped them to activate.

Leon checked her ears. "You need to push them more firmly inside."

When she did, he motioned for Eleanor to test it.

"Sofia. Stand on one foot and touch your nose with your finger."

A wide grin spread over Sofia's face. "You sound like a different person, and no, I will not stand on one foot."

"Awesome." Eleanor smiled. "Now take them out, and we will repeat the test. Maybe I'm just not strong enough of a compeller."

When the test was repeated without the earpieces, Sofia obeyed the command with a grimace. "I hate compulsion. It's really vile."

"I won't argue with you on that," Eleanor said. "Put the earpieces in the case, and let's rehearse your story."

For the next hour, Emmett and Eleanor refined the story and made comments about Sofia's acting, or rather her overacting. She sounded rehearsed, and no matter how many times she tried to get better, she still sounded as if she was reading a script.

She was either a really bad actress or an excellent one who was trying to convince them that she was bad.

"It's no use." She threw her hands in the air. "He's never going to buy my story."

"I have an idea." Marcel got to his feet. "Pretend that you are trying to convince me of your story. Talk to me as if I'm Valstar or Igor."

Sofia took in a deep breath, and as she looked at him, her expression sent chills down his spine. She seemed frightened and unsure, and as she spoke again, she sounded like a scared child who'd been summoned to the principal's office, or worse, a prisoner facing her prosecutor.

He hated to see her like that, especially since she was talking to him, but her performance was much better. She'd still mumbled and got lost for words several times, but that could be explained away by her anxiety.

"That might pass," Eleanor said. "I wish we had more time, but the longer he doesn't hear from you, the more difficult it will be to convince him that everything is back to normal and that you are no longer a suspect."

Sofia sighed. "Let's do this." She reached for the cat and cradled Cecilia in her arms. "She will give me courage." She kissed the cat's head. "Won't you, sweetie?"

Marcel felt his heart squeeze. The poor girl had no one to turn to for comfort other than the cat, and he was a jerk for not being more supportive of her.

Wrapping his arm around her narrow shoulders, he leaned and kissed her temple. "If she gets heavy, I'll carry her the rest of the way."

Sofia gave him a small smile. "It's okay. I can carry her. She gives me warmth."

Marcel knew that she wasn't talking about the physical sensation. The cat showed her more affection than he had since the whole thing exploded in Emmett's office, and she had no one else to lean on.

Sofia

Was Marcel warming up to her? Or was he just trying to be nice to boost her confidence for the call?

Probably the second one, and how sad was that.

Maybe she shouldn't pine for a guy that could form an instantaneous ice shield around his heart. Now that she was free to choose her man, she should find someone stable and free of emotional issues. Someone who would remain steadfast no matter what.

Yeah, dream on. As if such a creature exists.

Life was a long journey of disappointments and betrayals, and the sooner she resigned herself to that reality, the sooner her heart would stop bleeding. Every time she'd allowed herself to hope that someone other than her father and her aunts and cousins actually cared for her, she'd been disappointed. But perhaps instead of complaining, she should count her blessings for having a family who cared about her.

Some people didn't even have that.

When they got to her spot, she pulled the earpieces out of their case and stuffed them into her ears.

Marcel checked that they properly sealed her ear canal, and then took the cat from her.

"Do you need a moment alone?" he asked.

Hearing the male machine voice was jarring. It made her realize that Marcel's voice hadn't been completely devoid of emotion before.

Eleanor's pinched expression communicated that having a moment wasn't an option. She was there to ensure that Sofia didn't stray from the storyline they'd agreed upon, but since she had the earpieces in, all Eleanor could do if she strayed from the script was to stop the communication like she had done in Emmett's office.

Except, how would she know?

Sofia wasn't going to talk with her grandfather in English, and neither Eleanor nor Marcel had said anything about knowing Russian. Maybe they were wearing translating earpieces too?

Eleanor's long wavy hair was down and covered her ears, but Marcel wasn't wearing any.

"That's okay. Just give me some space so I can pretend I'm alone."

Nodding, he took a couple of steps back and motioned for Eleanor to do the same.

Sofia took a deep breath, pulled the earpiece from the pendant, and pressed it against the other device.

That had been the easy part. The hard part was pressing the picture to activate the communication. Her hand shook so badly that she had to close her eyes and focus on forcing her finger to move.

"Sofia," Valstar barked into her ear. "What happened?"

Even with the machine voice, she knew it was him. Igor's word choice would have been different.

"It was a close call. I didn't know that Emmett's girlfriend was listening in on the line from the other room, or that she was a compeller and realized right away what was going on. She knew that Emmett wouldn't have admitted to any wrongdoing, especially not to a stranger on the phone. She terminated the call and accused me of being an undercover journalist. I panicked. I didn't know what to do, but the tears did their job." She chuckled. "Marcel came in and calmed things down."

"They took away your pendant. How come they gave it back?"

"I came up with a great story." She repeated what she'd rehearsed with Eleanor and Emmett. "They brought a truth-teller to verify that I wasn't lying, and I thought that I was done for, but he didn't detect the lie. I don't know if he was a fake or if my Kra-ell heritage protected me, but somehow, he believed me, and I was so relieved.

Anyway, after that, they invited me to join their community and gave me my family heirloom back." She chuckled. "They might be paranormally talented, but they are not very technologically savvy. They didn't realize that the pendant is a communication device."

"Hold on for a moment," Valstar said. "Igor wants to speak with you."

"Of course."

Sofia closed her eyes and prayed to the Mother of All Life for the earpieces to work. If they didn't, the charade would end in a moment.

"Good afternoon, Sofia," the robotic voice said. "Valstar informs me that you managed to wiggle out of the situation you were in and even gain a foot up. Is that true?"

"Yes. I pulled out the best acting of my life. After they heard my sad story about my supernaturally talented parents and how desperate I was to have a useful talent like theirs, they felt sorry for me and invited me to join their paranormal community. I suspect that their goal is to crossbreed the various talents and produce even more enhanced humans. Not only that, but they also seem to have lots of money, so they must have rich backers. I would love to stay on and continue the investigation, sir. I don't know if any of this information will be beneficial to you, but in the long run, a new breed of enhanced humans might pose a problem. They have compellers, telepaths, empaths, remote viewers, and all kinds of other talents that are great for spying."

"Indeed. That was good investigative work, Sofia. Keep me informed."

Sofia's knees nearly buckled from the relief. "I will, but it's not safe for me to call every day. I managed to get away today, but I have a feeling that they will be watching me closely from now on. I can't do it anywhere near the lodge because I think they are monitoring outgoing signals. Every time I need to call, I go on a run or a walk of at least three miles. The exercise excuse worked before when I wasn't a suspect, but if I keep doing this every day, eventually, they are going to appoint a guard to accompany me, and I won't be able to communicate at all."

"Call whenever you can. The information you collect about those paranormal talents is important. Who else other than Emmett's girlfriend is a compeller?"

"I met a guy named Tom and another one called Malcolm, but they told me they have more. Not everyone is in Safe Haven. They have other locations."

She purposefully avoided mentioning that Emmett was a compeller. It just seemed like something Igor shouldn't know. The other names were meaningless to him, but he knew who Emmett was.

"Are they strong compellers?" he asked.

"No, sir. They must be very weak. Emmett's girlfriend and Tom tried to compel me to tell them the truth about my so-called father, but they weren't able to break through the shields you've built for me. I stuck to my story."

"Good job, Sofia. Find out what you can about their other locations and about the kinds of talents they have and the talents they intend to breed."

"Yes, sir."

Marcel

Sofia ended the call and pumped her fist in the air. "I did it!" She turned in a circle, leaned toward Marcel, and kissed the cat on the head.

Reaching for the pendant, he double-checked that the transmission had been terminated and ran a compact handheld device over it to make absolutely sure that it wasn't transmitting.

Sofia gave him a hurt look, but that hadn't been avoidable. He still didn't trust her a hundred percent.

His Russian was so-so, but it had been good enough for him to understand the conversation and approve of Sofia's act, but he might have missed some nuances of meaning that might have clued Igor in. Later, when they returned to Leon's office, he would listen to the translation of the recording that the earpiece had made.

Leon had been listening to it all along, and so had Eleanor through her translating earpiece, but neither of them spoke Russian with any fluency. Perhaps they should ask Morris to listen to it just in case the three of them had missed something.

"Good job." Eleanor clapped Sofia on the back. "That was your best performance yet. Do you think Igor bought it?"

"He had to. He used compulsion to get me to tell him the truth, and he's never had trouble compelling me before. I just hope he's not aware of the translating earpieces trick."

"He's not," Marcel said. "We developed the technology in-house."

Sofia took off the pendant and handed it to him. "Please, lock it back in the safe. I don't want it anywhere near me."

He put it in his pocket. "Let's head back. I'm sure you're hungry after all the excitement."

"What now?" She fell in step with him. "What am I supposed to do here?"

"There is one more thing." Eleanor handed her the cat.

When she cast Marcel a sidelong smirk, he wondered what she was plotting. With her gaunt face and small, dark eyes, that smirk looked evil.

"How do you feel about Marcel?" She shocked Sofia and him with the question. "And you have to tell us the truth."

"That's not fair," he murmured.

Eleanor shrugged. "All is fair in love and war. Or is it the other way around? War and love? I will have to look it up." She leveled her intense eyes at Sofia. "Talk, girl."

Sofia turned her face to him and swallowed. "Before everything went wrong, I could see myself spending the rest of my life with you. I was falling for you. But even though I had no choice in any of this, I don't think you can forgive me, and I don't want to give my heart to someone who can close his off so easily."

The pain in her eyes was unbearable, and the need to forgive her and take her into his arms was overwhelming, but he'd been in a similar scenario before, and the price he'd paid for his weakness was so monumental that it still haunted him. He could not allow himself to be vulnerable again.

"Our infatuation with each other is irrelevant at the moment. We are dealing with a crisis, and only when the crisis is resolved, can we revisit our feelings. For now, this has to stay on ice."

"Ice indeed," Sofia murmured. "What do you consider as crisis resolution? Capturing Igor and executing him?"

"He didn't commit any crimes against my people. It's up to the members of his community who he has wronged to decide how he should be punished."

"They are under his compulsion. They can't do a thing against him. If they could, Jade would have killed him a long time ago."

"Maybe that's the solution," Eleanor said. "We smuggle earpieces to Jade, and she takes care of Igor for us."

Marcel shook his head. "That's not going to help with the previous layers of compulsion she carries. We need to smuggle her out, have Tom free her mind, and send her back with earpieces."

Sofia nodded. "That could work. How are you going to smuggle her out, though?"

"We can capture her during one of her hunting runs. Does she ever go alone?"

"I don't think any of them ever go alone. Hunting is a social activity for them, and they usually go out in groups. But I'm not a good source of information on anything related to the purebloods or the hybrids. I've been gone most of the past seven years, and when I'm back, I spend my time with my family in the human quarters. You need a Kra-ell, preferably a male. Maybe you can capture one, question him, compel him to not say anything, and release him right away, so no one would notice that he'd been missing."

Those were all good ideas, but they were all fraught with difficulties and pitfalls that could have disastrous results. Turner was working on a plan, though, and Marcel trusted the guy to work the kinks out.

"That went well," Turner said after listening to the recording.

Being immune to compulsion and familiar with the Russian language, he was the best equipped to listen to the unfiltered version and ascertain that it had indeed gone as well as it seemed.

"Igor seemed doubtful at first, but when he thought that he compelled Sofia to tell the truth, his tone changed."

"What's your take on him?" Kian asked.

"That wasn't enough to form an opinion. He sounded calm and confident. He wasn't rude or obnoxious, and he didn't sound worried. He's pretty much emotionless, which makes him more dangerous, not less."

Kian chuckled. "It takes one to know one. But you are not entirely unemotional, just a little stunted."

Turner smiled indulgently. "I pride myself on my logical mind. The heart usually interferes with rational thought."

"Indeed, but I wouldn't trade places with you. My intuition is no less important to me than my analytical ability." In fact, he trusted his intuition more than he trusted his mind.

"Intuition is nothing more than your subconscious mind using all the information it has stored and making calculations behind the veil. There is nothing mystical about it."

"Says the man who invoked the Fates in this office the day before."

Turner shrugged. "We need to decide on our next step. As I see it, we have several options now that Sofia has bought us time with her great performance. We can up the ante and send the cat on a trip, see if anyone follows, and if they do, capture them. But that would cost us the element of surprise, and the time we gained will be wasted." Turner crossed his arms over his chest. "I'm just thinking out loud. If Sofia indeed has a tail and we capture it, the game will be up, and it will move into Igor's court. He will realize that something more than what Sofia told him is going on, and his next step will be to get Jade to admit what she's been doing. Sofia did well by not mentioning that Emmett was a compeller, and Igor didn't ask about him, so I assume that he didn't compel the truth out of Jade yet. I assume that he's not confronting her about it because he wants her to keep communicating with Safe Haven so he can find out who and what is involved."

"That has been his goal from the start," Kian said. "He knows something is up, but he doesn't know what, so he sends Sofia with a double purpose. If she finds out something, that's great, and if she doesn't and gets caught, he can follow the tracker inside of her and find out where she was taken. Right now, we have the advantage of him believing in a plausible story that leaves Jade out. As far as he's concerned, she might be interested in finding more about paranormal talents to see if she can enhance hers in some way and get free from his compulsion, or she's looking for information about other talents that might assist her in some way."

Turner nodded. "Another thing he might do if we capture the tail is retaliate against Sofia's family, or he might flee. He might also assume that we fed Sofia lies, and that she told him the truth as she knew it. If that's the case, he will send more people to investigate what's going on here."

"Isn't the same true for capturing one of his males during the hunts they go on?" Kian asked. "That will also serve as an alert and trigger the same chain of responses from him."

"I'll contact my guy in Russia and ask him to get one of those tiny bug drones. From what we've learned from Sofia, the Kra-ell are using old-school methods to hide, and they probably don't have sophisticated equipment to detect a small drone."

"Their eyesight and hearing are just as good as ours. They might be able to detect it without any equipment."

Turner didn't seem to share his concern. "If Navuh and his warriors didn't detect the one we sent to Areana, I don't think the Kra-ell will either. It's a risk, but of the several options we have, none is risk free. If Igor believed that everything Sofia told him was true, then the safest option might be to do nothing and fake her death. We can ignore Jade's communication attempts and close the case as is."

That was what Kian had proposed to do from the start, and Turner had been of the same opinion, but they both had been drifting closer and closer to choosing a confrontation.

Kian sighed. "I thought we agreed to send a team of Guardians to scope out the compound's area."

"It was one of the options, but it hasn't been done yet, so you can still change your mind."

"Should I?" Kian rubbed the back of his neck. "I really don't want to open this can of worms. On the other hand, it's always better to deal with a threat before it becomes even more menacing."

"I think that we should keep gathering information, but we should avoid doing anything rash. We can send the cat on a trip along with Eleanor, who can pose as Sofia, and we can see if she picks up a tail, but we don't engage with the tail. We start monitoring the tail's movements and collect more information."

"What if the tail notices our tail?"

Turner lifted his hands in the air. "As I said, every move we make carries a certain risk, but doing nothing is also risky in the long run. You need to decide what you want to do."

"As usual, you are right. We need to collect information."

"Can I take Cecilia with me to my dungeon cell?" Sofia held the cat to her chest as Marcel opened the door to the cottage.

"I think you can." Eleanor patted her arm. "I'll let Anastasia know that she is with you." She turned to Marcel. "You will need to stay around and let Cecilia out to do her business in the yard."

"I have to finish up a few things in the lab, but after I'm done, I can come back here."

Sofia glared at him. "If you don't lock me up, I can take the cat out to pee and poop myself."

Eleanor cast Marcel a pitying glance. "I'll get you two lunch and something for Cecilia. She's been a very good sport about all of this." She turned around and walked back the way they'd come.

Following Marcel down the stairs, Sofia rubbed her chin against the cat fur, eliciting contented purring from her.

If only it was so easy to please Marcel.

His nonanswer to her earlier admission of feelings toward him shouldn't have surprised her. He'd been cold and remote, with occasional flares of slight warmth that hadn't been enough to console her, but they had been enough to keep her hope alive. Marcel also hadn't said that it was over between them, only that the timing was wrong, so perhaps there was still a small chance that he would get over what he perceived as her betrayal, but he was slow to forgive, and she needed him right now.

Sofia was alone, frightened, and needed more than someone else's cat for comfort and support.

"Why do you have to lock me up?" she asked as they entered the bunker's living room. "Didn't I do everything you wanted me to do? Besides, it's not like I have anywhere to go." She grimaced. "And not just because Safe Haven is so isolated. I would have nowhere to go even if we were in the middle of Manhattan."

Looking uncomfortable, Marcel rubbed a hand over his jaw. "Where would you stay? You can't go back to sharing a room with Roxana, and I can't invite you to my bungalow."

"I can stay here. Just don't lock me up, so I can at least let the cat out."

"I need to ask the boss."

She rolled her eyes. "Seriously, Marcel. What am I going to do? Tell the guests of the retreat that I'm the progeny of aliens?"

He looked lost for words.

Sofia plopped down on the couch with the cat in her lap. "When do you need to go to the lab?"

Marcel sat next to her. "I'll go after lunch."

For a long moment they sat together in awkward silence, with the cat's purring the only sound.

"You know that I didn't want to do any of this," Sofia said as she stroked Cecilia's back. "I was compelled, and my family was threatened. If I didn't bring Igor good results, he would have taken it out on my family, and those were not empty threats. He's ruthless. I hated every moment of the deception. And just so you know, my instructions were to ask you to call Igor. I protected you by shifting his attention to Emmett and convincing him that Emmett knew much more than you did. Imagine how bad things would have been if I hadn't. He could have gotten you to reveal everything, and Eleanor wouldn't have been there to stop you."

He nodded. "The Fates must have intervened."

"The Fates?" He'd said something about the Fates before, but she had thought that he'd meant to say fate.

"I meant fate. We were saved by fate."

She huffed. "You were saved by Sofia. You are just too stubborn and self-absorbed to admit that."

The door opening at the top of the stairs saved Marcel from having to respond, which was a blessing.

Getting him to forgive her by insulting him was probably not a good tactic.

Smelling food, Cecilia jumped out of Sofia's arms and rushed up the stairs.

"I need some help here," Eleanor said. "And get the cat before she trips me up."

They both rushed after the cat, with Sofia grabbing the tabby and Marcel relieving Eleanor of half of the packages she was carrying.

"What did you do?" he asked. "Rob the kitchen?"

"More or less. Emmett is teaching a class, so I decided to have lunch with you two."

As Sofia set the cat's food down, Cecilia attacked it with vigor she hadn't seemed capable of before.

Once Eleanor and Marcel were done setting up the table, the three of them sat down to eat, or rather her two companions did. Sofia was too upset to feel hunger.

"You can't just keep me locked up down here," she said. "You can compel me to keep everything a secret so I can go back and enjoy the retreat. There is another whole week of it. I would also love to spend time with Roxie. I miss her."

She could really use Roxie's cheerful company.

"That's an option." Eleanor eyed Marcel. "You should talk to the boss. About everything."

He frowned. "What do you mean?"

Eleanor waved with her fork. "If you pulled the stick out of your ass for a moment, you would know what I meant."

Sofia gaped at the woman in stunned silence, and so did Marcel. Did anyone ever talk to him like that?

He shook his head. "I don't know what I did to court such a remark, but I don't appreciate being spoken to like that."

Eleanor rolled her eyes. "Yeah, yeah. You are so prim and proper, and I have the tact of a bull in a china shop. I just hate seeing you two tormenting yourselves needlessly. Sofia likes Marcel, and Marcel likes Sofia. Sofia is brave and admits her feelings, while Marcel is a chicken and refuses to pull said stick from that unmentionable place." She grinned. "There, I said it politely."

Sofia couldn't help the giggle rolling out of her mouth. "I think you've just become my favorite person." Well, perhaps her second favorite after Roxie, but Roxie wasn't there to call Marcel on his bullshit.

Eleanor laughed. "Sorry, doll, but I'm taken. You are a looker, though." She winked at Marcel. "Isn't Sofia beautiful? She's so graceful, so delicate, and such a fascinating contradiction of soft and hard, gentle and assertive. If I were a single male, I would be drooling all over her."

Marcel's cheeks turned crimson. "Would you stop it already? What has gotten into you?"

Eleanor pretended to sniff the air. "I guess it's the pheromones you two are emitting."

What had gotten into Eleanor? Why was she suddenly siding with Sofia?

She wasn't the type to forgive and forget.

Was it the affinity at work?

Was affinity even a thing between immortals and Kra-ell?

Or perhaps it was something else.

Up until not too long ago, Eleanor was an outsider who'd been brought in for the simple reason that they couldn't let an unscrupulous newly turned immortal roam free, so they'd been forced to keep her locked up in the village. Until she'd proven her loyalty and her worth to the clan, she had gone through her share of well-deserved mistrust and outward hostility. Was she empathizing with Sofia because she was now in a similar situation?

"This is not about you, Eleanor. When you were captured, you were just a single operator, and you were not a serious threat to us."

All levity left Eleanor's expression as she trained her dark eyes on him. "You're right. It's not about me, and my history is very different from Sofia's. What I did was of my own volition, not because I was coerced or threatened, and yet look at me today. I'm a proud member of the community, and Kian trusts me. If he can change his mind, so can you. Stop being so stubborn and look at the facts."

Her words struck a chord, and he didn't have a proper retort. Kian was the most suspicious and paranoid person he knew, and yet he'd welcomed Eleanor into the fold and trusted her with one of the clan's most important endeavors.

Running the paranormal program put her in charge of finding new Dormants.

"I'm confused." Sofia looked at Eleanor. "What did you do?"

Eleanor shook her head. "My case is different from yours, but it gives me perspective. I can put myself in both your shoes because I've been on both sides." She looked at Marcel. "I had a bad history that made me bitter, mistrustful, and selfish. I thought that the whole world was against me and that the best way to deal with it was to be a solo operator and look out for myself." She turned to Sofia. "I plotted to capture paranormals and sell them to the highest bidder. When I was captured, I became part of this organization not because they wanted me, but because they were stuck with me. I was a compeller with no morals, and it was dangerous to let me go. Most regarded me as the enemy, and rightfully so, and at the beginning, I resolved to learn all I could about them so I could find a way to escape or even profit from the situation. But then I had an epiphany, which was prompted by the kindness and selflessness of a person who had the least reason to be nice to me. I also realized that for the first time in my life, I was surrounded by other people who were like me, and even though most were hostile to me, I could see myself finally belonging somewhere. I set out to prove myself and become an asset to the community, and that's what I did. Some still look at me with hostility in their eyes, but most have accepted me."

Sofia shook her head. "I didn't set out to do anything bad or good to any of you. I was forced into the role."

"I know." Eleanor reached over the table and took her hand. "Which should make your assimilation much easier than mine. The advice I can give you is to not give up. You escaped a bad situation, and if you play your cards right, you can join us and start a new life. I didn't leave anyone behind, so that wasn't an issue like it is for you, but you basically don't have a choice. You're not going back, so I suggest that you embrace what fate has given you."

Sofia cast a quick sidelong glance at Marcel. "It's not all up to me."

"That's why I delivered my little speech to both of you." Eleanor pushed to her feet. "I'll leave you alone to talk it out." She lifted her hand and pointed a finger at Marcel. "My advice to you is the same. Rise above the past, embrace what fate has shoved in your face, and say thank you."

With that, Eleanor walked around the table and started up the stairs.

They both remained silent until the door at the top of the stairs opened and closed.

"She's a very opinionated lady," Sofia said. "What's her story?"

"She told you the gist of it. I can't say more without revealing details that I shouldn't."

"Who am I going to tell? She can compel me to silence."

"True." He got to his feet and walked over to the wine cabinet. "It's difficult for me to trust, and even more difficult to give my heart. I've been made a fool before." He pulled a bottle of Chardonnay and two glasses out of the cabinet.

"You told me about your ex."

"I didn't tell you even a fraction of the story."

"Is that also a secret that you are not free to share?"

He huffed out a breath. "Revealing this secret will only affect me. It has no bearing on the organization." He uncorked the wine and poured it into their glasses.

He needed a moment to think, or an hour, or a day, but Sofia was looking at him with a pair of pleading eyes, and he felt compelled to give her something. Instead, he lifted his glass. "Cheers."

"Cheers." She clinked her glass to his. "I promise that whatever you tell me will never leave my lips." She cringed. "Unless someone compels it out of me. I really dislike compellers, or rather what they can do. I like Eleanor a lot. She's such a straight shooter, and that's so refreshing."

Eleanor wasn't easily likable, and it had taken him a while to warm up to her. The shameful truth was that if she were a male, he would have accepted her abrasive personality a long time ago and focused on her impressive achievement record instead. But because she was a female, he'd expected her to be softer, kinder, and more careful about the way she expressed herself.

Talk about a double standard.

It dawned on him that he was applying the same double standard to Sofia. If she were a guy, he would have been much more forgiving and understanding, but because she was a female, and he had a bad history with women, she was a suspect despite the mitigating circumstances.

Nevertheless, being aware of his prejudice didn't help dissolve it. He didn't trust himself to think objectively where a female he was attracted to was concerned.

He put the glass down. "I want to believe you. I yearn to, but I've been burned so badly in the past that it's very difficult for me to trust. I haven't told this story to anyone, and I probably never will."

Sofia's face fell. "I understand. You don't need to tell me if you don't feel comfortable sharing your past with me." She looked up at him. "Would it help if I told you more about my own life?"

"Yes, please."

"Not all of it was bad. In fact, most of it was good."

Sofia

Sofia talked for what seemed like hours.

She told Marcel about her childhood growing up in the compound, about being raised by her father and her aunts, about her cousins and things they'd done together. Most of her stories included Helmi, and talking about her cousin had brought both a smile to her lips and tears to her eyes. The memories were mostly sweet, but knowing that she wouldn't have any more of them made her want to crawl into bed and cry until she fell asleep from exhaustion.

"I'd better talk about something else." She rubbed her eyes. "The university is a safer topic." She let out a breath. "I was so excited to get selected. It was a little scary to live outside the compound but not enough for me to turn the offer down." She chuckled. "Not that I had the option to say no. Igor's word is law. Thanks to my father and my aunts, I was fluent in Finnish, so language wasn't a barrier, and after the first semester, I felt at home there."

"But you still had to return to the compound once a month."

"I did, but it was no hardship. I wanted to see my family and friends, and the twenty minutes in Igor's office to reinforce his compulsion was a small price to pay."

"What about boyfriends? I'm sure you had many during your seven years at the university."

He hadn't told her about his girlfriends, so she wasn't inclined to tell him about her love life, but she didn't want to flat out refuse either.

"I dated a little, and I had a total of two serious boyfriends."

"What happened with them?" Marcel asked.

She caught his eyes glowing again and wondered what emotion had triggered the glow. He still refused to admit that they did that, but she'd noticed it was usually when he was excited, angry, or aroused.

"There isn't much to tell. It was difficult to develop meaningful relationships with guys when I couldn't tell them anything about my family or introduce them to my parents."

"You could have said that you were an orphan."

"Then they would have wanted to meet my adoptive parents. I said that I was estranged from my family and didn't provide a reason, but I don't think they believed me. They probably thought that I was embarrassed about them." She emptied her glass of wine and sighed. "It doesn't matter. I couldn't maintain those relationships anyway. At some point, I had to go back to live in the compound, and it wasn't as if I could bring someone with me."

"Yeah, I get it. It's the same in our community."

Sofia arched a brow. "No paranormal talent means no admission?"

"Something like that." Marcel refilled her glass.

They were on their second bottle of wine, and she was tipsy, bordering on drunk. Marcel seemed much more at ease and relaxed. Maybe it was because of the wine, or perhaps it was because her stories had entertained him. In either case, she liked seeing him smiling for a change.

"How did your father and aunts get to be in the compound?" he asked.

"They couldn't tell me. People never talked about their pasts before arriving at the compound, and as a kid, I thought that they were all just born there like me. Later, when I became aware that the rest of the world didn't know about the Kra-ell or live in blended communities with aliens, I started to wonder where the humans came from, and given that they were more or less slaves, I figured that they were captured and brought in against their will. I imagine that it started with the women." She grimaced. "The purebloods needed breeders because there weren't enough of them to provide genetic variety."

"You said that your father speaks fluent Finnish. He might have been brought from the outside."

She shook her head. "Not necessarily. My grandmother also lived in the compound, so she might have been the first to be brought in, or she might have been born in there as well. She died before I was born. They don't have a doctor for the humans in the compound, only a nurse, so if someone suffers a heart attack, they are not likely to survive."

"What about when they get sick?"

"For routine non-emergency stuff, they take people to a human doctor and compel their help."

"That's better than nothing."

"I know. The Kra-ell treat the humans they keep better than other humans would have treated their captives, and the Kra-ell are not kind-hearted creatures. They are brutal, and they don't believe in love. But they have a code of honor that they take very seriously."

Marcel chuckled. "According to their tradition, or maybe religion, Igor's community is an affront to the Goddess. Her chosen are females, and they are the ones who are supposed to be in charge of breeding. Not the males. The females' job is to select the best males to father the next generation, and I bet they use several criteria to determine who's the best. It's actually a better system. Males tend to be visual, and they choose the mothers of their children based primarily on their looks and level of attractiveness. If they focused on her intelligence, her drive to succeed, and her kindness and empathy, they might have produced a better next generation. I wonder if that's why the Kra-ell religion came up with the idea of giving females all the power. After all, life is about producing the best next generation."

"The Mother of All Life holds all of her children precious." Sofia smiled. "Until I got to the university, I didn't know how prevalent Christianity was. I read about it in books during my studies, but since everyone in the compound revered the Mother, I never gave it much thought. It occurred to me later that Igor must have compelled the humans to abandon their original religion in favor of the Mother."

"So, you were home-schooled?"

"I studied in the compound. We had a school for the children, and we got books and everything else we needed. Naturally, I got a fake high school diploma to get accepted into the university, but I had all the education I needed." She winced. "Except for everything that had to do with computers, but I wasn't the only one. There were other students who came from poor villages that didn't have free access to technology."

"I know that the compound has access to the internet."

"Igor and the others in charge have access. Jade probably got special permission because she teaches the Kra-ell children and needs to obtain new material from time to time."

"I'm surprised that she chose to be a teacher. She doesn't strike me as the nurturing type."

Sofia sighed. "I thought so too, but she has a soft spot for the little ones. I can't think of her without being overcome with sadness. She is so brave to keep on going despite what happened to her. It never occurred to me before that some of the Kra-ell also had been brought to the compound against their will. I did wonder, though, about the discrepancy between the ratio of boys and girls born to the purebloods and the ratio of adults. I thought that they were getting rid of the boys somehow." She shivered. "I don't know what's worse. What they actually did, or what I imagined."

"You have a good heart, Sofia." Marcel leaned toward her and kissed her forehead. "You are a good person."

"Do you really believe that? Or are you just saying it to cheer me up?"

He smiled. "I know that I'm not the best judge of character. You'd be surprised to know that my natural inclination is to see the good in people, but since that tendency has cost me dearly in the past, I'm very careful before I make up my mind about a person's character. Still, unless you are the best actress ever born, everything you've told me indicates that you are a good person despite having a lousy mother and growing up in an alien community. Your father and your aunts must be terrific to compensate for your mother's neglect and indifference."

"They are." Hot tears accumulated in the corners of her eyes. "I miss them so much."

Marcel

As Sofia's eyes misted with tears, the last of Marcel's resistance crumbled. She'd been so animated in her story of growing up among the Kra-ell and having a happy childhood despite living in captivity that he couldn't conceive of it being fake. He wanted to meet her father and tell him that he had done a great job, and that he should be proud of the daughter he'd raised.

But what right did he have to tell the man anything?

Could he promise him that from now on his amazing daughter would be taken care of? That he would protect her? Love her unconditionally?

Fates, how Marcel yearned for that to be so.

He wanted to embrace Sofia, to tell her that he had fallen for her as well, and to save her family so she wouldn't have to miss them. But he couldn't do that. He had no idea how to save her family, but he could love and protect her, provided that he managed to pull the stick out of his ass as Eleanor had so colorfully stated.

"Come here." He reached for her and pulled her into his arms. "You are safe now."

"Am I?" She looked at him with doe eyes.

"I will not let anything happen to you." He dipped his head and took her lips in a soft kiss. "And I promise to make it up to you for the sorrow I caused you."

"Am I forgiven?" she whispered against his mouth.

"You were never to blame. I'm sorry that it took me so long to realize that."

She chuckled on a sob. "It wasn't long. It just felt like an eternity."

"Am I forgiven?" he asked.

"I was never angry at you." She scrunched her nose. "Well, that's not true. I was angry, but I never hated you for how you were treating me because I can't turn off my feelings the way you do. I just couldn't understand how you could shut your emotions down on a dime like that. You knew that it wasn't my fault, that I was a victim in this as much as you were. I never stopped yearning for you, wanting you to look at me with the same fondness and desire you did before." She gave him a sad smile. "Some women are attracted to brooding unemotional guys, but that's not me. I don't find it attractive or sexy. I find it off-putting. I need warmth and affection."

"I didn't turn off my feelings. I just buried them to protect my heart, but the only things I was protecting it from were my own fears and insecurities. Deep down, I knew that you didn't set out to use me."

She winced. "I did, but not really. Valstar and Igor wanted me to find a man who worked in the retreat and seduce him for information. When you started flirting with me, I convinced myself that it could be you, even though I had no reason to believe that you had any useful information. You told me that you were not part of the staff and that you were working on an independent project. When you acted like a jerk, I made plans to seduce one of the teachers. But I wanted you, so when you pleaded with me to forgive you, I decided to play along. I gave myself a great excuse to seduce you so quickly. Usually, I don't move so fast. I take my time getting to know a guy before I get intimate with him." She smiled. "Not that I regret it even for one moment. It was the best night of my life."

And didn't that make Marcel feel like he'd just grown a couple of inches. His knee-jerk reflex was to scent her emotions to make sure she meant it, but the scent of her arousal was all the confirmation he needed.

"Was it now?" He cupped the back of her head. "Do you want to give it another go to make sure?"

"Are you offering?"

"What does it look like?"

"Do you always answer a question with another question?"

He loved to see her spunk and humor come back.

Sofia was a positive person by nature, the glass-half-full type, and if not for him giving her the cold shoulder, she would have weathered her ordeal better. Instead of being the rock of support she'd needed, he'd added to her sorrow and anxiety.

"Let's check out that four-poster and see what other goodies we can find in there. But this time, I'm tying you to the bed."

Her smile wilted. "I don't like those things. I've seen real implements of torture being used to punish Kra-ell who dared to step out of line, and it was horrible. I will never associate those things with anything pleasurable."

Talk about a cold shower.

"Then no restraints for you. I will just give you a little taste of the torment you inflicted on me. I will torture you with an abundance of pleasure."

Her smile returned. "I didn't say that about the restraints. Just about the flogger and the crop and whatever else is stored in that footboard."

"We don't need any of that." He pulled her into his arms, rose to his feet, and carried her to the bedroom. "I laundered the sheets, so we will have a fresh bed to play in."

It wasn't the most romantic thing to say, or the sexiest, but Sofia seemed to like it.

Wrapping her arms around his neck, she tilted her face up and kissed him. "That's very sweet of you. I love the smell of fresh bedding."

Sofia

As Marcel walked with Sofia into the bedroom, he didn't head toward the bed as she'd expected. Instead, he carried her into the bathroom and set her down on the bench in the shower.

They'd done a long walk on the beach and back, so a shower wasn't a bad idea, but it wasn't her idea of sexy reconciliation.

What did she know, though?

Her experience was limited, not just in practice but even in general knowledge. The romance novels she read were tame and sweet, and nothing overly sexually adventurous happened in them. Most of the love scenes were the fade-to-black kind without any explicit details.

"What's your plan?" she asked as he knelt at her feet.

"I'm going to treat you to something special." He took one shoe and sock off, tossed them on the floor outside the shower, and repeated that with the other.

Fearing that her feet didn't smell all that fresh, Sofia's cheeks heated with embarrassment, and she pulled her feet away from him even though he didn't look as if he had smelled anything unpleasant. In fact, given the glow in his eyes, he was excited about what he was planning to do.

"You still didn't tell me why your eyes glow," she said to divert his attention from her feet.

"They glow when I get excited." He lifted onto his knees, pushed his thumbs into the elastic of her leggings, and pulled them down along with her panties, baring her from the waist down. "Now the top." He reached for the hem of her T-shirt and tugged it up, urging her to lift her arms.

When she did, he pulled it off and tossed it on top of the leggings. Her bra was unceremoniously taken off next, and before she knew what was going on, his mouth was on her nipple, licking, sucking, and making her mindless with pleasure. When he switched to the other one, all thoughts about glowing eyes on a human receded to the corner of her mind where she stored other unexplained mysteries that needed further investigation.

"I'm sorry. I just couldn't help myself." He smirked as he toed off his shoes.

As Marcel got undressed so fast that she couldn't track the movements, Sofia added that to the list of mysteries to investigate later. Right now, she was enthralled by the beauty of Marcel's male body.

She'd seen him naked before and had gotten very familiar with his manhood, but seeing it again, fully erect and standing straight from his hips right in front of her face, she couldn't help but reach for it and give it a kiss hello.

With a groan, Marcel pulled away. "Save the thought." He reached for the handheld shower head and turned the faucet on.

After checking that the water was the right temperature, he offered Sofia a hand up and pulled her against his body. "Have you ever made love in the shower?"

"I haven't. Have you?"

"No." He grinned. "It's going to be the first time for both of us, which means that it's going to be clumsy and awkward but fun nonetheless."

She wrapped her arms around his neck. "I like having firsts with you." She pressed her aching nipples to his chest and lifted her thigh between his legs, rubbing it against his erection.

"Wicked woman." He cupped her ass and dipped his long fingers into the seam, testing her wetness.

She loved that his hand was so big that it covered her entire backside. She was a tall woman, and his size made her feel feminine and dainty.

Gyrating her hips to get more of those dexterous fingers, she lifted her leg and wound it around his torso.

He brushed his lips against hers with soft velvety touches, teasing her before licking into her mouth and taking possession of it. As he dipped two fingers into her wetness, pumping into her in sync with his tongue, she closed her eyes and moaned.

"Marcel," she breathed when he let go of her mouth. "Take me to bed."

"Not yet." He turned her around and pressed her against the tiled wall. "Put your hands on the wall above your head and spread your legs."

As she followed his command, a new gush of wetness prepared her for what was coming next.

"Are your eyes closed?" He pressed his hard body into her from behind.

"Yes."

"Keep them closed. If you open them, I'll punish you."

A smile tugged on the corners of her lips. "How?"

"Like this." He pulled back and lightly smacked her bottom.

It was oddly arousing.

"Is that supposed to be a threat?" She was tempted to open her eyes and taunt him to do it once more.

He smacked her bottom again, harder this time.

She laughed. "That's not a threat either."

"We shall see about that."

He didn't do it again. Instead, she felt the head of his erection nudging her entrance, and as she pushed back, he entered her with one swift thrust.

There was a moment of discomfort as her sheath stretched to adjust to his size, but it was over almost as soon as it began, and then she couldn't wait for him to start moving.

"Marcel," she whispered his name.

He didn't move.

Brushing her hair aside, he kissed her neck, and when she pushed against him again, he rocked in and out of her in shallow thrusts.

"Please," she groaned. "I need more."

Marcel was more than happy to oblige Sofia's plea, but making love in the shower had its limitations. He needed to be face-to-face with her, to see the lust and desire in her eyes, to kiss her deeply and pour his soul into hers.

There were also practical considerations.

Sofia was lithe and strong, but she was human, and with his passion awakened after being forcefully suppressed, he didn't know how gentle he'd manage to be, and pounding into her from behind while she was pressed against the tiled wall might get uncomfortable or even dangerous for her.

As he pulled out, she chased his retreating erection by arching back, but as he spun her around and lifted her into his arms, she wrapped her arms around his neck and smiled. "Where are you taking me?"

"Where you wanted to go before. To bed."

"We are wet," she protested as he lay on top of the covers with her on top of him.

He smiled. "I know. You said that you needed more. Take it."

Her puzzlement lasted a split second, and then she was straddling his hips. "Are you mine for the taking?"

"Always."

As doubt flitted through her eyes, he wondered whether it had to do with his attitude toward her during the past twenty-four hours or with him withholding his story about his life-altering experience.

If it was the first, he could fix it, but if it was the latter, it would remain untold.

Marcel feared that once Sofia learned what kind of a man he really was, her attitude toward him would change and never recover. She might not want him anymore.

When she angled his erection toward her entrance and started to lower herself on top of his shaft, all thoughts of the past receded to the corner of his mind where he usually kept them locked up tight, and when the tip breached her entrance, he gripped her hips and helped guide her, but didn't attempt to control her movements.

It was her show, and he was there for the ride.

The perfection of their fit was enough to chase the last vestiges of those terrible memories away, and he gave himself over to the marvelous creature riding him like a prize bull.

Sofia was gentle, keeping her rhythm slow and rocking side to side on each downward glide.

He loved that she wasn't in a rush to bring them both to completion. They were soaking in the intimacy, the closeness that was so much more than just sexual pleasure. With her, it was about love, about the connection, and the pleasure was a side effect rather than the goal.

Love, though?

Was he falling again into the same trap?

He shouldn't be thinking in terms of love until at least a year had passed, and Sofia had proven herself to him beyond a shadow of a doubt.

Except, there would always be doubt, wouldn't there?

As the saying went, once burned, twice shy. For now, he would just stick to liking her and lusting after her.

"Sofia," he murmured as his climax neared, his fingers digging into the soft flesh of her hips.

She slowed down even more. "Not yet. I want this to last."

Marcel wanted to smile, but his fangs were already elongated, and he didn't want to thrall her yet. "There are many more to come." He let go of one of her hips and reached between their bodies to gently tease her clit.

"Cheater," she breathed as she undulated on top of him. "That's not fair."

"All is fair in love and war." He kept circling the engorged nub while urging her with his other hand to keep moving.

When she closed her eyes and threw her head back, he kept going with his thumb and rocking up into her to prolong her climax, and when her tremors subsided, he wrapped his arms around her and flipped them around.

"I told you that there was more." He gripped her hands and pulled her arms over her head.

"Yes." She smiled up at him. "Give it to me."

"Yes, ma'am."

His own climax was hovering near the edge, and the need to pound into her was overwhelming, but the need to prolong the closeness and look into her eyes was even greater. Once he bit her, she would black out, and then he would lose the connection to her soul and would have to be satisfied with just holding her body until she floated back down.

He wasn't ready for that.

"Your eyes are glowing," she murmured.

He'd forgotten about that, but he was loath to command her to close her eyes. He couldn't get enough of looking into their blue depths.

It was time to tell her about himself, so he would no longer have to hide his fangs and his eyes, but he could never tell her everything.

"It's nothing. Ignore it." Reluctantly, he just closed his own eyes.

Sofia

As Marcel closed his eyes, Sofia mourned the loss of the window into his soul.

He wasn't a normal human. He had paranormal talents, so maybe somewhere down his ancestral line there had been a Kra-ell. Then again, his ability to make her forget things or remember things that had never happened wasn't one of theirs. They were compellers, some weak, some strong, but as far as she knew, none of them could erase memories or plant new ones in human minds.

That must have come from his human genes.

As her pleasure surged again, bringing her to the verge of climax, thoughts of genetics and the mystery of glowing eyes were forgotten, and all she could focus on was the male thrusting into her, and how good it felt to be in his arms.

Sofia had never enjoyed ceding control, and given the precarious situation she was in, that wasn't the wisest thing to do, but somehow, despite everything, she trusted Marcel like she'd never trusted any other man.

He would never hurt her, not intentionally anyway.

In the short time they'd known each other, he'd repeatedly hurt her feelings, but he hadn't set out to do that. He was just inept romantically, and he'd been hurt in the past, so he was being careful.

Was she making excuses for him?

Maybe, but having him hold her arms over her head and thrust into her like he was a sex god with boundless stamina felt too good to question.

When his thrusts became furious, and the bed groaned in protest under them, the tightly wound coil inside of her got released without warning, and as she cried out her climax, she instinctively turned her head to the side, exposing her neck.

On some subconscious level, she knew what was about to happen next, but when the pain from twin incisions registered, it was a shock nonetheless.

She cried out, and her eyes popped open, but all she could see was the top of Marcel's blond head, and then the pain disappeared as if it had never been, and she was orgasming so hard that she felt like passing out from the pleasure.

The euphoria washing over her stole her breath away, and she felt as if she had died and her spirit had left her body.

She was weightless, soaring up over the clouds, and as she looked down, she saw all kinds of ethereal creatures roaming around an idyllic landscape. Beautiful and insubstantial, they looked up at her, acknowledging her passing through their world by smiling and waving.

Were they real?

Had she passed through the veil separating different realities? Or was she in the human heaven?

Those weren't the fields of the brave or the valley of the shamed, and there was no Kra-ell in sight. Was it a near-death experience? Or had she died from too much pleasure, her heart giving out?

The floating, peaceful feeling was too extraordinary to waste on wondering the why and the how of it. Instead, she let go of her earthly concerns, and let herself forget all that she had been told about the human God and the Kra-ell Mother of All Life.

Soaking up the sensations, she was at peace with the universe.

Syssi

"How do I look?" Kian walked into the family room wearing a charcoal suit.

He looked like a god, and if they weren't expecting Amanda, Dalhu, and Vivian to arrive in a few moments, Syssi would have shown him how good she thought he looked.

"You look dashing, my love."

"Da-da," Allegra said in confirmation.

"Your daughter agrees." She kissed her sweet cheeks, twice on each side, but on the third pass, Allegra pushed her away.

"That's it? That's my quota of kisses?"

"Da-da." Allegra lifted her arms, making it clear who she wanted kisses from.

Syssi laughed. "She's her daddy's girl."

Kian lifted their daughter and spun her in the air, eliciting a string of adorable giggles. "That's because I do fun stuff with her."

Syssi shook her head. "It's dangerous. She's still human."

The smile slid off Kian's face, and he hugged Allegra to him. "She should spend more time with my mother."

"She's still too young to transition."

As the doorbell rang, Syssi walked over to open the door.

"Good evening, darling." Amanda leaned to kiss the air next to Syssi's cheek. "I don't want to leave lipstick stains on you."

"You look amazing." Since Syssi hadn't put on any, her lips actually made contact with Amanda's cheek.

"Careful of the makeup." Amanda tilted her head back, avoiding the second kiss coming her way.

"Sorry." Syssi backed away.

Amanda gave her a once-over. "You look stunning yourself."

Syssi looked down at her pale blue cocktail dress. "I love getting dressed without worrying about food stains for a change."

"Good evening." Dalhu pushed the stroller through the doorway, looking dashing in a navy suit. "I can't say the same. I mean about getting dressed for fancy dinners. Most of my clothing is covered in paint stains."

Amanda laughed. "Stuffing Dalhu into a suit was not an easy task. He only did it because he loves me and because I insisted that he couldn't attend Callie's opening night in a pair of jeans and a paint-stained T-shirt."

"I wasn't going to wear a T-shirt. I was going to wear one of those ridiculously expensive dress shirts you got me."

Amanda waved a dismissive hand and walked over to Kian and Allegra, treating each to an air kiss.

When the doorbell rang again, Okidu beat Syssi to the door and opened it for Vivian. "Good evening, mistress. Thank you for coming to watch over the little ones."

Was it Syssi's imagination, or did he sound hurt?

He was perfectly capable of babysitting both babies, but Syssi and Amanda still didn't feel a hundred percent confident leaving him with their daughters. Not because of safety concerns, but because Vivian was so much better qualified for the job, and she didn't mind doing it. In fact, she was jubilant every time she was asked to watch the girls, not that it happened often.

Okidu was there in case Vivian needed help.

"I'm happy to do it." Vivian walked over to the stroller and picked up Evie, who cooed happily at her. "Hello, beautiful people. You all look like models on a cover of a fashion magazine."

"Thank you." Amanda leaned and kissed the air next to both of Vivian's cheeks. "I'm looking forward to my first gourmet meal in the village."

When Okidu cleared his throat, Amanda lifted her hand. "In a fancy restaurant, darling. I adore your cooking. You know that."

That seemed to mollify him.

"Shall we?" Kian put Allegra down on her play mat.

"Da-da?" She looked at him with questioning eyes.

"Dada and Mommy are going to Aunt Callie's new restaurant, and you are going to have fun with Aunt Vivian and Evie until we come back."

Allegra cast Evie a resigned glance and then looked at Vivian and smiled. "Da-da," she said, making it sound like *okay, you can stay.*

"It's amazing how well she can express herself just by changing her tone." Kian straightened his tie. "Thank you, Vivian. Call us if they give you any trouble."

"They won't." Vivian sat on the floor next to Allegra. "They are both wonderful little girls."

"It's a little chilly outside." Okidu handed Syssi a shawl as she stepped out the door.

"Thank you." She draped it around her shoulders.

The restaurant was only a few minutes' walk away, and the warmth coming off Kian's body as he wrapped his arm around her was enough to keep the chill away, but the shawl complemented her dress and made her feel more dressed up.

"How many people did Callie invite to her opening night?" Dalhu asked.

"Thirty-six," Syssi said. "She can't handle more than that until she can get more people to work for her. For the opening night, she invited the council members and their mates, Toven and Mia, and Jackie and Kalugal."

"Are they coming?" Dalhu asked. "I was told that they were isolating themselves to protect the baby."

"Bridget talked some sense into Kalugal," Kian said. "She told him that they were doing the baby a huge disservice by isolating him from human germs. Darius will remain human until puberty, and they can't keep him in a bubble until he transitions. They need to expose him to germs so he can build up his immune system. Once his human body is infected by a specific virus, it will learn how to make antibodies to fight it. The next time he's exposed to the same virus, his body will fight it off without getting infected."

"I hope he listened," Syssi said. "I spoke with Jacki yesterday, and she wasn't sure whether they were coming."

"Who is babysitting for them?" Amanda asked.

"Shamash." Kian chuckled. "I have no idea what the guy knows about babies, but if Kalugal trusts him with his son, who am I to say anything?"

"Welcome." Callie looked nervous as she addressed the small gathering. "Thank you for being my first guests. I hope you enjoy tonight's menu."

They were all seated in individual two-person tables, which felt weird given how well they all knew each other. Callie had designed her restaurant for romantic evenings, but the opening night was different, and Kian had the urge to get up and start combining the small rectangular tables into one long banquet table.

"Say hello to your servers." She motioned for Lisa, Parker, and Cheryl to come forward. "I'm glad that they agreed to work in my restaurant in the evenings and save me from having to do everything myself."

The three took a coordinated bow that elicited a few chuckles and some applause.

"As I explained in the invitation, the menu for tonight is set. It's a five-course meal." She looked at Kian. "Your, Syssi, and Amanda's menus are slightly different to accommodate your vegan and vegetarian preferences."

Amanda chuckled. "The problem kids."

"I can't wait to sample your cooking," Onegus said. "I've heard so much about it."

"Good things, I hope."

"The best." Cassandra adjusted her napkin over her lap.

Annani rose to her feet. "Congratulations on your new restaurant, Callie. I would like to make just one suggestion for tonight." She put her hand on Brandon's shoulder. As the only two singles, they were seated together at the same table. "As much as I love your company, I would love to enjoy everyone's. Can we combine the tables?"

"Great idea." Kian jumped to his feet. "I was thinking the same thing."

As everyone rose to their feet and started moving the tables together, Callie wrung her hands. "I'm sorry. I should have realized that the regular setup wouldn't work tonight. I just wanted everyone to enjoy the place as I envisioned it."

"It looks beautiful." Annani smiled. "Tomorrow night is the couples' mixer, correct?"

Callie nodded.

"They will surely appreciate the intimate setting," Annani said. "When we are done tonight, the boys will return everything back to the way it was."

When the eighteen tables were set in one long row and they had all sat back down, the young servers brought out the appetizer course.

Anandur did the honors of uncorking the champagne bottles and pouring the bubbly into everyone's flutes. "Let's make a toast." He lifted his glass. "To Callie's place. May it succeed and prosper."

"To Callie's!" they all echoed, filling the room with clinking sounds.

As Callie and Brundar sat down, she unfurled the napkin and draped it over her knees. "The advantage of preparing everything in advance is that I can sit with you and enjoy my creations. I wish I had the staff to do everything, though, so I could offer a selection of items like a regular restaurant."

"I offered a solution for that," Turner said. "But Kian didn't like it."

"What's your solution?" Bhathian asked.

"You have a mighty workforce buried in the catacombs, and now that several strong compellers have joined the clan, we can resurrect them and compel them to behave. I think no one here has any objection to using them as a slave workforce. They owe the clan for their actions against it, and for not executing them but putting them in stasis instead. They should be grateful to be allowed to live again."

For a long moment no one said a thing, not even Annani, who Kian had no doubt loved Turner's crazy idea.

"I don't know about that," Anandur said. "The Doomers we captured and put in stasis were murderers and rapists. They weren't like Dalhu or like Kalugal's men." He looked at Kalugal. "What do you think?"

Kalugal put his fork down. "I wouldn't do that. I selected my men one by one, and it wasn't an easy task to find males who were not completely corrupted by my father and who retained a shred of decency. After I relieved them from his compulsion, I worked with them for months, sometimes years, to undo his indoctrination." He sighed. "Don't forget that the human males Navuh used to breed with the Dormants were ruthless, dumb lowlifes. He chose the strongest, the most brutal, and the most mentally limited. His goal was to produce powerful immortal warriors who would obey him blindly. Occasionally, the mothers' genetics triumphed and produced thinking, decent offspring, but since the mothers themselves were the daughters of lowlifes, most of them weren't nice people either." He cast a sidelong glance at Bridget. "Nature trumps nurture, and nurture in Navuh's war camps was even worse than the genetic makeup of those males. I doubt you would find even ten percent of them are worth saving."

"Ten percent is more than zero," Annani said. "Even if one of them is worth saving, we should not dismiss it. I wish we could design a test that could determine that. We talked about it before. We could resurrect a small number of Doomers at a time, test them, and put back in stasis those who failed."

Kian gave her an indulgent smile. "As soon as we have nothing better to do, and no new crisis comes up for a year or two, we can give it a test run."

Yamanu laughed. "That's like saying never. I can't remember any stretch of time that was longer than a few months without something happening that required us to mobilize some kind of defense or evasive tactics, and most of the time, it wasn't even the Doomers' fault."

"Now we have a new enemy to add to the mix," Onegus said. "Or a potential enemy. It still remains to be seen whether Igor of the Kra-ell is our enemy or just a general threat we should be aware of but not actively try to eliminate."

Annani

"That's another reason to use the Doomers," Turner said. "The enemy of my enemy is my friend."

Kian chuckled. "It is true that the Kra-ell might pose a threat to the Doomers as well, but since the Doomers are a much bigger force, they have nothing to worry about from the Kra-ell."

"We don't know that," Turner said. "In pure numbers, you might be right, but we still don't know anything about them. Who knows, maybe they will become our allies against the Doomers."

The dinner was turning into a council meeting, and Callie was probably not happy about that, but since she had chosen to invite the leadership of the clan to her opening night, she should have expected it.

"What is being done in that regard?" Annani asked.

Kian pushed away his empty appetizer plate, which Cheryl rushed to collect. "Turner's contractor on the ground is procuring a miniature drone to fly over the compound, and Monday, we are sending a team of Guardians to Russia to scope the area. Their mission is just to observe. Sofia says that the purebloods and the hybrids go hunting in the area, but since they are all under strong compulsion not to attempt an escape and have location collars around their necks, we can't just grab them." He looked at Toven. "Given your experience with Sofia, do you think you can release them from the compulsion via video call?"

Toven pursed his lips. "Perhaps with Mia's help. Frankly, I didn't expect her enhancement to be so significant, but once she added her power to mine, it became much easier to override Igor's compulsion, and it was also easier on Sofia. When I used just my own power, she got a severe headache and needed to rest before we could continue."

"Go, Mia," Amanda said. "I know you will be a great asset to the clan."

Mia blushed. "I wish I knew what I was doing and how."

"Do you need someone to blow things up?" Cassandra asked. "I've gotten much better at that, both in accuracy and power." She smiled. "My type of explosives won't alert airport security."

Onegus wrapped his arm around her shoulders. "We can use conventional explosives if needed. It's not difficult to smuggle them in or even obtain them locally. In Russia, money talks louder than anything. We don't even need to use compulsion or thralling."

Edna sighed. "How the world has changed, and at the same time, it hasn't. No matter what the political regime is about, it's always about money. Communists, fascists, dictators, monarchs, autocrats, you name it, they are all after wealth and power, and the people they govern are fed fantasies and lies about ideals and morals to keep them compliant, or they are terrorized into toeing the line. Regrettably, we see the same thing happening in democracies, which used to be a little better before they adopted similar tactics of mass control."

As the soup was served, the political talk thankfully moved on to Callie's culinary skills, and the atmosphere lightened.

"This is the best butternut squash soup I've ever had." Syssi scraped the last drops off her bowl. "Would it be too presumptuous of me to ask what's the secret?"

Callie put her spoon down. "You have to bake the butternut squash first, along with carrots and sweet potatoes, and the ratio between the vegetables is critical. I keep adding them in small quantities until I get the right taste."

"Don't you follow a recipe?" Kaia asked. "Like one of each?"

"You can't do that because you never know how flavorful the particular vegetable you are working with is. As a general rule, I use one sweet potato and one carrot for each medium-sized squash, but if you want the flavor to be just right, you need to keep tasting."

Annani listened to the back and forth about cooking methods with a smile on her face, but her mind was somewhere else.

Turner was onto something with his idea about resurrecting the Doomers and using them to benefit the clan. They were a neglected asset. The problem was that compulsion was not enough to change them from the inside out.

Was it possible to turn murderers and rapists into good people?

Given Wonder's transformation, maybe it was. Gulan had been a timid girl who had hated her size and her physical strength. She had been raised as a servant, and if not for Esag breaking her heart, she would have never run away. She would have lived out her life as a servant without ever thinking that there was anything more she could do.

The woman who had awoken thousands of years later was a different person. Not an ounce of servitude had remained in her, and she could not even stand her old name because it reminded her that she used to be a servant. She was a warrior, if a reluctant one, but she had used her strength to save herself and other innocents.

Gulan had been the product of her upbringing. Wonder was the woman she had been born to be.

Then again, Gulan's parents had not been monsters like the fathers of those Doomers. But who was to say that those fathers had been born like that? Maybe they had become monsters because of the way they had been brought up?

Biology and genetics were complicated fields that Annani understood only superficially, but what if what was encoded was not only what was inherited from the parents but also one's life experience? Was it possible to reprogram that somehow?

Her eyes shifted to Kaia.

Fate had sent the girl to the clan for a reason, and it might not only be to provide William with a wonderful life companion or to decipher Okidu's journals. Her unique set of skills and her sharp mind made her the perfect person to figure out how to reprogram genetic behavior anomalies, especially since she had all the time she needed to explore and test her ideas.

Kaia did not suffer from humanity's biggest limitation, which was time.

"Do you want to go to your auntie?" Karen handed Darlene one of the twins.

She still couldn't tell them apart. To her, they looked identical, but she could get away with it by calling them sweetie, honey, or handsome baby boy.

"I'm heading out tomorrow." Gilbert bounced Idina on his knee as if she was a baby, but she didn't seem to mind. "I wanted to fly out, but Kian suggested that I take a moving van with a couple of Guardians to help me pack, and I took him up on his offer."

"Which ones?" Eric asked.

"I forgot their names. Max brought them over and introduced us. One of them is going to rent the van, and the other one will drive me to the rental place, and we will continue from there. I figured that driving over wouldn't make my trip that much longer than flying."

Darlene tensed at the mention of Max's name. Tomorrow was the Guardian's day off, and they'd made plans to give Eric's idea a try. She'd gone over the scenario in her head a thousand times already, and she still wasn't comfortable with it even though Max's role would be minimal.

She would wear a modest, voluminous nightgown, and she would be on top of Eric with it covering everything so he couldn't see anything, but it still freaked her out and not only because she was about to get bitten for the first time, and not by Eric.

For some reason, having Eric bite her scared her less than getting bitten by Max. She loved Eric, and he loved her back, and anything that happened between them was done with love and care. Having Max at her throat would feel like a violation despite her agreeing to it, and despite him doing them a favor.

It was silly.

So many women who were in a loving relationship got artificially inseminated, and it wasn't to save their lives, but to have the incredible joy of having a child with their partner. The only difference was that instead of having it done at a clinic, she was going to do it in the privacy of her bedroom, with the donor administering the donated venom himself.

"The drive is about six hours long," Eric said. "Between driving to the airport, going through security, and then driving from the airport there, it would have taken you three hours or so. That's half the time it'll take for the ride, but you will gain the help of two guys who can work like machines to help you pack and load the van."

"I know," Gilbert said. "That's why I accepted Kian's offer."

Darlene suspected that Kian had suggested the arrangement because he wanted Gilbert monitored. Given that his family was staying behind in the village, the precaution was unnecessary, but Kian was a little paranoid.

Or a lot.

"Are you coming back with them?" she asked.

"They're driving the van back the next day. I need to stay longer to prepare the house for rental and to visit my job sites. I'll probably be back on Friday." He looked at Karen. "Sooner if I can help it."

"I wish I could come with you," Eric said.

Surprised, Darlene arched a brow at him. Had he forgotten their plans for tomorrow?

"You can come if you want to," Gilbert said.

Eric sighed dramatically. "I'm still too weak to help you pack. Besides, Darlene will miss me too much." He winked at her.

Gilbert nodded. "That's okay. I prefer that you stay in case Karen needs help with the kids. Cheryl got a part-time job at Callie's restaurant, so she won't be much help, and Kaia has her hands full with the research."

"Did you make reservations at Callie's?" Karen asked Gilbert.

He shook his head. "I checked the waiting list on the clan's virtual bulletin board, and it looked like the entire clan, including Kalugal's men, are on that list. She can only handle forty guests at a time, so it will be a while before she has an opening."

Karen gave him an incredulous look. "Then you should have put our names down before everyone signs up for a second round." She picked her tablet off the coffee table. "I'll do it right now." She cast a glance at Darlene. "How about you? Are you and Eric on the waiting list?"

"We are. We have reservations for Wednesday two weeks from now."

Eric regarded her with a conspiratorial smirk. "If for some reason we can't make it, we can give our reservation to Karen and Gilbert."

"Why wouldn't you be able to make it?" Karen asked.

"Oh, I don't know. Darlene might come down with something. After all, she's still human."

As Marcel lay awake, savoring the feel of Sofia's warm body in his arms, he tried to remember if he had ever felt like that toward the woman he'd thought he loved all those years ago. Had it felt so right, so good?

He couldn't recall. The anger and guilt had long ago erased any tender feelings he could have had for her. He remembered the lust, his obsession with her, his need to be near her, but her closeness had never brought him peace. He was sure about that. Being with Cordelia had been turbulent, exciting, excruciating. He'd had to work so hard to gain her affection, and in retrospect, he knew that he never had. She'd been with him because he'd been a tool she'd wanted to use, and she'd wielded him like a mindless weapon.

No, not mindless.

Eager to please, eager to do anything that would make her welcome him into her arms and give him what he'd thought was love.

She'd never loved him. She'd been a sociopath incapable of love, a master manipulator who'd used her beauty and her fake charm to enthrall him as surely as if she'd entered his mind and thralled him as an immortal would.

She'd been a human with an evil mind.

But the truth was that his anger was mostly directed at himself. He could have walked away, he should have realized that she'd been manipulating him, but at the time he'd been incapable of rational thought, and all he'd cared about was making her happy.

How convincing she'd been with her fake tears, with her fake pleading for him to end her suffering and eliminate the cause of her torment. And like a fool, he'd believed every lie and had felt honored to be her knight in shining armor.

Sofia stirred in his arms. "Is it morning yet?" she murmured with her eyes closed.

"Not yet." He caressed her slim back. "Go back to sleep."

"Okay." She yawned, smiled, and cuddled closer to him.

Heaven. That was what being with her felt like.

Sofia didn't want anything from him other than his love. She didn't expect him to go to war for her, to betray his people for her, and in her own way, she'd protected him.

He would have loved to believe that she'd been sent to him by the Fates, but he didn't deserve a boon. He was a sinner, and he deserved eternal condemnation from them, not a reward.

Still, she was a daughter of a hybrid Kra-ell female, and if the Kra-ell were indeed a race similar to the gods, he might be able to activate her.

They'd had unprotected sex several times, and he'd bitten her twice. If it was at all possible to activate her, she could enter transition. And if they kept at it, which he planned on, then her transition might be imminent.

Should he warn her?

The clan had clear guidelines on that, and a potential Dormant needed to be told about the possibility of her immortal genes getting activated by having sex with an immortal male. Well, in Sofia's case she would only be long-lived, not immortal, but he would take a thousand years over her human lifespan.

Maybe that was his punishment.

Perhaps she was his one and only, but she wouldn't live as long as he did, and he would have to mourn her death or find a way to join her on the other side of the veil.

He had to find out whether it was possible.

Aliya was a female Kra-ell hybrid, and yet no one was sure whether her children could be activated, or so he'd heard. Perhaps Bridget had looked into that already?

Would Kaia know? She was a bioinformatician, and she was researching Okidu's journals, so maybe she'd gleaned some information that might shed light on Sofia's prospects?

Pulling gently out of Sofia's arms, he slid out of bed and padded to the bathroom. After taking care of his bladder, he washed his face, brushed his teeth, and pulled on his pants.

Checking that his phone was in the pocket where he'd left it, he walked into the living room, sat on the couch, and sent Kaia a message. *Are you busy? I need to ask you a couple of questions.*

Jade

The summons from Igor took Jade by surprise. There were no official rest days in the compound, but things slowed down on the weekends, and she seldom visited his office on Saturdays or Sundays.

A long time had passed since she'd sent the fable to Emmett, and she hadn't dared to send anything more. She'd spent some time reading through the submissions by other contestants on the Safe Haven website and had even found one that could potentially mean a request for more information, but even if Igor followed her every move on the internet, which he most likely did, he wouldn't have found anything suspicious.

If she couldn't be sure that the fable had been directed at her and what it meant, he certainly couldn't.

Besides, other than his initial response to her winning the contest, he'd acted as if nothing was amiss.

Still, she wasn't in her fertile cycle, and he sure as hell didn't enjoy her company for anything other than breeding, so why had he summoned her?

Her nerves in turmoil, she strode toward the office building and contemplated stopping by the human quarters and purchasing one of the home-brewed elixirs they concocted over there.

One of the young humans was studying chemistry, and he was mixing potent drugs and selling them to humans and Kra-ell alike. They were less effective on the Kra-ell, especially the purebloods, but they still carried a kick, and some of the other females swore by them as an antidote to frayed nerves and a general feeling of ennui.

Jade wasn't a fan of chemical mood enhancers, and she handled her bad moods with intensive training and hunting, but now and then, she was tempted to take the edge off with the help of those drugs. Hell, sometimes she was tempted to buy copious amounts of them and imbibe as much as it took to end it all.

How long could she continue living with the rage, with the grief, with the humiliation of sharing her body with the murderer of her people? The rage was the antidote to the grief and self-loathing, but she'd been consumed by it for so long that there was not much left to burn.

She felt empty, resigned, and Mother forgive her, ready to call it quits.

It was a sin in the eyes of the Mother to give up. Her chosen daughters were supposed to fight till their last breath. But lately, Jade felt as if her last breath had been expelled a long time ago, and she existed as a wraith. Not dead yet, but not alive either.

Death would be a liberation, but unless she died honorably, she wouldn't ascend to the higher spiritual realm of heroes and would be sentenced to forever walk the valley of the shamed.

The guard didn't stop her as she walked past him, and as she knocked on Igor's door and walked in, she found him sitting on his couch, not behind his massive desk as he usually did.

"You summoned me?"

For a change, he didn't react to the lack of honorific. "Yes." He motioned for her to join him on the couch.

"I'm not in my fertile cycle." She sat as far away from him as possible.

"I know. Can't I enjoy your company regardless of your fertility or lack thereof?"

She arched a brow. "I didn't know that you were a masochist."

He barked out a laugh, which was more frightening than if he had scowled at her. "If anything, I am a sadist. But I find your sharp mind and sharp tongue entertaining despite your sour attitude."

That was a first. He had never admitted his sadistic inclinations, but the truth was that she didn't think he was a sadist. Igor didn't take pleasure in anything other than power, and inflicting pain on the helpless was not a power play. He punished cruelly to set an example and scare others from daring to rebel in any way. He didn't derive pleasure from their pain, but he wasn't affected by it either. He just didn't care one way or another.

"What can I do for you?" Jade asked. "Or let's rephrase it. What do you want me to do for you?"

"I have a story that I think you will find interesting." He uncorked a bottle of some liqueur she didn't recognize, poured it into two glasses, and handed her one. "After you showed so much interest in Safe Haven, I got suspicious, and I sent a spy to investigate."

Jade forced her features to remain schooled and raised an eyebrow. "That must have been a colossal waste of money and resources. It's a silly spiritual retreat sham that swindles stupid humans out of their money. I was only interested in it because it has a treasure trove of material that I can use to teach the little ones about morals and striving to do their best. It's useless for sensible adults."

"Surprisingly, it turns out that there is more to it. The paranormal retreats that they started running were not just another product to enhance their portfolio. My spy discovered that a very well-funded organization purchased the resort, and they are running those paranormal retreats to find more humans with paranormal talents. She also discovered that they have several compellers in their community. Did you know that?"

She'd been shoring up her defenses in case she needed to lie to him, but she could honestly say that she hadn't known. "I had no idea. What do they need the paranormal talents for?"

"Sofia suspects that they are trying to breed an enhanced next generation of humans with paranormal abilities."

"Sofia? The girl who studies languages? That's who you sent to spy on them?"

He shrugged. "I needed someone with a solid human background in case they checked, and I needed someone with perfect English. She's also Valstar's granddaughter, so I figured she wasn't an entirely worthless human."

Not daring to even think about Emmett and how he was connected to the paranormal conspiracy Sofia had discovered, Jade decided to continue in that vein. "Are you worried about the enhanced humans?"

He regarded her with his penetrating gaze. "Should I be?"

"You tell me. What can those paranormals do?"

"They can compel, but Sofia reports that they are all weak, so they are not a threat to me." He kept looking into her eyes, but there was nothing to see.

Other than Emmett, who was no match for Igor, she hadn't known about compellers in Safe Haven. "Of course not." She grimaced. "You must be the most powerful compeller ever born. Are you related to the royals?"

She'd asked that before, but he'd never given her an answer.

Today wasn't any different.

"I told Sofia to stay as long as she can pull it off and find out what they are plotting over there. If they are only planning on producing a new crop of enhanced humans, I have nothing to worry about. But I want her to keep digging in case there is something more interesting going on."

"Maybe you should do the same." Jade threw the liquor down her throat. "Breed the most powerful Kra-ell with each other."

He chuckled. "Why do you think I tolerate you? You are a strong compeller in your own right. Our child would be unstoppable."

"Drova is not a compeller."

"Drova is a girl." He gripped the back of Jade's neck. "I'm still waiting for you to give me a son."

Kaia's call came a few minutes after Marcel had texted her. "Good morning, Marcel."

"Thanks for calling back."

"Sure. I assumed that it must be important if you were texting me so early. I heard you had a lot of excitement over at Safe Haven. I bet no one even remembers William's and my whirlwind romance."

She wasn't wrong. It felt like they had left Safe Haven months ago.

"I assume that you know all about Sofia."

"I don't know much her. I heard that she was sent by Jade's captor, a dude named Igor, who is a powerful compeller, and that Toven managed to override his compulsion with Mia's help. Also, that she's willingly feeding him false information until we figure out how to free Jade and her people."

"There is more. Sofia's mother is a hybrid Kra-ell, and her father is human, which is very rare because the hybrid females usually only want to breed with pureblooded males. I was wondering if it might be possible that she's a Dormant and can be activated."

"If their longevity is passed through the mothers like immortality is for us, that should be possible in theory. I don't know if the Kra-ell's venom has the special mojo needed for activation, or if an immortal male can activate one of theirs. You should talk with Bridget. She has a lot of experience with transitioning Dormants and the various factors that contribute to it, but I would wait an hour or two. You know it's six in the morning, right?"

He hadn't checked the time. "What are you doing up so early?"

"Do you really want me to answer that?"

He chuckled. "I'll assume that you were consumed by the need to work on Okidu's journals and got up to do it. Speaking of the journals, I thought you would have more insight into our genetics after working on them for so long."

She sighed. "So far, I've only scratched the surface. Besides, I'm new to this world, and I'm still learning. One of the things William kept bringing up is the affinity and how fast we have fallen for each other. Is that how you and Sofia feel?"

Marcel closed his eyes. "I think we both felt the connection immediately, but our story was so fraught with issues that things got derailed. I was suspicious of her motives and tried to pull back, she felt guilty about manipulating and using me, but at the end of the day, it just feels right to be with her."

"Then go for it. What's the worst that could happen? She will just not transition."

"Yeah, but I need to obtain her consent, and to do that, I need to tell her about us, and I haven't yet."

"You need to talk to Kian and get his permission first."

"I will after I talk with Bridget. If she says that there is no way I can activate Sofia, there is no point in me asking Kian's permission."

"True. Good luck, Marcel."

"Thanks. And thanks again for calling me back so early in the morning."

"You're welcome." She ended the call.

It was six o'clock Saturday morning, and the doctor was probably enjoying a lazy time in bed with her mate, but Marcel was going to pretend that he'd forgotten it was the weekend and that he hadn't noticed how early it was.

"Marcel," Bridget answered after several rings. "Why are you calling me this early? Did something happen?"

"My apologies. I didn't realize what time it was. I can call later."

She sighed. "That's okay. I'm already up. What can I help you with?"

He explained the situation and what Kaia had said.

"I agree, but I need to add that we know that Kra-ell males cannot activate Dormants. At least not immortal Dormants. Emmett and Margaret are proof of that. They were intimate many times over the years, and he still failed to activate her. That being said, he kidnapped Peter because he believed that immortal males could activate Kra-ell Dormants. But since all the human children born to the Kra-ell had human mothers and hybrid fathers, that wasn't going to work. Sofia is the exception, so there might be a chance that you can activate her. You should ask her if she ever had unprotected sex with any of the hybrids or the purebloods. If she did, and they failed to activate her, then it's either because the Kra-ell can't activate their Dormants, or because even the children born to hybrid mothers and human fathers don't inherit the longevity genes."

"She told me about her boyfriends, and they were human, but she might have omitted having been coerced into breeding with the purebloods or the hybrids. She didn't mention that, and I didn't ask. She was in a good mood, and I didn't want to spoil it.'

"You should find a gentle way to do that. We need to know."

"I will."

It wasn't going to be an easy conversation, but Bridget was right. They had to know.

"Come to think of it," Bridget said. "Perhaps Mey and Jin's mother wasn't an immortal Dormant. She might have been a Kra-ell hybrid that somehow escaped or just left her tribe. She might have fallen in love with a human male, had two daughters with him, and, for some reason, couldn't raise them. Or maybe something happened to her and her mate."

"Yeah. Maybe Igor and his cronies found her and killed her and her male. Anything is possible."

"The attack on Jade's tribe happened several years after they were born, but we don't know when they were placed in the orphanage, so perhaps that's possible. If they are of pure Kra-ell descent, though, they are not immortal, which is bad news for them and Yamanu and Arwel. On the other hand, Mey and Jin have very distinct paranormal talents, and from what I heard, Sofia's talent is questionable, which favors the hypothesis of their mother being one of our Dormants."

"I haven't spoken to Sofia about her talent. She can supposedly determine a person's true nature from their reflection in the mirror. There is some mention of that in human literature, so perhaps there is something to it." He sighed. "If Mey and Jin are indeed of pure Kra-ell heritage, and they are still Yamanu and Arwel's truelove mates, then maybe the Fates have some grand plan in mind for the Kra-ell and us."

What he meant by that was that he hoped Sofia was his truelove mate, and that his venom might somehow make her immortal.

Bridget let out a breath. "Who knows? I used to scoff at those who invoked the Fates, but I'm no longer dismissive of their part in what's going on."

"Same here. I love being an engineer and finding scientific solutions to problems. But now that I've found a woman who I feel can be my one and only, I'm finding myself hoping for divine intervention."

"As the saying goes, there are no atheists in the foxhole. Good luck, Marcel."

"Thank you."

Marcel wasn't in bed when Sofia woke up. The door to the bedroom was closed, but she knew he was in the bunker. He wouldn't have left her alone without telling her that he was leaving.

Last night was spectacular, and with the residual pleasure still pulsing through her body, she wanted to find him and drag him back to bed for another round.

What better way to start the day than making love, right?

Except, she didn't know what mood she would find Marcel in today. Would he be as loving and as sweet as he had been last night? Or would he go back to being broody and remote like he had been since that fateful call in Emmett's office?

Sofia had done everything they had asked her to do, she'd explained why she'd had no choice, and he should have forgiven her. He'd even said so last night. But she'd been hurt by him before, and she didn't trust his feelings not to change again.

Maybe if she went back to sleep, she would wake up with him holding her in his arms and murmuring sweet nothings in her ear, and they would live happily ever after. The end.

She smiled at her own girlish fantasies. Life didn't work like that. It wasn't fair, good things didn't come as a reward to good people, and evildoers like Igor got their way.

Kind of made her question her faith in the Mother.

The goddess wasn't the benevolent god humans believed in. She was vengeful and demanding. The Mother was supposed to reward the worthy and punish the unworthy, but that wasn't how it worked in the real world. Now that Sofia knew that Igor was definitely unworthy, that he spit in the face of Kra-ell traditions, turning them on their head, she doubted that the Mother was a real force in the universe.

The thing was, Igor's murderous ways were not an affront to the Mother. The Kra-ell were warlike people, and to die in battle or in a duel was considered an honorable death. Deadly duels weren't allowed in Igor's compound, but he hadn't disallowed stories of them to circulate like he suppressed the truth about females being the Mother's chosen leaders.

As the bedroom door opened and Marcel walked in, shirtless and barefoot, her mouth watered. "Come back to bed." She lifted the blanket, inviting him in.

"I wish I could." He sat down and leaned to kiss her lips. "I didn't go to the lab yesterday as I was supposed to, and I need to do it now. It shouldn't take long, though."

Once again, he seemed awkward and remote with her, but she had a feeling it was about something other than mistrust. Something was troubling him, but it might be about the things he needed to do in the lab.

As her aunt used to say, not everything was about her, and the people around her could have other things troubling them that had nothing to do with her.

Sofia sighed. "What am I supposed to do while you do whatever you need to do in the lab?"

"I made coffee, and Eleanor will bring you breakfast later. I can send a book with her. What do you like to read?"

"Do you have any romance novels?"

He winced. "I have some thrillers and detective stories, and I think that in one of them there is a love interest, but I wouldn't call it romance."

"That's okay. I have a book that I brought with me and didn't finish yet." She put her hand on his knee. "Can I ask Eleanor to compel me to keep quiet about everything that went down so I can rejoin the retreat? I cooperated, and you said that you trusted me. Besides, where am I going to run? There is nowhere to go."

Marcel sighed. "I need to ask the big boss's permission. I sent him a message, but he hasn't answered me yet, and I don't want to bug him. He's not the friendliest of guys, and especially not to those who disturb his Saturday morning with his family."

"Is he the one who was listening through Julian's tablet?"

Marcel nodded.

"Is he angry at me?"

"Not at all. He's a grumpy fellow, but he's not a bad guy. He knows that you had no choice, and he doesn't blame you."

Sofia let out a breath. "That's a relief. Isn't Eleanor teaching a class today, though?"

"Not until later in the day. She can come down and spend some time with you." He cupped her cheek. "She's not the friendly type either, but she seems to really like you. I think the two of you could be friends."

"I think so too. She's a little bit like the Kra-ell females. She's no-nonsense, assertive bordering on aggressive, and she looks like a hybrid Kra-ell. Well except for the eyes. They are the right color but the wrong size. The Kra-ell and the hybrids have big eyes."

He smiled. "Emmett doesn't."

That was a shock. "Emmett? What are you talking about?"

"I'm surprised that you haven't figured it out yet. Emmett is a hybrid. He used to be a member of Jade's tribe, but he left many years before Igor attacked her compound. Jade must have recognized him from his picture."

"Dear Mother of All Life. How could I have been so blind? It's just that he's so not Kra-ell in the way he acts. They are all so macho and severe and all about honor, while Emmett is a performer who lives for drama." Her hand flew to her mouth. "It would have been a real disaster if he told Igor his real name. His Kra-ell name. It would have been the end of Jade. Igor would have killed her."

Marcel nodded. "That's why I didn't tell you before. But since I trust you, and since we both know that you can never go back, I figured you would feel a little less homesick knowing that there is a hybrid Kra-ell right here in Safe Haven."

"I need to talk to him. Maybe he can tell me more things about the Kra-ell. They told us so little in Igor's place. Perhaps Jade was more forthcoming."

Marcel shook his head. "He doesn't know much either. Jade was just as tight-lipped, and I'm starting to wonder what they were hiding from their own people."

"They don't consider humans their people, and they consider the hybrids a necessary evil. Not that anyone has actually phrased it like that, but it's evident from how they treat us."

"I need to ask you something." Marcel took in a breath. "And I need you to answer it truthfully because it's important. Have you ever had sex with a pureblood or a hybrid male?"

She'd told him about her boyfriends. Was he doubting her again? He'd just told her that he trusted her.

So much for that.

"I didn't." She crossed her arms over her chest. "Why is it important to you?"

"I can't tell you yet, and I don't want you to feel embarrassed if you did. I know that you were not free to reject unwanted advances."

So that was why he was asking.

Marcel wanted to find out how highly she was regarded as the human granddaughter of a pureblooded male, and that would tell him her grandfather's position in Igor's organization.

Valstar being Igor's second-in-command was one of the few pieces of information she'd withheld from him.

"Rape is not condoned in our community. I didn't have to accept anyone's invitation if I didn't want to."

"Good morning, Syssi," Turner said as she opened the door for him. "I'm sorry about conducting business in your home on a Saturday."

She chuckled. "Being married to Kian, I'm used to that, and I prefer him being here than in the office. That way, at least I get to see him." She closed the door behind him. "I hoped Bridget would accompany you. Okidu prepared breakfast for four."

"Then I shall call her and ask her to hurry over. I thought it would be just Kian and me."

Syssi let the unintended insult slide.

"Allegra is at Annani's this morning, so I figured I would join your breakfast meeting."

Turner was a brilliant man, but his social skills were even worse than Kian's, and he surely hadn't realized how dismissive that had sounded.

She wasn't an official member of the council, but Kian didn't do anything without consulting her, and she knew everything that was going on, security-wise as well as business-wise. Kian trusted her opinion, mainly because she didn't express it unless she had something to contribute, and also because her second sight gave her a paranormal advantage.

She wasn't always aware of its influence, and sometimes it was difficult for her to tell the difference between things that her mind conjured up and things that her foresight was trying to hint at. The best example of that were the Kra-ell. She'd created a fantasy world for the Perfect Match studios with creatures called the Krall, thinking that it was a product of her creative imagination, but as it had turned out, it had foreshadowed the appearance of the real Kra-ell, a divergent species of new Earth occupants who most likely had come from the same corner of the universe as the gods.

"Bridget will be here in a few minutes." Turner returned the phone to his pocket.

"Wonderful." She motioned for him to take a seat at the dining table. "Can I offer you some coffee while we wait?"

"Yes, please. Thank you."

"Black, right?"

He gave her a smile. "I'm honored that you remembered."

Syssi laughed. "Coffee is my thing. I remember everyone's preferences."

"You remember every kind of preference." Kian walked into the dining room and pulled her into his arms. "You care, and you pay attention. That's why you remember. I bet you know what Turner likes to eat as well."

That was true and kind of odd. Generally, her memory wasn't great, and unless she made a conscious effort to remember a person's name and attached some visual mnemonic to it, she would forget it almost as soon as she'd learned it, but she remembered personal things about people without putting any effort into it.

"That's easy. Turner is competing with Roni for the title of the best barbecuer in the village. Ribs are his favorite."

"They are." Turner rubbed his stomach. "But lately, I've discovered that baking them in the oven is better than barbecuing them. I cover them with foil and bake them on low heat for a couple of hours. They turn out delicious."

As the doorbell rang, Okidu beelined for the front door and opened it for Bridget. "Good morning, Doctor."

"Good morning, everyone." She gave Okidu a small smile before walking over and joining them at the table. "I planned on catching up on some work while Victor was gone, but I couldn't refuse an invitation to breakfast cooked by Okidu." She turned to him. "Are you serving your famous Belgian waffles?"

Okidu straightened to his full height of five feet and eight inches. "But of course, mistress."

"Wonderful." Bridget unfurled the napkin and draped it over her knees. "I spoke to Marcel earlier." She turned to Kian. "Did you speak with him?"

"He sent me a message earlier, but it was marked as not urgent, and I didn't have a chance to call him back yet. Is there a problem?"

Bridget hesitated for a moment. "Usually, I don't like to discuss health concerns that clan members ask my advice about, but since Marcel's questions could be construed as general in nature, and they are relevant to what we are about to discuss, I feel that I should. Marcel asked me whether a human child born to a hybrid Kra-ell mother and a human father would be a Dormant who could be activated."

Kian frowned. "Didn't we conclude that the Kra-ell Dormants couldn't be activated?"

Bridget pursed her lips. "According to Emmett and Vrog, hybrid females don't produce children with humans. The Kra-ell philosophy is to choose the best possible male to father their offspring, so naturally, they choose pure-blooded males to impregnate them. They might dally with humans out of curiosity, though. Since we assumed that their longevity is passed through the mothers, we concluded that children born to hybrid males and human females didn't possess the longevity gene. Based on Emmett and Margaret's sexual history, we also knew that a hybrid Kra-ell male could not activate an immortal Dormant female. Sofia is a rarity. She's the daughter of a hybrid female. The question we need to ask her is whether she had sex with any of the purebloods or the hybrids, and if she did, then we will know that they can't activate their Dormants. That still leaves the possibility that our males can do that."

Syssi frowned. "Hold on. We also know that the pure-blooded females don't have sex with humans, so the hybrid females are the product of pureblooded males and human mothers. How would the longevity gene get passed? It should end with the hybrid daughters."

"Not necessarily." Bridget leaned back in her chair. "We made the mistake of thinking of the purebloods as equivalents of immortals, when in fact they are the equivalent of gods, and if that's so, both the males and the females pass on the longevity genes."

Syssi shook her head. "If the purebloods are genetically equivalent to the gods, they are a much more primitive version. If the two societies interacted, I bet the Kra-ell were treated as second class."

"Again, not necessarily," Turner said. "We suspect that the gods were experts in genetic manipulation. They might have created the Kra-ell to serve them as workers and soldiers. The Kra-ell are physically stronger than the gods, they produce many more males than females, and they live by a code of honor that celebrates death in battle as the ultimate achievement. They are the perfect warriors."

"They might have taken an existing species and altered it." Syssi shivered. "They were far from the benevolent creatures they tried to portray themselves as."

Kian chuckled. "We already know that. But I still think that the Kra-ell are just a more primitive form of the gods, not their creation. The gods wouldn't have given them such incredible power of compulsion."

Syssi shook her head. "Most of the Kra-ell have a very limited ability to compel, and it's possible that the original species had it before the gods altered their genetics. Perhaps some are just born with a stronger ability. I wouldn't dismiss the possibility that they were created by the gods to serve them."

Leaning over, Kian took her hand and planted a kiss on the back of it. "I never dismiss anything you say, my love."

She gave him a smile. "That's sweet."

"It's not sweet. It's smart. You're always right."

Turner nodded. "Especially when she supports my opinion."

"I should call Marcel." Kian took a sip from his coffee. "But first, tell me what your guy in Karelia found."

Turner put his fork down. "They followed the map, used a raft to cross three of the rivers, but they got stuck on the fourth. The rapids are too strong to use a raft, and it's too wide to cross any other way. They need more equipment, and it's on the way, but it will take time to get to them."

"How do the Kra-ell deliver supplies to the compound?" Bridget asked.

"They could have built tunnels under the riverbeds," Turner said. "My guy's team looked for the entrances, but they must be very well camouflaged. They couldn't find them. Sofia mentioned tunnels, but for some reason, Toven dropped the subject. We need to question her again and use compulsion to get her to answer truthfully and fully. She must know where they are."

"Unless she was driven there," Bridget said. "They probably employ the same tactics that Navuh and we do. We have special vehicles to allow clan members to travel freely to and from the village, and Navuh uses windowless planes piloted by humans who are compelled to keep the island's location a secret."

Turner nodded. "We also need Sofia to draw the layout of the compound, the patrol schedules, how often the purebloods and hybrids leave the compound to hunt, and at what times of the day."

"What about the miniature drone?" Kian asked. "Did your guy manage to get one?"

"He ordered it, and it should get to him tomorrow."

"I'm still not a hundred percent sure that a drone is a good idea, even a small one."

"There is another option," Turner said. "If we manage to find the tunnels, which we should with Sofia's help, we can use a crawling bug instead of a flying one. They make less noise, require less energy, and get into tight spaces. We can send several spiders in at once and have them crawl all over. They might be able to get into the weapons storage, which a flying bug won't be able to do."

This should have occurred to Kian before, but he'd been too fixated on the miniature drone. "Great idea. Make it so."

Turner sighed. "It will take time. Normally, I prefer to go slow and collect as much information as I can before I even begin to plan a mission, and technically, we are not in a rush. The sense of urgency is due to Sofia's presence and to how long we can drag out the misinformation campaign. The moment Igor realizes that she's been captured, he's going to react, and we will be out of time. A faster way to get information on the compound is to capture a pureblood and compel it out of him, but that might show our hand prematurely."

"Can't we fake her death?" Syssi asked. "But it needs to be very convincing, or it would look suspicious and produce the same undesired result."

"We can use the misinformation for that as well," Bridget suggested. "She can start reporting that the stress is getting to her, and she's feeling faint. Then she'll say that she visited the clinic and was told that she might have a heart problem. The doctor recommended a bunch of tests, but she doesn't have insurance, and they will cost a fortune." Bridget chuckled. "American healthcare costs are legendary around the world. Everything here costs ten times as much as it costs in Europe, so they will believe it. A simple MRI exam would run several thousands of dollars."

"I like it," Kian said. "The answer she gets will show how much they care about her, if at all. If they authorize the expense, then they deem her valuable and not a disposable pawn. If not, she will be even more motivated to cooperate with us. In a week or two, we can send an email to her emergency contact informing them of her death from heart failure and ask them to pay for transporting the body to Finland. If they refuse, we will inform them that the body was cremated."

Syssi shivered. "That sounds so gruesome. Poor girl."

Kian put his hand on her shoulder. "She will not really die, love. We will just make it look like it as convincingly as we can."

"I know, but it's sad. She's all alone in the world, and those who care for her can't help her. I hope that she's a Dormant, that Marcel can activate her, and that they can live happily ever after."

"Speaking of Marcel. I need to call him." Kian pulled out his phone and looked at Turner. "Any other suggestions before we talk to him?"

Turner crossed his arms over his chest. "Marcel's questions to Bridget indicate that he wants to induce Sofia. Since the protocol is to get the Dormant's consent before attempting it, he probably wants to ask your permission to tell her about us."

"Yeah, I figured as much."

"What are you going to tell him?" Syssi asked.

"I don't feel comfortable telling her anything, but that's just my knee-jerk response. She's supervised at all times, so she can't tell Igor anything, and she's not going back to him. She can also be compelled to keep quiet about us and thralled to forget if need be." He looked at Turner. "What do you think?"

"I think it's a great opportunity to find out whether hybrid Kra-ell mothers and human fathers can produce Dormant children who can be activated. The thing is that for us it's just curiosity, while for the Kra-ell, it could be a game changer, and not one we are interested in."

Kian pinned him with a hard stare. "You're not being helpful."

"I'm just thinking out loud. It's not in our best interest for the Kra-ell to find out that we can activate the Dormant children born to their female hybrids. On the other hand, the Kra-ell we know about, the ones who are holding Jade, only have one such possible Dormant, and Sofia is not going back, so how are they going to find out?"

"True," Syssi said. "But since we invited Aliyah and Vrog into our community, we need to find out for their sake. What if they have children, and they are born human? They would need to know whether their children can be activated."

Marcel

Marcel collected everything that the team of bioinformaticians had been working on, scanned it, emailed it to William, and destroyed the documents.

After that was done, he disconnected all the servers, locked up the lab, and headed back to Emmett's cottage.

Kian's call caught him when he was entering the cottage.

"Hello, Kian."

"Where are you now?"

"I'm about to enter the bunker. Why?"

"We need to question Sofia again. Turner's team wasn't able to reach the compound with the map she drew for Toven. The fourth river has strong rapids, and they are waiting for more equipment to cross it. She mentioned tunnels, and we believe that she knows where to find the entrances. We also need her to draw us a layout of the compound. Once we have the locations of the entrances to the tunnels, we plan on sending spiders to collect information. Between the layout she draws for us and what the spiders transmit, we will have a better idea of what we are dealing with. Get Eleanor and have her compel Sofia to cooperate."

She wasn't going to like it, but it was necessary.

"What are you planning to do?" he asked.

"Nothing yet. We are debating the benefits versus the pitfalls of capturing a pureblood and pumping him for information, and we haven't decided yet whether the risks outweigh the benefit or vice versa. If we could manage to do that without Igor being any the wiser, then it's a no-brainer, but it doesn't seem feasible. The moment he gets a whiff of anything being amiss, he could flee, or he could retaliate against Sofia's family, and we promised her not to endanger them."

"I see. I wish I had some insight to offer, but I don't."

"You're not a strategist, Marcel. I only shared our deliberations with you because of your involvement with Sofia."

That was the opening he needed to ask Kian's permission to tell her the truth about them, but it was bad timing to bring it up. Nevertheless, he had to do it. He might have induced her already, and if Kian didn't allow him to tell her about her potential transition, he should start using protection and make up a good reason for why it was suddenly needed.

"Thank you for keeping me informed. I also have something I need to discuss with you."

"I know. You think that Sofia might be a Dormant, and you want to try to induce her transition."

That was a relief.

Kian had probably spoken with Bridget, and even if he hadn't, it must have occurred to him that the rare daughter of a hybrid mother and human father might be a Dormant.

"I wouldn't have brought it up if it weren't urgent, but we'd been intimate twice before it occurred to me that Sofia might be a Dormant, and since she's on birth control, we didn't use protection."

"Bridget told us that you called her, and we decided that it's a good opportunity to find out whether a child of a hybrid Kra-ell female can be induced by an immortal male. Did you ask her if she had sex with any of the purebloods or hybrids?"

"The same thing occurred to me, but when I asked her, she insisted that she didn't. She said that rape was not condoned in the compound, and that she had the right to refuse, but I don't think she told me the truth. Sofia emits very little in terms of emotional scents, so I can't tell by that, but she averted her eyes when she said that. It was either a lie or a half-truth."

"She might have special status in the compound," Syssi said in the background. "Because of her being a rare daughter of a hybrid female. It's also possible that her mother and or her grandfather are important members of Igor's community."

"That's possible." Marcel rubbed the back of his neck. "The same thought had occurred to me, but I was afraid of being biased and looking for explanations that would validate Sofia's statement."

"Refusing a female's invitation was considered a great affront in Jade's community," Kian said. "I assume that to refuse a male's invitation in Igor's carries the same stigma. I don't see how human or even hybrid females can refuse without suffering the consequences. You can ask Eleanor to make Sofia answer that truthfully."

Sofia was going to hate him for it, but they had to know. "What about telling her about us? Do I have permission to tell her our history and why I think she can be induced?"

"As I said, we want to find out whether that's possible, but we don't want to do that without her consent or her knowledge. We all know the law, and I don't think Edna would let it slide if we forgo asking for Sofia's consent, even taking into account the special circumstances. Besides, Sofia is not going back whether she transitions or not. She already knows too much, and we can't release her. We will have to fake her death, and she will have to be confined to the village. Like it or not, you are stuck with her for as long as she lives."

"I don't have a problem with that, but Sofia might, especially after I get Eleanor to interrogate her about her sex life. She might not want to have anything to do with me ever again."

"If she's your truelove mate, she'll forgive you. It is what it is, though, so let's make the best of it. If she refuses to be with you, we will get her accommodations elsewhere, and find her something to do. There are plenty of jobs available in the village for anyone willing to do them."

"How are we going to fake her death without it looking suspicious? She's twenty-seven and healthy."

After Kian had told him about the heart condition idea, Marcel had to agree that it sounded plausible. "Sofia told me that healthcare is practically nonexistent for the humans in the compound. Her grandmother died of heart failure, so that will fit perfectly. They will assume it was genetic. If I haven't unintentionally induced her already, perhaps it would be a good idea to fake her death before giving it a try. If she enters transition, she might be out for a few days, and she won't be able to communicate with her contact."

"That's not a bad idea. Tomorrow, have her contact Valstar and start the story. If she enters transition, we will implement the heart failure scenario and send our condolences along with a bill."

Sofia put her book back on the nightstand and pulled the blanket over her head. The Spanish romance novel was all about rich people hopping on private jets, traveling from one exotic location to another, and staying at luxurious hotels. The love talk was too flowery, the love scenes too unrealistic, and it all made her feel like Cinderella before meeting the prince.

She was stuck in a bunker, her so-called prince had left her hours ago and hadn't returned yet, and before leaving, he'd asked her about her lovers and hadn't believed her when she'd told him she'd never had sex with a pureblood or a hybrid.

Her story wasn't a fairytale, and it wasn't going to turn into one.

Maybe if she fell asleep, she could dream about a different world where the prince didn't doubt her, where she could keep her job at the university, where both of her parents loved her and cared for her, and where an evil overlord didn't threaten to torture those she cared about if she failed him.

Dream on.

She chuckled. *That's what I'm trying to do.*

When the knock sounded on the bedroom door, she tossed the blanket aside and got to her feet. "Coming."

"May I come in?" Marcel said from the other side.

Had she just dreamt him up?

"Sure. Prisoners don't get to refuse their jailers entry."

He opened the door. "What got you in a bad mood?"

Her sour expression must have given him pause because he didn't even attempt to get closer.

Sofia was in no mood to smile to make him feel better. "Nothing. What's up?" She straightened the blanket over the bed and tucked the corners in to make it look nice.

Being mad didn't mean she wanted her prison space to look messy. Keeping it neat was the only thing she could control right now.

He shook his head. "Even I know that *nothing* is not a good answer. Did Eleanor say something to upset you?"

"Not at all."

Eleanor was the only friend she had right now, and out of all Sofia's jailers, she treated her the best. She'd promised to bring Emmett with her later so they could all have dinner together and talk about Kra-ell stuff. But dinner was many hours away, and until then, all Sofia had for company was that damn romance novel that she really didn't want to keep reading. It only made it painfully obvious that her own romance story was severely lacking.

She finally understood the appeal of bully romances.

Compared to the jerks in those books, average guys like Marcel looked better than they actually were.

Not that he was average. He was handsome, intelligent, and deep down, he had a good heart. But he was still no prince.

"So what is it?" Marcel asked. "Is it something I said?"

She sat on the bed and picked up her book. "Did you talk to your boss about allowing me to attend the retreat?"

The sheepish expression on his face was her answer. "I forgot. I'll do it right now." He turned on his heel and walked out of the bedroom.

Sofia let out a breath and let her shoulders sag. It wasn't smart to antagonize her jailer. Sometimes he was nice to her, so maybe if she was nice in return, she would get more nice out of him.

But that wasn't how it was supposed to work between lovers.

They were supposed to float toward each other on a cloud of love and admiration, embrace each other passionately, and hop on a jet to Buenos Aires, where they would make love in the bedroom of their private jet, three thousand meters above the Earth.

Right.

Damn romance novel and the unrealistic expectations it had planted in her head.

But what was the alternative?

Expect abuse of the verbal, emotional, or physical variety and call it life?

She'd had enough of that in Igor's compound.

Marcel returned a couple of moments later. "He said it was okay as long as Eleanor compels you to keep everything that happened since you were caught a secret."

Sofia grimaced. "Eleanor can't make it until dinner. She has a class she's teaching."

Marcel lifted his hand and rubbed the back of his neck. "I asked her to rearrange her schedule and come as soon as she could. She will be here in a few minutes."

As Sofia's heart made a happy flip, she put the book aside, rose to her feet, walked over to Marcel, and wrapped her arms around his neck. "Thank you. I appreciate you going to all that trouble for me."

Marcel knew that he was in trouble, and he didn't know how to avert the storm that Sofia was about to unleash on him.

He could pretend that he'd called Eleanor over only to compel Sofia so she could rejoin the retreat, and perhaps she would hold her tongue while Eleanor was compelling her to reveal more information about Igor's compound. But then her wrath would be even greater.

Would she forgive him once he told her about her potential Dormancy?

Not in the mood she was in. She would probably throw him out of the room without giving him a chance to explain.

Gently removing her arms from around his neck, he took her hand and led her to the living room. "Just as you had to follow commands from your boss, I have to follow commands from mine. It's true that he doesn't have to compel me to do that, and I follow because I trust his leadership and his judgment, and I know that his motives are good, but I'm still a cog in this machine, just like you are in yours."

She frowned at him. "Now I'm worried. What was that preamble about?"

"I asked Eleanor to come over after my initial conversation with the boss. He needs you to disclose more information about the compound and how to get there. We have a team on the ground in Karelia, and they were not able to traverse the last river on your map because of the rapids. You mentioned tunnels, and we need to know where they are."

Her face fell. "And here I thought that you were making an effort for me."

"I'm making a tremendous effort for you. I asked permission to do something that I would have never asked for anyone else."

"What is it?"

"I'll tell you tonight. It's not something that can be covered in a two-minute conversation, which is all we have before Eleanor gets here."

"I have to admit that I'm curious, but I'm even more curious, or rather worried, about what your boss wants to do with the information he's about to force me to reveal." She smirked. "By the way, I don't think that Eleanor will be able to get it out of me, and Tom is not here. Tom freed me to say what I want to say, but since I don't want your people invading my community, and I don't want to tell you where the tunnels are, Igor's compulsion might hold."

Marcel was afraid of that as well, but he was glad that Sofia had inadvertently admitted to knowing where the tunnels were.

"I hoped that Eleanor's services wouldn't be needed. My boss, whose name is Kian, is just collecting information. We don't have enough people to offer Igor and his warriors a challenge, but we need to know who and what we are dealing with. And in case your family needs rescuing, we need to have a contingency plan for that."

That seemed to finally penetrate her stubbornness. "I believe that you sincerely believe that, but what if your boss is not telling you the truth?"

"We don't operate like that. Kian is not a dictator, and he's not operating in a vacuum. We have a council, and if he does something that's not justified, the council will have his head. On top of that, he's not the ultimate authority. We have several establishments, each with its own regent, and the lady who is in charge of our entire organization is the most loving, compassionate person you will ever meet."

That put a sparkle in Sofia's eyes. "Am I ever going to meet her?"

Marcel grinned. "There is a very good chance of that."

Sofia took in a deep breath. "I'm sorry for giving you a hard time. I know it's futile, and I know that with Tom's help, Kian can get me to do anything he wants, the same way that Igor could. But I can't help fighting this. My family's safety is on the line, and so far, Igor hasn't harmed any of them. If he does, it's going to be my fault, either by failing to provide him with the information he wants, or by providing you with the information you want. As the saying goes, I'm between a rock and a hard place."

Sofia

When Eleanor came down with Emmett and Leon, they had with them a stack of large printouts.

"Those are enlarged maps of Karelia." Leon spread them on the dining table with Marcel's help.

"Are the tunnel entrances near the rivers?" Eleanor asked.

She hadn't imbued her voice with compulsion, which Sofia could have kissed her for, but she knew it would only last as long as she cooperated and gave them all the information they wanted.

"The tunnels are well-guarded. Since it's impossible to get to the other three tunnels without going through the first, it is the most heavily guarded, usually by one pure-blood and two hybrids. The others have two hybrids each. The paved road ends here." She marked the spot with a Sharpie. "There is a dirt road that continues from here, but it's not marked on the map, and there is a really rough patch between where the paved road ends and the dirt path begins. My old car gets a beating every time I force her through it. It's not easy to find the dirt path, and since it rains so much over there, and it's so overgrown with vegetation, leaving tracks is not a concern. The same goes for the paths between the tunnels."

“I bet the tunnels have cameras and are boobytrapped,” Leon said. “If someone manages to get to the first tunnel entrance undetected and eliminates the guards, they can collapse the secondary tunnels.”

"What happens if you get stuck?" Eleanor asked.

"I have a cell phone. I can call for help."

Leon and Eleanor exchanged glances.

"We forgot about your phone," Eleanor said. "It's still in the safe in the office." She looked at Leon. "Should we tell Kian about it?"

"There is nothing to tell. When we fake Sofia's death, we will mail it back along with the rest of her belongings."

Sofia felt the blood drain from her face. "I can't do that to my father. He will die from a broken heart."

Eleanor patted her arm. "Better a broken heart than a broken back. You don't want Igor to torture him."

"That's not helpful," Emmett murmured. "Maybe we can put something in the stories to let Jade know that you are alive, so she can tell your father."

"Did she send another email?" Eleanor asked.

"She didn't, but I know that she read my fable. William set it up, so I know who visits which page. It's something called cookies, and all the websites have them these days. She either didn't understand what I was trying to say, or she's afraid to answer."

"It's better that way," Leon said. "We can't help her anyway, but we can send her encoded messages." He narrowed his eyes at Emmett. "Maybe you should sharpen your writing skills, so she can actually understand what you are trying to tell her."

Emmett glared at him but didn't say a thing.

Leon turned to Sofia. "Please mark the dirt road for us."

"I'll try. I'm not good at judging scale. But here is the first river, and I know that the dirt road terminates half a mile or so before it. The first tunnel entrance should be somewhere here." She marked the spot with an X. "They have cameras on the dirt road, so when I get near, they move the bushes aside and roll the fake stone door aside."

"Where are the three other entrances?" Leon asked.

“I can only estimate.” Sofia marked the spots.

“They are not far from each other.” Leon leaned his chin on his fist. "But it’s still a long way for the spiders to cross. I’m not worried about the cameras in the tunnels detecting the spiders, even if they are using infrared. Their heat signature is minimal. But we will need to study the terrain and find a shorter path for them. We might have to use a drone to drop them closer to the compound."

"Spiders?" Sofia arched a brow. "What do you need spiders for? Are they poisonous?"

"These are not real spiders," Marcel explained. "Leon is talking about mechanical devices that look like spiders and carry a tiny camera and transmit sound and images. We can send them to film the compound and even listen to conversations."

Her eyes widened. "Are they remote-controlled?"

"Some are, why?"

"Perhaps we can deliver a message to my father with one of them." She winced. "I just hope he doesn't squash it before it delivers the message."

"We can send a message to Jade as well," Eleanor said. "I wish those bugs could carry earpieces, but then they would be too big. Just imagine what Jade could do if she was free of Igor's compulsion."

"We can drop earpieces with a small drone," Leon said. "The problem is the distance. We will have to deploy a larger drone with the small one piggybacking on it, have it glide over the compound with the engine off, and drop the small one to free-fall somewhere that is not heavily patrolled."

"The human quarters," Sofia said. "We have a large grassy area with a playground for the children, and the Kra-ell hardly ever visit it. You can drop the small drone there, but first, let my father know that it's coming with one of those spider communicators so he will know to look for it."

"Will he cooperate with Jade?" Eleanor asked.

"That might be a problem." Sofia let out a breath. "My father works in the laundry, and he has no reason to seek Jade out or vice versa." She tapped her lips. "But my aunts work as maids in the Kra-ell quarters, so they can slip her a note while they clean her room."

"We've gotten sidetracked," Leon said. "Our first concern is gathering intel, and since the only way to get to the compound and its immediate area is through tunnels that are guarded twenty-four-seven, our best option is to capture the guards securing the first one instead of waiting for a hunting party to come out. We can easily disable the cameras on the dirt road or circumvent the road altogether." He flipped one of the printouts around. "We need you to draw the layout of the compound and mark all the areas according to function and security level, and by that, I mean the frequency of patrols."

She nodded. "Can I get a ruler? I'll try to draw it to scale as best as I can."

From not seeing any options to free the compound, they suddenly had several, and one of them was helping those who opposed Igor's rule to rebel against him. Sofia still didn't know how they were going to accomplish that, but if they kept working on it, they might figure out a good plan.

"I'll get a ruler from my office." Emmett rose to his feet. "I'll be back in a couple of minutes."

Eleanor got up as well. "I'll make coffee while we wait."

"I'm excited," Sofia said. "It seems like we are starting to develop a plan, but I'm not sure for what. Are we going to start a rebellion?"

"That's one option," Leon said. "After we are done, I'll share what we discussed with Turner. The guy is a strategic genius, and he should be able to put this new information and the ideas we came up with to good use."

"Is it okay?" Max threaded the tongue through the buckle on the cuff around Eric's left wrist. "Or is it too snug?"

"It's fine." Eric tugged on the chain. "But I think you went overboard with those titanium chains. I'm not a gorilla." He moved his hips to adjust the blanket covering his privates.

"I got them from Brundar. I guess that's what he uses himself."

Eric chuckled. "I didn't know that Callie was that strong."

Max cut him an amused glance. "They are not for Callie."

"Brundar doesn't strike me as the submissive type. Come to think of it, neither does Callie, but I don't know much about that lifestyle and its rules of engagement."

"Neither do I." Max took hold of Eric's right wrist and pulled the leather cuff over his hand. "Maybe they take turns being tied down. It takes a lot of trust to be at the mercy of another person like that." He lifted his eyes to Eric's. "I appreciate it that you trust me to do this."

"I trust Darlene with my life. You are just the help."

Max snorted out a laugh. "Thanks a lot. Now I really feel special."

"You are, and I'm grateful." Eric let out a breath. "I use humor and sarcasm to alleviate the stress." He glanced at the closed bathroom door. "If I'm nervous, I can imagine how hard it is for Darlene. All I have to do is lie here like a slab of meat while she has to do all the work."

Darlene was hiding in the bathroom.

She was still uncomfortable about having Max bite her, and although she refused to admit it, Eric suspected that she was also scared.

Her standard answer was that if all the immortal females who had immortal partners enjoyed it, it couldn't be too bad.

Except, those females were doing it with males they loved, and that made a difference.

Max tightened the strap, threaded the tongue through the buckle, and put Eric's arm down on the mattress. "It's going to be alright. After I'm done, I'll put on soft, romantic music, light up the candles, dim the lights, and leave. You can forget that I was even here."

Hardly, but Eric knew that the moment Darlene touched him, it would become all about her, and he would have no problem getting aroused.

The reverse, though, was going to be more challenging. He was tied up, so there was little he could do as far as foreplay, and Darlene wasn't the type of woman who liked to take control. Seeing him chained to the bed would not turn her on.

He had a plan, though. He would tell her to straddle his face, hold on to the headboard, and let him bring her to orgasm once or twice with his tongue alone. By the time he was done with her, she would be so anxious to ride his shaft that she would hopefully forget all about Max jerking off in the next room.

Eric had asked Max to get a good bottle of wine for Darlene, so she could let go of her inhibitions, but she'd been too nervous to drink it, claiming that her throat was too tight to swallow, and his joke about her giving him a blow job to loosen it up hadn't helped.

She hadn't even smiled, and given that she always laughed at all of his corny jokes, no matter how stupid they were, that spoke volumes about her mental state.

Darlene was freaking out.

"All done." Max finished the last buckle on Eric's ankle. "Comfortable?"

"No. My nose itches. Can you scratch it for me?"

Rolling his eyes, Max did that not too gently. "Anything else? Do you need me to fluff you up too?"

Eric laughed. "The only hands I allow on my yoke are Darlene's, but thanks for the offer."

"It wasn't an offer." Max cast a glance at the bathroom door. "I'd better finish up so she can come out."

When Max was done with the music, the candles, and the lights, Eric asked, "Can I ask you for just one more favor? Can you add another pillow under my head?"

"Sure, buddy." Max lifted Eric's head and stuffed the pillow under it. "All good?"

"Yeah. Thank you. You are a really good friend."

"I know, right?" Max grinned before turning toward the bathroom door. "I'm leaving now! Count to ten and come out!"

The soundproofing of the house was excellent, but the bathroom door wasn't as fortified as the bedroom door, so it didn't block out all sounds.

"Thank you," came the muffled reply.

Darlene waited until she was sure that Max was no longer in the room before opening the door and peeking into the darkened bedroom.

The illumination came from two small, scented candles, soft music was playing, and the door to the bedroom had been left slightly ajar.

There was no helping it. The soundproofing was so good in the village that a closed door would have prevented Max from hearing when was the right moment to come in, and for some reason, Eric and Max thought it was important that the venom and the semen entered her body at the same time.

Darlene didn't think it mattered. If semen could stay viable in a woman's body for forty-eight hours and fertilize her egg, the same should be true for its other properties. Max could come in whenever he was ready and bite her.

On the other hand, it was better if she was climaxing when it happened, so she would be flooded with endorphins, and it wouldn't hurt as much.

"Are you just going to stand there?" Eric said. "Come out and let me see you."

Feeling a blush rise on her cheeks, she opened the door wider and stepped into the bedroom. "Hello." She smoothed her hand over her voluminous cotton nightgown before daring to look at Eric.

He was sprawled over the bed, heavy chains securing him to the four-poster and a blanket spread over his groin to protect his modesty.

His body began shaking, alarming her, but then he burst out laughing. "What the hell are you wearing?"

She let out a breath. "You scared me. I thought you were having a reaction to the titanium chains or something."

"I'm not a werewolf. Did you get that travesty of a nightgown from a costume shop?"

It was a Victorian-style nightdress, with a high neck that tied with a string at the throat, plenty of lacy embellishments, and a wide cut that could hide an orgy going on under it. Not that an orgy was about to happen. She was going to ride Eric, Max was going to come in at the critical moment, bite her, and leave. She was making sure that he saw nothing of her body while he was at it.

"I got it at Macy's, and it's perfect for what we have planned. Do you want Max to see me nude while I'm riding you?"

Eric growled. "I don't. Now, come here and lift that two tons of fabric so I can see your beautiful legs."

Sauntering toward the bed and trying to look sexy despite what was covering her, Darlene smiled. "You are not in any position to issue orders, my love."

"That wasn't an order. That was a request." He tried to push higher on the pillows.

The chains rattled, but there was very little give. No more than an inch or two.

Was Max really that afraid of Eric attacking him?

Darlene bunched the skirt up as she climbed on the bed with her knees, exposing her legs like he'd asked. "Let's see what goodies are hiding under the blanket." Given that it was lying flat against his groin, he wasn't aroused, and she couldn't blame him.

Darlene felt as sexy as a fish left to dry on the sand.

"Climb up and straddle my face. Just keep that night-gown up, so I don't suffocate."

"Are you sure? What if Max misinterprets the sounds and comes in too soon?"

"He won't. Come here." He wiggled his tongue, and his eyes started glowing. "You know how much I love tonguing you. This will get us both in the mood."

As if to prove his words, the blanket lifted a bit, the outline of his shaft making Darlene's mouth water.

"Maybe we can put each other in the mood simultaneously?"

He shook his head. "Not tonight, love. I don't want to accidentally come in your hot mouth."

"You're an immortal now." She gripped the sides of her gown and pulled it up as she flipped one knee over his torso and climbed up to his face. "You have more than one load in you now."

"I had more than one for you even before I turned immortal." He kissed the top of her mound.

She'd had it waxed to be as bare as that of the immortal females, and it had been so painful that she hoped never to have to do that again. Going through the awkwardness with Max might be worth it just for that.

"Come up a little closer." Eric blew air on her heated flesh. "I want to taste that sweet pussy of yours."

His tongue gently circled the nub at the apex of her thighs with feather-like strokes to get her started.

Eric knew her so well by now, having memorized every response to every stimulus. He knew that she was sensitive there and if he started too fast and too aggressively, it would be a turn-off for her and not a turn-on. It would become painful in seconds.

It had taken Eric one time to learn that, while Leo hadn't learned that lesson even after nearly three decades of marriage. He'd just conveniently assumed that she wasn't into it and stopped offering.

Not that he'd offered to pleasure her much to start with. He'd been much happier to be on the receiving end while complaining that she was no good at it despite coming down her throat every freaking time.

Darlene shook her head.

This was no time to think about damn Leo and the damage he had done to her. He was ancient history, and she was in the process of being reborn, of rebuilding herself from the ground up, figuratively and materially.

"Stay with me, love," Eric murmured before moving his talented tongue to her entrance and slipping it inside for a few greedy licks. "Cup your breasts for me," he murmured against her moist petals. "Let me see those ripe nipples of yours as you play with them."

Easier said than done while holding up ten pounds of fabric, but she was determined to make it work. Pulling the nightgown all the way up to her throat, she tucked the sides under her armpits and folded her arms to reach for her breasts.

"Yeah." Eric's eyes cast a glow on her naked skin. "Just like that."

Feeling the heat radiate up from her core, she fondled her breasts and pinched her nipples as Eric alternated between thrusting his tongue into her wetness and flicking it over her engorged clit.

Darlene breathed through the pleasure, her hips bucking uncontrollably against Eric's mouth, but she kept her lips tightly pressed together, muffling the moans that begged to be let out.

She didn't want to share any of this with Max.

When the first climax tore through her, she had no choice but to open her mouth, or she would have suffocated on the cry that needed an outlet.

The chains rattled as Eric strained against them, reminding her that this pleasure had been one-sided and only the start, and that much more was awaiting her under the thin blanket covering him.

Eric

Darlene's sweet, fragrant pussy hovered above Eric's face, her hips undulating with the aftershocks of her climax, and as he licked her clean, he was so damn aroused that he was afraid he would shoot his load the moment she touched his painfully stiff shaft.

Panting, she let the hideous nightgown flutter down around her, restricting his airflow, but a moment later, she shifted down, dragging the fabric with her.

"I think you're ready for me, lover boy." She gripped what was covering him and tossed it aside. "Oh, my. Ready and then some." She dipped her head.

"Don't. I'm about to blow."

She looked at him over her shoulder and smirked. "Normally, that wouldn't be a problem, but we don't want to waste your most potent load."

Gripping him lightly, she positioned him right at her entrance, and holding him in place, she lowered herself on top of him.

Eric bit down hard on his lower lip, commanding his seed to recede and wait for the right moment.

When Darlene pushed down, and her heat enclosed him, he realized that he was never going to get enough of it. They could make love thousands of times, and he would still want her, on top of him, taking him, taking her pleasure from him. He would look at her beautiful face and feel the love swelling in his chest for this amazing woman who had saved him from a life of coasting but not living.

"Let me see you," he begged.

She folded the nightgown over her knees but left where they were joined covered. "Close your eyes," she whispered. "Imagine that I'm naked."

Darlene started moving, her hips swaying as she pushed down and lifted and then pushed down again, getting a rhythm on.

Needing to touch her, his fists opened and closed, opened again, and gripped the sheet under him, tearing into the fabric as he struggled to hold on and not come right away.

He wanted her to climax again, and not from Max's venom bite.

As the aggression surged in his chest, his muscles tightened, and he pulled on the chains, but they held him firmly. All he could do to distract himself from thinking about the Guardian in the next room was to focus on Darlene's hips going up and down and how much he wanted to grip them.

"Lift that damn skirt. I need to see you riding me."

When she did as he asked, what he saw mesmerized him. Every time she moved up, he saw his glistening shaft, and each time she lowered herself on his length, seeing it disappear inside of her filled him with lust and possessiveness that was almost too much to bear.

Gritting his teeth and wishing that they were fangs, he hissed. "Come for me, Darlene."

With a groan, she threw her head back, and as her sheath tightened around his shaft, he started coming.

He was still drunk on her and semi-conscious when the door banged open, and a monster with long fangs and crazed eyes rushed toward his woman.

Eric's instincts roared to life, and the need to leap from the bed and protect his female was overwhelming. As he pulled on the chains, the wooden poles groaned but held, and he could do nothing but watch helplessly as the monster gripped Darlene's head.

Darlene

As Darlene heard the door bang open, she let go of the nightgown, so it covered her and Eric. Keeping her eyes closed to keep Max out of her awareness, she had a moment of fear as the chains rattled and the bedposts groaned, and then a powerful hand gripped the top of her head, yanking it to the side.

She expected Max to tear the top of her nightgown to expose her throat, but he just bit her through the fabric.

The pain was intense, a burning sensation that had her hiss, but it didn't last long. A cooling sensation followed, flooding her with a wave of euphoria, but the peace didn't last long either. A wave of lust followed, and she was coming again and again. No longer mindful of keeping quiet, she heard herself screaming, but had no idea what syllables were leaving her hoarse throat.

When a loud crack sounded, pulling her out of her euphoric trip, her eyes flew open, and she had a brief

"Do you need help?" Max asked from the doorway.

"Stay out," Eric hissed. "I've got it."

"Don't be an idiot. You might have broken your back, and you are squashing Darlene. Let me lift the bedposts and unlock the restraints."

Max's words managed to penetrate through the crazed haze that had overpowered him when the guy had bitten Darlene.

Eric hadn't been thinking straight when he'd pulled on the chains and brought the massive posts down. Thankfully, he'd had enough presence of mind to pull Darlene under him, so they wouldn't crash into her. But now, he was on top of her, and with the added weight of the posts, he must be crushing her.

The pain had started to register as well. Did he have broken ribs?

Lifting on his forearms, Eric relieved Darlene of some of the weight and turned to look at the Guardian. "Fine. But leave after you unlock the restraints."

Max smirked. "I should wait for later to say this, but I can't. I told you so."

He started on Eric's left wrist. "I can't lift the posts without freeing you first because the chains are still attached to them on one end and to you on the other."

"Got it." Eric gritted his teeth as the need to attack Max assailed him again. "Those damn immortal instincts are such a nuisance."

"I know. I told you so."

If this one time didn't do the trick, he didn't think he could go through it again. Not after experiencing it. If he hadn't been chained to the bed, he might have tried to kill Max. The Guardian wasn't a foe easy to overcome, he was immortal, and Eric didn't have fangs and venom yet, so he couldn't have killed him even in his crazed state, but he would have inflicted pain on a friend who'd just been trying to help.

Yeah, right. As if Max didn't enjoy biting Darlene.

Don't go there, idiot.

When Max was done freeing Eric, he carried the clanking bundle of chains out of the room, and by the sound of it, dropped it on the hallway floor.

He returned to lift one of the bedposts and carried it outside the room as well. "It's good that the mattress is sitting on its own support, or it would have crashed to the floor as well. This bed is going to the dumpster." He lifted the next one and carried it out too.

When he was done with the fourth one, he looked at the floor. "Don't let Darlene walk barefoot here before we vacuum the place. The floor is covered with wood chips."

"Got it. Can you leave now, so I can assess the damage?"

"I'll be in the living room if you need me."

"Thanks." Eric waited for the door to close before daring to look down at Darlene.

She had a smile on her face, which alleviated his anxiety, and when he pulled out of her and lifted her nightgown to check for bruises, he was relieved to see that there were none on her body. There was a small bruise on her right wrist where it had been pressed against one of the chains, but other than that, she seemed fine.

"I really hope it worked, my love." He dipped his head and pressed a soft kiss to her parted lips. "If we have to do it again, we will need to do it in a dungeon where the chains can be embedded in concrete." He flexed one arm to look at the muscle. "I turned into a damn gorilla."

How he hadn't caused her more damage than that one little bruise was a mystery. One thing was for sure. He needed to be careful with Darlene from now on. She was still human, and he was much stronger than he'd thought he was.

As he carefully lowered one leg to the floor and then the other, the pain wasn't too bad, and when he straightened up, it got just a little worse. Hopefully, that meant nothing was broken. There was no blood either. When he checked in the bathroom mirror, the red marks that the posts had left behind on his skin were already fading.

"The advantages of being an immortal." He washed himself in the sink, wetted a few washcloths, and returned to the bedroom.

The room looked like a war zone, and after he'd cleaned Darlene up, he covered her with the blanket, pulled on a pair of pajama pants, and went to the kitchen to grab the Dyson.

"Is she okay?" Max asked.

Now that Eric was back to his normal self, his animosity toward Max was gone, and he was grateful to his friend for his help.

"She's out like a light. I wonder if the noise from the vacuum cleaner will wake her up."

"Not likely." Max grinned. "I pumped her with enough venom to knock her out until tomorrow."

Eric's lips pulled back from his teeth. "Do me a favor, and don't talk about that? I was just thinking that I'm calm enough to appreciate what you have done for us, and now I'm back to raging."

Max lifted his hands in the air. "I will never mention it again. Whiskey?" He rose to his feet.

"Definitely, and a lot of it." Eric started toward the bedroom.

"Coming up," Max said.

Kian

It was nearly nine o'clock at night when Leon and Marcel called to report what they had learned from Sofia.

"Did she give you a hard time?" Kian asked.

"Not at all," Leon said. "She was very helpful, and you are going to love some of her ideas. In fact, you might want to get Turner on the line if it's not too late."

Kian hadn't expected Sofia to contribute ideas. In fact, he'd been sure that she would resist providing them with more information about her people. Perhaps she'd fed them misinformation? Then again, Emmett and Eleanor had been right there with her, and she'd known that they could verify everything she'd told them, so it wasn't likely that she'd fed them lies.

"Before I do that, did you get the location of the tunnels from her?"

"There are four tunnels that she knows of," Marcel said. "She marked the map, but naturally, the entrances to the tunnels are guarded, the dirt road leading to the first entrance is peppered with cameras, and the last tunnel doesn't go inside the compound. It spills right outside its walls, and there is another gate to go through. Bottom line, getting to the area around the compound where the Kra-ell are hunting in order to grab one is not feasible, but we can grab the guards from the entrance to the first tunnel. It will require tampering with the cameras, but that's not a big deal. Sofia says that the guard shifts last about twelve hours, so that gives us plenty of time to grab them, pump the pureblood in charge for information, thrall them or compel them to forget that they were interrogated, and put them back at their posts before their replacements arrive. That gives us a much longer window of time to work with than kidnapping a pure-blood during a hunt. They might communicate with the other guards at certain intervals throughout the day, so that should be the first thing we address when we capture them."

"Just as an aside," Leon interjected. "Sofia bases her assessment of their shift length on what Igor's personal guard told her about his own schedule. That doesn't mean that the guards at the tunnels operate on a similar one."

"We also came up with a way to use a combination of spiders and mini drones to kickstart a resistance," Marcel said. "The spiders can deliver messages back and forth, and the drones can drop earpieces. Sofia says that the human quarters are rarely inspected, and that we can safely drop earpieces in the children's playground. She sketched a layout of the compound that's to scale and is very detailed. She doesn't know what's inside the Kra-ell quarters, but she's familiar with the office building where Igor and the other purebloods in charge spend most of their time. I'll scan it and send it over to you."

That was excellent intel. If need be, they could launch a missile at the office building and eliminate the Kra-ell leadership while minimizing civilian casualties.

"Let me get Turner on the line and bring him up to speed."

Turner answered immediately. "Hello, Kian."

"I have Leon and Marcel on the line. They have interesting new information."

After listening to Kian repeat what they had reported, Turner asked, "Did Sofia volunteer the information, or did Eleanor compel her to talk?"

"She volunteered it," Marcel said. "She was so excited about the possibility of contacting her father and letting him know that her death would be faked and that she was not really going to die. I didn't have the heart to ask Eleanor to verify that she'd told us the truth. It would have been insulting."

Turner chuckled. "I can see why you are no longer a Guardian. You think with your heart and not your head. She could've fed you all a bunch of lies."

Kian felt offended on behalf of Marcel. Guardians were not cold-hearted. Hell, he wasn't cold-hearted either. Did Turner suggest that having emotions made him an ineffective leader?

"Come on, Turner. Emmett and Eleanor were right there with her. Sofia knew that they could force her to tell the truth, and if they caught her in a lie, that would have looked really bad for her, and she would have been forced to tell the truth anyway."

"That might be true, but I would have verified the information, nonetheless. Are you willing to risk the lives of your men because you don't want to hurt the girl's feelings?"

"Good point." Kian sighed. "Emmett or Eleanor should verify the information. You can tell Sofia that I demanded it."

"It will be done," Leon said. "I'll have Eleanor go over everything with her tomorrow."

"I have no problem being the bad guy," Turner said. "Tell her it was me, and make me look really cold and ruthless. She's terrified of Igor, and it wouldn't hurt to let her believe that there is someone just as ruthless on our side."

Kian chuckled. "Am I not intimidating enough?"

Turner was cold, but he wasn't ruthless. After all, he was in the business of saving people, and he derived satisfaction from that, and not just because he was good at what he did.

"Using Turner as the bad guy will work better," Marcel said. "I've spent a lot of effort convincing Sofia of our moral superiority, praising our leadership for the good work it does, and emphasizing the checks and balances we employ. I think that was instrumental in her volunteering information, and I would hate to see all that work go to waste. I would much prefer to have her on our side voluntarily."

"It's good that you did that," Turner said. "You showed her the carrot. But it's also good to have a stick. It makes persuasion much more effective."

Marcel

Marcel didn't want to show Sofia the stick. When he returned to the bunker, he planned to tell her who he was and what he could potentially do for her. If that didn't pull her fully over to their side, a stick wasn't going to do it either. But he couldn't disobey Kian.

"What are we going to do with this information?" Leon asked. "Are we going to start a rebellion?"

"A plan is starting to formulate in my head," Turner said. "It's a combination of what you suggest, Merlin's potion, and Toven. The question is what we are going to do once we liberate the compound. Are we going to leave Jade in charge? Who's to say that she wouldn't turn out to be just as dangerous of an adversary as Igor? So far, they don't know that we exist. Once they do, will they consider us a threat?"

There was a long moment of silence as everyone contemplated his statement.

"We still don't know how many Kra-ell communities are scattered around the globe," Kian said. "What they were sent here for, and if any more are scheduled to arrive. Jade might know the answers to that, and if we help her liberate her people, she will owe us. Emmett and Vrog claim that she's an honorable female, so she might feel obligated to share the information with us, and if not, we can have Toven get it out of her. The bottom line is that we can't leave things as they are and hope the Kra-ell will never discover us." He chuckled. "Worst case scenario, we can let the Doomers know about them. They would take care of the problem for us."

"I didn't think I would live to see the day when we cooperate with Navuh," Leon said.

Kian huffed. "Who said anything about cooperation? I will never trust that fucker not to turn around and stab me in the back. But he's a known entity, and he has the force to deal with the Kra-ell. If they pose a threat to us, I would be very happy to get them to fight each other while we stand back and watch."

So many suggestions had been flying back and forth that Marcel was confused as to what step they were about to take next.

"What is the play, then?" he asked. "What's our next move? Does Sofia keep feeding Igor nonsense about a paranormal community and its breeding program? Are we grabbing the guards?"

"Grabbing the guards might be one of the first steps," Turner said. "Or we might employ a shortcut and drive the cat around. If we are lucky, the tracker we took out of Sofia has a pureblooded tail, and we might be able to collect the information from them before Onegus's team even leaves for Karelia. For that to work, though, we would need Toven to return to the area and be on standby. It's imperative that Igor doesn't find out that we captured and interrogated his men, and no one other than Toven is capable of compelling them into pretending that nothing happened and keep reporting as usual. He would probably need Mia's help to override Igor's compulsion."

"That's risky," Kian said. "If Toven fails, or if they manage to send a signal before we incapacitate them, we won't be able to implement any of the other ideas we discussed. Igor will lock down his compound, and if he's a coward like most despots, he might escape with his inner circle."

"That would be a good thing, right?" Marcel asked. "Maybe we want him to find out, so he leaves the compound, and we just walk in and take over."

Kian huffed. "He might blow it up to prevent us from taking anyone alive, and he would either kill Jade or take her with him."

"He would take her," Marcel said. "Sofia says that they have a daughter together and that he wants a son from her. Apparently, Jade is the most powerful pureblooded female he has, and that's why he keeps her as his main breeder even though she makes no secret of the fact that she despises him."

"He still might kill her if he believes that she betrayed him," Turner said. "And since his men will be captured while trailing Sofia's tracker, he will rightly assume that it had to do with Jade."

"We need to knock the men out and search them for listening devices and embedded trackers," Leon said. "We will need strong tranq darts."

"Give me a couple of days to work on a plan," Turner said. "In any case, Monday, the Guardian team is leaving for Karelia, and their first order of business should be to scope the dirt road leading to the first tunnel, check what kind of surveillance equipment they are using, and watch the guards to find out their schedule."

"Are we going to drive the cat around first?" Marcel asked.

"I'll get back to you on that," Turner said.

Sofia

Long after Marcel and Leon had gone to talk with the boss, and Eleanor and Emmett had said their goodbyes, Sofia was still buzzing with excitement.

Pacing the bunker's long hallway, she replayed the ideas they had come up with and the hope they offered.

Jade was a powerful female, and if she had the earpieces to protect her from Igor's compulsion, maybe she would be able to overcome the many years of it and kill the guy.

Would his inner circle have to be taken down with him?

Would that mean that her grandfather had to be killed as well?

Did she care?

There had been moments during the weeks leading to her assignment when she'd felt closer to him, moments when she'd believed that he cared, that he was proud of her, but those hopes had been shattered when she had realized that he'd sent her to be captured so she could lead him to Safe Haven's real leader.

To Kian.

Who was that guy?

Marcel sounded fond of him, respectful and appreciative, and if Kian had to answer to a council, then he wasn't a dictator like Igor. She needed to meet him in person and see for herself to believe it, though.

When the door at the top of the stairs opened, she stopped her pacing, walked over to the foot of the stairs, and looked up.

"How did it go?" she asked.

Marcel came down with boxes from the kitchen. "It went well, I think. Turner is working on a plan."

"Is Turner Kian's right-hand man?" She followed Marcel to the dining table.

"Not officially." Marcel put the boxes down. "He runs an independent hostage rescue operation, but when Kian needs help with a difficult situation, he asks for his advice." He pulled a chair out for her.

"What kinds of difficult situations does a community of paranormally talented people run into?"

She had a strong feeling that Marcel and the others hadn't been telling her the truth about that. Listening to Leon and Marcel discuss ways of infiltrating the compound and using all kinds of sophisticated spy gear made it obvious that at least part of their organization was military in nature. There was no reason for a bunch of paranormally talented people to have commando teams and know about miniature drones and spy spiders.

Maybe they were a spy organization?

Many of the paranormal talents Eleanor had talked about in her lectures could be used for spying, and it made sense for them to use those special abilities for profit. It would explain how their organization had so much money.

Marcel sighed. "That's just a cover we use. It's not really what we are about."

"I knew it. What are you about?"

He walked to the wine cabinet and pulled out a bottle and two glasses. "You'll need a drink to hear that story."

She tensed. "Are you a spy organization?"

He laughed. "No."

Then what were they?

Marcel's glowing eyes and exceptional night vision could be some strange manifestation of a paranormal talent, or, as she'd suspected all along, he and the others were like the Kra-ell. They looked human, but so did some of the hybrids. Except, none of the Kra-ell hybrids were blond like Marcel. The dark coloring of the pureblooded Kra-ell was dominant.

"Are you a different kind of Kra-ell?"

"In essence, yes."

Sofia's breath caught in her throat.

Marcel uncorked the wine and poured it into two glasses. "We are the descendants of the mythological gods, who we suspect came from the same place as the Kra-ell. Another hypothesis is that the gods and the Kra-ell have a common ancestor. We are genetically similar, and both species are compatible with humans."

Her heart beating at double speed, Sofia emptied the wine down her throat. "In what way are you similar? And who are the mythological gods you are referring to?"

"I know that you didn't attend regular school, but to be accepted to the university, you must have been taught the regular school curriculum." He opened the two boxes and pushed one toward her.

"I can't eat." She pushed it away. "Are you talking about the Greek pantheon?"

"The Greek, the Roman, the Norse, and many others have their roots in the Sumerian, as does the Bible. They are all talking about the same gods. Those stories are mainly fantasies, but they are based on real people." He smiled. "My ancestors."

"Why are you telling me this now? What has changed?"

"I'll get to that in a moment." He pushed his box away as well and leaned to take her hand. "You noticed that my eyes glow, right?"

Sofia nodded.

"I also have fangs. But my fangs are not for drinking blood like the Kra-ell's. They are to inject venom. Did you notice that you black out after we make love?"

Her other hand flew to her neck. "Yes."

"That's because of my bite. My venom contains a powerful euphoric and an aphrodisiac, and it's responsible for the strings of orgasms you've been enjoying, as well as for the floaty, dreamy feeling that followed them."

It was just like Marcel to deliver his little lecture on the benefits of his venom as if he was explaining the operating manual of some gadget he'd developed.

She shook her head. "Why can't I remember you biting me?" She rubbed a spot on her neck. "Was it here?"

Nodding, he reached with his finger and tapped the other side of her neck. "I bit you here too. You can't remember it because I thralled you to forget it. Remember what I told you about my special ability to make you forget things that happened and remember things that didn't?"

"Like the necklace that you bought your ex-girlfriend, only it wasn't a necklace, but something else that you refused to tell me."

"Correct. But it's also not an ability that's reserved just for me. Nearly all immortals can do that, just as nearly all Kra-ell can compel."

Sofia's heart dropped to the pit of her stomach. When she'd suspected that Marcel wasn't entirely human, it hadn't crossed her mind that he might be long-lived.

He wouldn't want to tie himself to a woman who was going to get old in a couple of decades, while he still looked as young as he was now.

Was he young, though?

"Immortals? Is that what you call yourselves?" She couldn't keep the bitter tone from her voice.

"We are immortal. We can be killed, but it's difficult to do, and if no disaster befalls us, we can live forever. Our bodies don't age, they don't get sick, and we have phenomenal self-repairing capabilities."

Marcel

Marcel had a feeling that he was botching it. He'd prepared his speech while waiting for his takeout to be packaged, and he'd thought he had it covered, but Sofia's response wasn't what he'd expected.

She wasn't excited.

In fact, she seemed upset.

"Do you live even longer than the purebloods?" she asked.

He nodded. "Emmett and the other hybrids assume that the average lifespan for the purebloods is about a thousand years. Is that what you were told as well?"

She nodded. "No one knows how long the hybrids will live. The oldest in our compound is about eighty." She let out a breath. "I still don't understand why you are telling it to me now. Is it because I'm not going back, and you are tired of telling me stories?"

Perhaps when he got to the point and told her the real reason, she would cheer up.

Lifting her hand to his lips, he kissed her knuckles. "What if I told you that I can make you live at least as long as the hybrids?"

Her eyes widened. "How?"

"That requires a bit of an explanation, so bear with me." He took in a breath. "When the gods took human partners, their children were born immortal. However, when those immortals grew up and took human partners, their children were born human."

"It's the same for the Kra-ell. My mother is a hybrid, but I'm a human."

He smiled. "I'm not done. They later discovered that the children born to immortal females still carried the godly genes, and that those genes could be activated with an immortal male's venom. We produce it in response to two triggers, and the composition of the venom depends on the type of trigger. One is arousal, which makes us produce less potent venom that does all those wonderful things like orgasms and euphoric trips, and the other trigger is aggression, which produces a potent venom that is potentially deadly because it can stop an immortal's heart. Both types can activate the dormant genes. We use the one produced by arousal to activate females, and the one produced by aggression to activate males."

Sofia shook her head. "The Kra-ell don't have venom. They use their fangs to suck blood. That's what they eat."

"Actually, they do have venom, and it has similar properties to ours in that it makes the bite pleasurable and has healing properties. But since it's produced in much smaller quantities, it can't activate Dormants, not immortal Dormants anyway. But we suspect that our venom can activate Kra-ell Dormants, which means that I might be able to activate your longevity genes."

Sofia's hand flew to her mouth. "Am I going to grow fangs?"

He laughed. "You might. But the important part is that you might live a thousand years or even longer, become stronger and faster, and all the other good things that the Kra-ell hybrids enjoy."

For a long moment, she gaped at him in stunned silence. "Do the Kra-ell know about you?"

Marcel shook his head. "We don't think they know we even exist, and we would like to keep it that way. But if we liberate Igor's compound, our secret will be out. Not only that, if I manage to activate your dormant genes, the Kra-ell will have a big incentive to either cooperate with us so we can activate their Dormants or try to use us to propagate their species. Since we are compatible, our females can provide them with immortal offspring, and our males can activate their second-generation hybrids who are born to hybrid mothers."

"Why just the mothers?"

"The longevity is passed through the mothers. Compulsion ability seems to be passed by the fathers for reasons we are not clear on."

Leaning back, Sofia closed her eyes. "How many times have you bitten me?"

"Twice. Usually, it takes several bites for the transition to start. I didn't know that you had Kra-ell blood in you. It only occurred to me that you might be a Dormant after you told me that your mother was a hybrid. We knew that the Kra-ell couldn't activate their second generation with humans, and we also knew that a hybrid Kra-ell male couldn't activate one of our dormant females. It took me a little while to go through the mental exercise and realize that maybe I could induce your transition. Once I did, I knew that I couldn't keep biting you and having unprotected sex with you without obtaining your consent to induce you. It's a monumental decision, and it needs to be yours."

"What does unprotected sex have to do with anything? I'm on birth control."

"Our doctor believes that insemination boosts the power of the venom. Most of what we know about how it works is by trial and error." He chuckled. "I think that the geneticists who engineered us made it in such a way that the catalysts would remain a mystery."

Sofia looked puzzled. "What are you talking about? Who engineered you?"

"Not me specifically. We speculate that the gods engineered themselves, humans, and other species."

"That's a lot of speculation and very little proof."

"I know. We hope that Jade will be able to tell us more."

"Is that why you are willing to help free her?"

Marcel rubbed a hand over the back of his neck. The conversation wasn't going the way he'd hoped, and he needed to get it back on track.

"As I said before, I'm not the one making those kinds of decisions. Let's get back to the issue at hand. You need to decide whether you want me to try to induce you or not."

"What's to decide?"

He chuckled. "Maybe you'd rather remain human than grow fangs, which by the way, our females don't have. But seriously, the transition is not easy, and many transitioning Dormants lose consciousness. Some are out for a day or two, while others are out for weeks. There is also a very low risk of death."

She narrowed her eyes at him. "How low?"

"We haven't lost a transitioning Dormant yet, and the younger and healthier you are, the less risky it is. You really have nothing to worry about, but I would be remiss if I didn't warn you of the risks."

"Makes sense, and I appreciate that you are not trying to sugarcoat it. I have a question, though. How do you know that a Kra-ell male can't activate one of your Dormants?"

"Emmett had been having sex with a dormant lady for many years, and he failed to activate her despite biting her numerous times. She transitioned after falling in love with one of us. Still, he's a hybrid, so perhaps a pure-blood can do that."

She nodded. "That's why you were asking me whether I had sex with any hybrids or purebloods."

"Yes. Did you?"

She glared at him. "I've already told you that I didn't."

He lifted his hands. "Just double-checking. You might have felt bad about being coerced."

"I haven't been coerced." She winced. "At least not as far as I know. If some of them can make people forget things, they could have done that to me, but I really doubt that."

"Good. Since no one aside from me had ever injected you with venom, there is a chance that mine can activate your dormant genes."

Hope surged in Sofia's chest, but she didn't allow it to soar too high.

What Marcel was proposing had never been done before, and it probably wouldn't work. They weren't even the same species.

Both of them were half-human, or three-quarters in her case. Was his mother a goddess? Were gods from mythology still around?

"I have so many questions."

"That's what I'm here for. Ask away."

"How old are you?"

"Three hundred and twenty-seven."

"Oh, wow. That's old."

He chuckled. "Thanks."

"Is your mother a goddess?"

"My mother is an immortal, and so was her mother before her, and so on. The females of our clan kept us from going extinct by having children with human fathers. But unlike you, we didn't grow up with those fathers. To keep our existence a secret, long-term relationships with humans were discouraged, or rather disallowed, and the men who sired us were not even told about having us."

She scrunched her nose. "So your blood must be heavily diluted. Are you sure you can activate me?"

Marcel nodded. "If you can be activated, I can surely do that. Our doctor says that eventually our genes will become too diluted to produce Dormants, but we still have a long time until that happens. You need to change your thinking from the Kra-ell's ability to produce just one generation of hybrids to the immortals' ability to produce them in perpetuity."

"Your people's genetics must be superior to ours."

"As I mentioned before, the theory is that the gods were genetically enhanced. The Kra-ell might have been the original. We are all dying to get a pureblood in our hands so we can finally learn the truth about our past. The gods were just as bad about keeping information from the next generation of even their own pureblooded children as the Kra-ell are. I wonder if that has to do with cultural issues or if they both share such a shameful past that they prefer to keep it where it belongs?"

"Are any of the gods still around?"

"None of the original ones, but a few of their pure-blooded children survived. The head of our clan is a goddess. Kian is her son, and he leads the American arm of the clan. There aren't many of us, but there is another group of immortals who are led by a god's son, and who have many thousands of warriors. We are not on good terms with them, and that's putting it mildly, but if the Kra-ell turn out to be a bigger threat than we anticipate, we might get those other immortals involved. As the saying goes, the enemy of my enemy is my friend. Maybe having a mutual enemy would finally end the animosity between our two groups, although I doubt it. Our feud has been going on for thousands of years."

That was all fascinating, and Sofia wanted to learn much more about his people's history, but that wasn't what was at the forefront of her mind right now.

"What happens if I don't transition?"

"You will live out your human life in our village, hopefully as my mate." He cupped her cheek. "But I have a strong feeling that you will transition. The Fates wouldn't have brought us together and dangled the perfect mate in front of me only to deny us a long life together. The Fates are fickle, and they have a wicked sense of humor, but they are not cruel."

This was the closest Marcel had ever gotten to telling her that he loved her, but it wasn't good enough. Calling her his perfect mate wasn't the same as calling her the love of his life.

Sofia sighed. "I'm touched that you think I'm perfect for you, but I'm not a great believer in fate. I believe in the Mother of All Life, and she's not a kind goddess. She's demanding and vengeful, and she doesn't grant happy endings. The best I can hope from her is that when I die, I ascend to a place of honor on the field of heroes, but since I'm human, I'm not likely to get there. So, in fact, the best I can hope for is not to be sent to the valley of the shamed."

Marcel arched a brow. "Is that like the human hell?"

"There is no fire or brimstone, so no, but it's the place all cowards go to."

"You're not a coward."

"Oh yes, I am. I've spent most of my life being afraid."

"That doesn't make you a coward. We are all afraid of one thing or another. It's what we do despite our fears that defines us as either cowards or heroes."

As Marcel reflected on his own life, he realized that he'd spent most of it being afraid of making mistakes, of trusting people who would later disappoint him, of choosing the wrong path, and he'd been a coward because he had let those fears keep him in a sort of suspended animation.

He'd chosen to be a coward.

He'd dedicated himself to his work, learning as much as he could about machines and their language because machines were predictable. They weren't manipulative, they weren't temperamental, and they gave back in direct proportion to what was put into them.

With William at the helm, Marcel had been shielded from having to make decisions or deal with their consequences, and the only responsibilities he'd had were to perform his job well, which he had done.

It had been a safe and comfortable life, devoid of turmoil, and then Sofia had shown up and had blown it to smithereens.

On the one hand, he loved the exhilaration, the novelty, the challenge, and the way she made his heart beat erratically, but on the other hand, he yearned to go back to his calm and orderly life where every day was more or less the same as the one preceding it.

"How do you know that I'm your perfect mate?" Sofia asked. "Maybe it's just a passing infatuation." She smiled sadly. "I'm a novelty that you will eventually grow tired of."

He briefly closed his eyes. "I'm not a great romantic, or at least I'm not anymore, and even when I was young and naive and fell in love left and right, I didn't know how to express myself. I still don't. But there is a simple test that I dare you to try. Close your eyes and imagine a life without me. If the thought doesn't squeeze your heart, then perhaps I'm not the one for you."

She shook her head. "That's such a simplistic approach. If I do it now, I'm sure that's precisely how I would feel. But if you hurt me badly enough, those feelings would die the same way as your feelings for your ex-girlfriend died after she'd hurt you. People say that true love is unconditional, but that's untrue. Everything is about give and take." She chuckled. "Look at who is decisively unromantic now. I bet you've never heard a woman say those things."

He smiled. "The Kra-ell don't believe in love. I guess growing up among them rubbed off on you."

"I believe in love. I just don't believe in unconditional love. If you treat me right and love me, I'll treat you right and love you in return. But I will never love a man who abuses me or treats me with disrespect." She averted her eyes. "My biggest fear living in the compound was being forced into becoming a breeder. The way I dealt with the fear was by minimizing it. The purebloods didn't seek out human women to have a relationship with. They only wanted to produce hybrid offspring to grow their numbers. I figured I could tolerate having sex with them as long as I didn't need to feel anything for them. Thankfully, my being related to Valstar afforded me some protection. None of the purebloods have approached me."

"I assume that he's someone important in Igor's organization."

Sofia nodded. "He's Igor's second-in-command."

Marcel's good mood took a nosedive.

Sofia had failed to disclose her relationship to the most important member of Igor's inner circle, painting herself as an innocent victim, compelled into doing the evil dictator's bidding.

Was it his lot in life to fall for women who disappointed him?

Marcel let out a breath. "Turner asked me to have Eleanor or Emmett verify the information you provided by compelling you to tell the truth. I told him that you were cooperating out of your own free will and that it wasn't necessary. But he was right."

She frowned. "What are you talking about?"

"You've just let slip that you're related to Igor's second-in-command. You're not the innocent victim you portrayed yourself to be."

Throwing her hands in the air, Sofia pushed to her feet. "You're insufferable, and Eleanor is right. You have a giant stick up your ass, and until you pull it out, don't talk to me about being your perfect mate. In fact, don't ever talk to me again." She marched into the bedroom and slammed the door behind her.

Marcel pushed to his feet.

Her tantrum didn't affect him. He retreated into his shell, which was crafted of logic and impervious to emotions.

But the fact remained that Sofia hadn't mentioned Valstar's position in Igor's organization, and it couldn't have been an oversight. She'd done it on purpose.

Then again, could he blame her?

Would he have done things differently in her position?

It all depended on how being related to Igor's second-in-command affected her standing in the compound.

The easiest way to get the answers he needed was to ask Eleanor to compel them out of Sofia.

The problem was that she might never forgive him for doubting her again.

Sofia threw herself on the bed but refused to cry.

Marcel had once again turned against her, but this time it hurt even more because it had come right on the heels of him declaring her his "perfect mate."

What a joke.

Couldn't he understand why she hadn't mentioned her grandfather's position before?

It was because she'd known that was how he would react despite what she told him about her relationships with her mother and her grandfather.

She was nothing to them.

She was a nobody in the compound, and her relationship to Valstar only provided her with the slightest advantage, maybe not even that. Perhaps her don't-mess-with-me attitude had been effective enough to keep unwanted advances at bay.

The Kra-ell were not rapists per se. Other than Igor, who must have a personality disorder, she hadn't noticed any obvious mental issues among the Kra-ell males. Like any normal men, they still wanted the females they invited to their beds to desire and want them.

It was true that many of the human females did that to remain in good standing and avoid courting undesirable consequences, of which there could be many, but she hadn't heard anyone complaining about being physically forced.

Then again, with all of the purebloods capable of compulsion to a lesser or greater degree, it was possible that the women just couldn't talk about it. Sofia hoped that wasn't the case, but she no longer knew who to believe.

Marcel still treated her like she was the enemy despite all of the information she'd voluntarily given him and his people—immortals who were much more dangerous than she could've ever suspected.

They weren't a community of paranormally talented humans. They had military capabilities, and they could enlist the help of their so-called enemies to destroy Igor and everyone else in the compound. Once again she'd been a pawn, but this time, of her own volition and to the detriment of her own loved ones.

How could Marcel have the audacity to accuse her of withholding information?

The nerve of the guy.

He'd gotten her to reveal the entrances to the tunnels, to admit that there were surveillance cameras along the dirt road leading to it, and to draw him a damn layout of the entire compound to scale.

It was true that Eleanor, or Emmett, or Tom could have gotten the information out of her with compulsion, but then she would at least not have felt like an idiot for volunteering it.

Seething with anger, Sofia grabbed the romance novel off the nightstand and chucked it at the wall, but it did little to channel the negative energy bubbling inside of her. The lamp looked like a much bigger projectile, but as she jumped to her feet and lifted it, intending to send it flying, logic managed to seep in and she put it back.

She would just have to clean up the broken glass, and she would have one less comfort item in her prison cell.

Exasperated, Sofia sat on the bed, braced her elbows on her knees, and let her head drop down.

When a knock sounded on the door, she ignored it, barely able to contain the words "go to hell" from leaving her mouth. It took tremendous effort to keep her lips pressed tightly together, but she knew that anything she said right now would only make things worse, so it was better to shut up.

Would it get better in a few hours?

Usually, her anger was quick to rise, quick to explode, and just as quick to subside, but not this time. She was too hurt, and frankly, there was nothing Marcel could say to make it better.

In fact, anything he said would just make it worse.

When the door eased open, she didn't even look at it.

"May I come in?" Marcel asked.

She shrugged. "It's your jail. I can't stop you."

He walked over and sat on the bed next to her. "Can you stop brooding for a moment and see things from my perspective?"

Oh, he was asking for it.

She cast him a baleful look. "Can you see things from mine? I thought that I was cooperating with humans who had paranormal abilities. Now I know that I sold out my people to another species of beings who have military capabilities and can enlist an army of immortal warriors. So you tell me who deceived whom and why."

Marcel

Sofia had a point.

"What I said before is still true." Marcel scooted a little closer to her. "We don't mean your people harm. If we can, we would like to liberate the compound, and for our own safety, we need to accumulate as much information about the Kra-ell as we can. Until recently we didn't know that they existed. We still don't know why they came, what their plans are, and if they know that we are here. If they came from the same place as the gods, they also might have information about our origins."

She shrugged. "That's a good story, but it doesn't change the fact that you can compel any information you want out of me, while I can't verify anything you say. I'm at a disadvantage, and you have the nerve of accusing me of withholding information right after you make the absurd claim that I'm your perfect mate and that you can make me long-lived or immortal. Excuse me if I'm skeptical."

"Why would I make false claims if I can force you to do anything I want?"

She turned a pair of angry eyes at him. "Just leave me alone. I don't want anything to do with you. From now on, I'll only talk with Eleanor. That way, I won't get accused of lying."

How had he messed this up so badly?

"I can't leave you alone. I've fallen in love with you, and I want to have a life with you. What can I do to fix this?"

She hesitated for a split second, but then shook her head. "Nothing. The damage has been done. Go away."

"No."

"Suit yourself." She rose to her feet, walked into the bathroom, and slammed the door shut behind her.

Despondent, he sat on the bed and waited for Eleanor to arrive.

A few moments later, he heard the door at the top of the stairs open, and then he heard Eleanor's light footsteps as she descended the stairs.

"Where is she?" Eleanor asked as she walked into the room.

"She's in the bathroom. She won't talk to me."

Hand on her hip, Eleanor cast him a glare. "What have you done?"

"I don't know. She's being unreasonable."

"Right." Eleanor walked over to the bed and sat down beside him. "That's what men say when they mess up and don't want to admit it. Is she mad that you called me to verify that what she told us before is legit?"

"That too. Evidently Valstar, who is Sofia's pureblooded grandfather, is not just a cog in the machine. He's Igor's second-in-command. Sofia just conveniently failed to mention that. She's not the innocent victim she's been portraying herself to be, and now she knows that we are immortals and that our ancestors and hers are somehow connected."

"So what?" Eleanor crossed her arms over her chest. "She's not going back, so it doesn't matter what she knows, and if she tries to breathe a word of this to her grandfather the next time she communicates with him, we will stop her. If anyone has a reason to be mad, it's her. She was keeping one little secret from you. You were keeping a very big one from her. You both had good reasons for that, and you both should get past that. It's not worth getting upset over."

"Tell that to her." He pointed at the door. "She won't listen to me, and she doesn't want to see me ever again."

Chuckling, Eleanor shook her head. "She wouldn't be so mad if she didn't care about you. Let Auntie Eleanor broker a peace." She motioned for him to get up. "Wait for us in the living room."

"That's ridiculous. I just told Sofia that she's the one for me and that I want to induce her transition. Any reasonable female would have been overjoyed."

"Oh, boy." Eleanor pushed him on his back. "You have a lot to learn about women."

"Tell me something I don't know." Marcel rose to his feet. "It's the story of my life."

The bathroom door opened, and Sofia stormed out. "And that's one more thing that you haven't told me because you don't trust me. I told you everything about my life, but you just keep hinting about the horrible thing your ex-girlfriend did, but you don't trust your so-called perfect mate enough to tell me about something that happened who knows how many years ago, and that doesn't affect anyone in the present. You're full of shit, Marcel." She stormed out of the room.

"Did you close the door upstairs?" he asked Eleanor.

"Of course. It locks automatically." She rose to her feet. "You really have to work on your trust issues."

Sofia

As Sofia paced the living room, she struggled to hold back the tears. The space was too small and too crowded with furniture to allow proper pacing, especially with her long legs, and the hallway would mean passing by the room Marcel was in, and she didn't want to look at him.

Was she overreacting?

No, she wasn't.

He was such a self-righteous prick.

What did he expect?

For her to fall on her knees and thank him for offering her a long life?

For what?

So she could spend an even longer time with a man who didn't trust her and caused her anguish?

No, thank you.

She'd rather live out her short human lifespan with someone who cherished her. Not that any such fantasy was going to materialize for her, but that didn't mean that she should compromise.

It was okay to be without. It was less painful than compromising on being with someone who made her miserable.

"Come on." Eleanor wrapped her arm around her shoulders. "Let's get out of here and breathe some fresh air."

That was a surprise. "Am I allowed out?"

Eleanor had promised to compel her into silence about everything that had gone down since that moment in Emmett's office, so she could rejoin the retreat, but she hadn't done so yet, probably because she'd known that Marcel was going to reveal more stuff, and she wanted to do it in one shot.

"I'm taking you with me, so you are under my supervision."

"What if anyone sees me?"

"Then we will tell them that you just came back, and if they ask where you have been, you can say that you're not allowed to talk about it."

Sofia sighed. "I like how simple you make everything sound. I wish Marcel was more like you."

Eleanor grinned. "Most people don't like my direct approach, so it means a lot to me that you do."

She led her up the stairs, punched the code into the keypad so fast that Sofia's eyes couldn't follow, and opened the door.

When they were out of the cottage, Sofia took in a deep breath. "It feels so good to be outside."

Eleanor nodded. "The Kra-ell need the outdoors to thrive. Emmett was wilting when he was kept in captivity. You have their blood, so being underground must affect you negatively."

It hadn't occurred to her. Sofia had thought that the lack of freedom and the isolation were making her agitated and restless, but it was also being cooped up in an underground bunker with no windows and no fresh air.

"What time is it?"

"It's almost midnight. We can probably sneak out to the beach without anyone noticing you."

"Except for the guards."

"They are called Guardians."

"Are they your military branch?"

"They are part an internal police force, part defenders, and part rescuers of trafficking victims. Do you know what that is?"

"The term is confusing, so I'm not sure. Does that refer to women who are kidnapped and sold into sexual slavery?"

"By and large, yes. But most are not kidnapped, just manipulated or sold by their families, and some are forced into menial job slavery instead of forced sex service, which is only slightly less horrific, and not all are women. Girls and boys are also taken."

"Why is it called trafficking?"

Eleanor snorted. "Don't ask me. It's one of the idiotic terms that politicians come up with. It makes an abomination sound like a speeding infraction. But anyway, that's the clan's humanitarian project. They raid the cells, free the victims, and rehabilitate them. The clan is not big, so their impact on the global problem is negligible, but every life matters, right? At least they are doing something."

Sofia nodded. "It's admirable."

"It is, and that's why I told you about it. The goddess leading these immortals made it her goal to assist humanity to become a more enlightened civilization, where everyone's human rights are respected, where people are given equal freedoms regardless of anything other than being born under the sun and given equal chances to succeed. She instilled those values in her children and grandchildren and their children and so forth. The clan is a force for good, and they made a convert even out of me, the most cynical, jaded woman you ever met."

"I'm sure you're exaggerating. You can't be that bad if I like you."

Eleanor snorted. "Perhaps compared to the Kra-ell females, I'm a sweetheart. Anyway, I haven't met anyone worse than me, so I can't be sure of that statement. But I can assure you that I'm a changed woman, and in my case, it wasn't because of a man. I met Emmett long after deciding that I was going to work with the clan and not against it."

They'd walked around the lodge rather than through it, so they'd made it to the beach without anyone stopping them, and as Sofia stood in front of the vast expanse of water, her agitated nerves reduced their firing speed. "I missed being out here at night."

Eleanor stood next to her. "The Kra-ell compound is not near the ocean?"

"There is a lot of greenery inside the compound as well as around it, and there are many bodies of water in Karelia." She smiled. "Over the last seven years, I lived mostly in Helsinki, but I made sure to spend as much time as I could in nature. It's probably the Kra-ell part of me that craves it."

It was almost two in the morning when Eleanor and Sofia returned, and Sofia looked like a different person. She even gave him a tentative smile.

"She's all yours." Eleanor winked at him. "Don't mess it up." She turned and walked toward the stairs, but then stopped and looked at him over her shoulder. "All the information is verified, and there is nothing to add. You can take it from here."

"Hi." Sofia remained standing. "I'm sorry about blowing up before," she said as the door at the top of the staircase closed. "Eleanor explained a lot of things, and I know now what the clan and the goddess who heads it are about. I find it admirable, and I wouldn't mind becoming part of it. I wish that my family could join me, but Eleanor explained that wouldn't be possible even if they were free. Kian rarely admits humans into the village."

If Eleanor was still there, Marcel would have given her a big thank-you hug and kissed her on both cheeks.

Instead, he walked over to Sofia, hesitating for a moment before wrapping his arms around her. "I'm sorry too. I shouldn't have doubted you."

Letting out a sigh, she rested her head on his shoulder and sagged into his embrace. "You had your reasons, and I had mine. Eleanor explained it all. But she left one thing for you to explain." She lifted her head and looked into his eyes. "She said that you need to tell me about fated mates and what it means."

Clever woman.

"She's right. I did a bad job of it. Hell, I made a mess out of everything. I was not blessed with the gift of gab." He led her to the couch, sat down, and pulled her into his lap.

"What's that?"

"Gab? It's the ability to express oneself eloquently, which I don't have. Everything I say sounds as if I'm reading an instruction manual."

Sofia chuckled. "I kind of like that about you. It makes you different."

"I am different, but not necessarily in a good way."

"Tell me about fated mates, and I don't mind how dry you make it sound. I'll add embellishments in my head."

"You see, that makes you my perfect mate. What other woman would have said that?"

She rolled her eyes. "Enough preamble. Just get it out already."

He nodded. "We believe that those who've earned the right, whether through sacrificing for others or suffering greatly, are rewarded by the Fates with a truelove mate. It's not what humans refer to as falling in love, and it's not like other loving relationships that the immortals might have. The attraction is immediate, resisting it is impossible, and once the bond is formed, it's unbreakable. Fated mates never look at another person with desire in their eyes. They love each other exclusively and forever."

"That sounds beautiful. Is it real?" She looked doubtful.

"I've seen it happen time and again to people I know, people who are not prone to flights of fancy, and who are not romantics at heart. The best example is Kian. He used to be a jaded, grumpy man who devoted his life to leading the clan and cared nothing about his own happiness. Then he met Syssi, and he fell in love with her right away. The same is true for her, and they are incredibly happy together. She changed him for the better. They also have a little daughter, who's the cutest little girl you'll ever see. She's beautiful like her mother, but at seven months old, she already has Kian's domineering personality, and on her, it's adorable. On him, not so much."

"I would love to meet her," Sophia whispered. "She sounds endearing."

"She is. But that's more or less what a truelove mate is. The thing is, I never sacrificed a lot for others, and my suffering was my own doing. I don't deserve a boon from the Fates."

"Neither do I, and besides, I'm not one of their subjects. I'm under the Mother of All Life's jurisdiction."

"The Fates do not belong exclusively to the clan. They are a universal force, and so is the Mother you speak of. Who knows, maybe they sit around a table in another realm, sipping on wine and coordinating their moves. They might be in cahoots."

Sofia laughed. "I love the image you're painting. What do the Fates look like?"

He caressed her back. "They can take any form they want, but I imagine them as three portly, human grandmothers with kind smiles and cunning eyes. How do you imagine your goddess?"

Sofia closed her eyes and rested her cheek on his chest. "Like an older Kra-ell pureblooded female who is ethereally beautiful and severe. She doesn't smile kindly, and her eyes are angry."

Marcel shivered. "Not my kind of deity. I prefer the three older ladies with big, soft bosoms."

"I bet." She chuckled. "Eleanor told me that immortal males are a lot like human men. You like soft females who treat you with love and kindness like your mothers."

"Perhaps that's the type other men prefer, but it's not mine."

She lifted her head and looked into his eyes. "Am I your type?"

"You are, but with a twist. I'm a sucker for delicate damsels in distress. That's my Achilles' heel. But you just look the part. On the inside, you are strong, assertive, and you are self-reliant, and I admire that."

"What about your ex? Was she a damsel in distress?"

He let out a breath. "She played the part to perfection, and I fell for it. Back then, the myth of a truelove mate was just that, a myth, but I was a romantic at heart, and I chased after it in all the wrong places. That's how I got in trouble."

"Are you ever going to tell me what really happened?"

"Do I have your consent to induce you?"

Sofia rolled her eyes. "Do you always answer a question with another question?"

"Not always, but this time I have to have the answer to that first. I will not tell this story to anyone other than my truelove mate."

"My consent will not prove it one way or another."

He put a hand on his chest. "I already know that you are in here. Your consent will mean that you accept it as well."

"Then I consent."

Sofia had planned to consent regardless of Marcel's confession.

Eleanor had told her so many good things about the clan that she would have to be stupid not to want to be part of it, and she trusted the woman.

Eleanor had nothing to gain by convincing her, she'd been sincere, and she hadn't sugarcoated anything.

After using compulsion to verify everything that Sofia had told her and the others and ensuring that she didn't have anything relevant to add, Eleanor had told her so many things that Marcel hadn't. She'd told her about the clan's powerful enemies and that it was unlikely they would ever join forces. Eleanor had also told Sofia about her struggles when she'd first transitioned, and about the unlikely help she'd gotten from the sister-in-law whom she'd abandoned in her time of need, but who had taken care of her nonetheless.

As a newcomer to the clan herself, Eleanor didn't know much about Marcel's past. She'd heard that he'd been burned by love in his youth, but she didn't know any details. Her advice had been to let it go and not press him to talk about it. Eleanor had said that she preferred not to dwell on her own past mistakes but to look forward to a better future.

Sofia disagreed.

She wanted Marcel to tell her about it, not just to satisfy her curiosity, and not just as a way to prove his devotion to her, but because he needed to unburden himself from the guilt and self-loathing that were dragging him down.

"It's not easy for me to tell this story." He leaned his forehead against hers. "You might not want anything to do with me once you hear what I have done."

"I doubt it. You are a good man, Marcel, and we all make mistakes. I bet you've been beating yourself up over whatever that was for far too long."

"It happened a very long time ago when I was still a young man."

He was three hundred and twenty-seven years old. If he'd been a young man when he'd been burned, it must have been about three hundred years ago. The world had been a very different place back then.

She leaned back and looked into his eyes. "It's definitely time to unburden yourself. Tell me."

"Cordelia was a married woman, but I didn't know that when I started seeing her. Her husband was a naval officer, and he'd been stationed on a warship. She was beautiful, delicate, and she carried sadness around her like a shawl made of gossamer. I was drawn to her like a moth to a flame. She made me feel special, as if I was the only one who could make her laugh, make her happy, and when we made love, she made me feel as if I was the best lover in the world."

Having an affair with a married woman was not a good thing, but it wasn't such a terrible offense either. Three hundred years ago, her husband might have been partying with prostitutes every night, and the only reward the poor wife could expect for waiting for him to come home had been a sexually transmitted disease.

If that had been so, then kudos to her for finding happiness in the arms of another.

"When did you find out that she was married?"

"At first, I assumed that she was a widow. A large portrait of her husband in naval uniform hung over the fireplace in the living room, but it was draped over with a semi-sheer black cloth, which indicated that he was deceased, and that the household was in mourning. None of her servants ever mentioned the master of the house, and combined with her sadness, it all pointed to one conclusion, albeit a wrong one."

"Didn't you think to ask her?"

He shook his head. "It seemed like a painful subject, and since none of the servants breathed a word of him or gave me the stink eye for spending night after night in her bedchamber, I saw no reason to ask." He closed his eyes for a moment. "I gave her expensive jewelry, not because she demanded it, but because I was a fool in love. Every time I brought her an extravagant gift, she was so happy, and it made me feel like a prince."

"Did you spend all of your money on her?"

"I did. I was a Guardian back then, and Guardians were well paid. Still are. I didn't need the money, but I could have spent it on feeding a hungry village or two instead of wasting it on a manipulative woman. I later found out that I wasn't her first lover, and that she used the same tactics with others to collect riches and pay for her extravagant lifestyle."

Sofia pursed her lips. "So you were played. Big deal. You loved her, you were blinded by her beauty and her acting, and you spent all of your money on her. It's not like you murdered anyone."

He huffed out a breath. "I'm not done. The story gets much worse."

Marcel

Marcel took a deep breath. "One day, I came to her house and found her crying."

This was the worst part, and he dreaded to see Sofia's reaction to his confession.

"'What happened?' I asked.

"'My husband is coming home,' she said.

"I thought that she meant that they were bringing his casket home, so I took her hand, looked into her eyes, and asked if she wanted me to be there when the coffin arrived, and if she needed my help with the funeral arrangements. She looked at me with her doe eyes.

"'He's not dead. But I will be when he finds out about you. He threatened to kill me before.'

"Tears were streaming down her eyes as she told me about the years of abuse she'd suffered. She pulled up her sleeve and showed me an old scar that I had seen before.

"He did this to me. The bruises have faded, the broken bones healed, but this cut is a reminder of what a monster I'm married to.'

"I was stunned. I asked her how come she'd never mentioned him before, and why none of the servants had spoken his name. She told me with teary eyes that the servants did that out of love for her.

"'They know how terribly he has been treating me, and they don't want to upset me by speaking his name. They all cower before him, his anger is explosive, and he's not averse to using his fists or even the crop. One of these days, he will finish what he started and end me. We cannot see each other anymore. If he finds out about us, he will kill us both.'"

Marcel's hands were sweaty as he lifted them to rake his fingers through his hair. "I was enraged. I couldn't understand how any man could raise his hand in anger at a woman, and especially not a delicate, gentle flower like Cordelia."

"What did you do?" Sofia asked, but the horrified look in her eyes told him that she'd already guessed.

"I promised to liberate her, and I did."

"You killed him?"

He nodded. "I waited at the docks for his ship to arrive, followed him home, and watched the reunion through the window. If he aggressed on her, I was ready to barge in and end him. He didn't act as badly as I expected, though, which should have given me pause, and Cordelia greeted him with smiles and hugs. The servants were cordial as well. I thought that it was an act meant to appease the monster. I waited until Cordelia retired to their bedchamber. She was all smiles for him, but I still thought that it was all an act, and my rage only grew because she had to pretend to love him so he wouldn't strike her, that she had to put up with him to appease him. When the husband was left alone in the salon, enjoying a drink and a pipe, I got in through one of the back patio doors. I was trained to walk soundlessly, so he didn't hear me as I walked up behind him, paralyzed him by seizing his mind, and sank my fangs in his neck. I pumped him full of venom until his heart stopped, and then I left the same way I came. He was found the next day by the maid, and the cause of death was determined as heart failure. No one suspected a thing, including Cordelia."

Sofia's hand flew to her neck. "Your fangs don't leave any marks."

"They don't. My saliva contains healing properties, and so does the venom. There was no sign of foul play."

Sofia's big eyes turned even larger. "Did you tell her that you did it?"

He shook his head. "She would have wondered how I managed to kill him without leaving any evidence. I just showed up the next day and acted as if I was shocked and relieved by the news."

"What did she do?"

"She donned mourning garb and sat in the living room crying and dabbing at her eyes. I knew it was an act, and I guess I started suspecting her then. Only the servants and I were in the house, so she had no reason to put on an act for anyone. I sat next to her and told her that she was free now, that she didn't need to live in fear anymore. She gave me a cold, accusing look.

"'To think that I invested that much work in you only to have nature take care of the problem for me. What a waste of time.'

"Her voice was as cold as ice, and so were her eyes. There was none of the warmth she used to shower me with. I knew then that I had been played."

"I can't believe you did that." Sofia rubbed her eyes as if by doing so she could erase the images that Marcel had painted in her mind. "I expected you to beat him up, to warn him never to lay a finger on her again, but you just went ahead and killed him." She took in a deep breath. "And her response. I can't wrap my mind around it. Maybe she was filled with remorse for having an affair with you?"

He laughed mirthlessly. "The woman didn't know the meaning of remorse."

"Perhaps by killing him, you saved her life?"

"I didn't."

"You can't know that. Do you know that the number one cause of death for young women is murder by their boyfriends or husbands?" She lifted a finger. "Number one. And I bet it was even worse in the days when women didn't have any rights."

Marcel shook his head. "The story gets worse. Later, I found out that he never physically abused her. He'd lashed out at her verbally on occasion, but it was well-earned. She loved to live lavishly, and she spent money beyond their means. She made up the abuse to make me get rid of him for her."

Sofia couldn't believe that Marcel had been played like that. How could he have been so gullible?

And where was that passion that had driven him to commit murder?

Had it been smothered by the guilt?

"How did you find out?"

"The way I should have done before I committed murder. I entered the minds of the servants. It turned out that I was just one more idiot in a long string of lovers, and that she told the same lies to all of them, hoping one of them would get rid of her husband for her. He was a couple of decades older, unattractive, and came from a wealthy family. She wanted to be a rich widow and spend his money without having to answer to anyone. The inheritance laws of the time were very different than they are today, and since they didn't have any children and he was much older, he put all his possessions in a trust so she would be taken care of. She must have manipulated him to do that as well."

Sofia let out a breath. "She was a sociopath like Igor. Why didn't you enter her mind to verify what she told you?" It suddenly occurred to her that he could have entered hers instead of having Eleanor compel her to tell the truth. "And why haven't you entered mine? You would have known that everything I told you and the others was true."

"It's not that simple. Memories are not objective, and people often believe the lies they tell. Also, if they are very passionate about the lies, it's difficult to differentiate. Besides, I was a Guardian back then, and I obeyed clan law which states that we are not allowed to enter a human's mind without proper justification." He snorted. "And then I went ahead and committed the worst crime imaginable."

"You must have been madly in love with her, and it clouded your judgment."

Pain lashed through her insides at the idea that he'd loved that monster so much, and it didn't matter that it happened three centuries ago. Worse, that love affair had tainted him forever and made him cold. He seemed to be warming up, but after what he'd told her, she knew that he was capable of much more feeling than what he had shown her.

Would she ever be able to scrape away the layers of guilt he'd covered himself with and uncover the man he used to be?

"I was stupid." He smoothed his hand over his hair. "Naive and trusting. I swore never to let myself fall in love again." He smiled at her. "And then you showed up, and centuries of building walls around my heart started to crumble."

Perhaps the outer walls were crumbling. The inner layers would take much more work to scrape away, but for that to happen, he needed to forgive himself first.

"From what Eleanor told me, there weren't any immortal females you could have hooked up with, so I assume that Cordelia was a human and is long dead. Do you know what happened to her?"

He shook his head. "I didn't keep tabs on her. I left on the first ship sailing to America and joined Kian's arm of the clan."

"Did you really never tell anyone but me about it?"

He shook his head. "I'm a murderer, Sofia. Why would I admit that to anyone? I didn't mind the whipping I would have gotten or even entombment, but I couldn't stand the idea of people thinking of me as an evildoer. I was supposed to be a good guy."

What a terrible burden to carry, and he was right. He was a murderer, and she had no right to absolve him of his crime. He'd made a terrible mistake.

"I don't know what to say."

Marcel sighed. "There is nothing to say. If you want to rescind your consent, I'll understand. There are many other immortal males who would be very happy to attempt to induce your transition."

As if she wanted anyone else.

Marcel looked so broken that all Sofia wanted to do was wrap her arms around him and tell him that it was okay, but it wasn't, and it would never be. He would carry the guilt of what he had done for the rest of his never-ending life.

Talk about suffering.

"I still want you, Marcel, and to be frank, I don't hold what you did against you. You did what you thought was right. I just wish there was something I could do to ease your guilt." She closed her eyes. "You've been repenting for centuries, and you've carried this terrible guilt with you, living half a life because you were afraid to let yourself feel. Maybe it's punishment enough?"

"I wish."

Suddenly, she remembered his explanation about who was deserving of a perfect mate, and it gave her an idea. "If the Fates rewarded you with a truelove mate, they must think that you are done with your penance, right?"

He smiled sadly. "Or they chose to punish me by dangling you in front of me but not making it possible for me to induce you. I really hope that's not their plan because it's not fair to use you like that."

"I've done nothing to earn their punishment."

A flicker of hope ignited in Sofia's heart. If she transitioned, Marcel would believe that he'd been forgiven.

Leaning over, she cupped his cheek. "Then I must transition to prove to you that your penance is over and that you've earned your right to live a full life again. You don't know the Fates' grand plan. Maybe the husband needed to die to prevent some major bad thing from happening, and you and Cordelia were just the pawns they moved on the chessboard to orchestrate that."

One corner of his lips lifted in a sad mockery of a smile. "I wish I could believe that."

"Believe it. I was a pawn as well, so I know all about being used by forces greater than me. I felt guilty for coming here and manipulating you, and then I felt guilty for providing you information about the compound that might endanger my family. But after talking with Eleanor, I realized that my purpose might be greater than I've given myself credit for. She pointed out that the unassuming pawn is more powerful than most pieces on the chessboard. If the pawn makes the right moves, she has the potential to become a queen and lead her army to victory." She smiled. "In my case, I want to lead an army to liberate my people, and since I don't know much about strategy or about leading armies, I need your help. Can I rely on you?"

Marcel's eyes started glowing. "Always."

She took his hand and kissed his palm. "Then let's start working on that transition. I want to be immortal when I liberate my people."

SOFIA & MARCEL'S STORY CULMINATES

The Children of the Gods Book 67
Dark Gambit Reliance

TURN THE PAGE TO READ THE EXCERPT—>

JOIN THE VIP CLUB

To find out what's included in your free membership,
flip to the last page.

Dark Gambit Reliance

Marcel takes a big risk by telling Sofia his greatest sin.
Can he trust her to keep it a secret? Or maybe it's time to
confess his crime and submit to whatever punishment
Edna deems appropriate?
Three miserable centuries of living with guilt and
remorse are long enough.

Once the dust settles on the Kra-ell crisis, he will gather the courage to put himself at the court's mercy.

Marcel

As Marcel lay awake, holding Sofia tightly against his body, wave after wave of anxiety swept through him.

When he'd told her his greatest sin, his crime, she'd been so supportive, so understanding, but would she feel the same when she woke up?

Would she want to tie herself to a murderer?

Cordelia's husband wasn't the first human Marcel had killed, but the others had been invading marauders, and he'd been defending his people. Those killings had been in the line of duty, sanctioned and justified.

Cordelia's husband had been a different story.

He'd murdered the man in cold blood. Well, in hot blood, but that was irrelevant.

Marcel had taken a life that hadn't been his to take.

He'd appointed himself the judge, jury, and executioner, and he'd convicted the man based on the words of a beautiful liar who'd had him wrapped around her little finger. He'd never stood trial for his crime, and his only punishment had been his self-inflicted flagellation and dreary existence.

What if Sofia decided to reveal his secret?

Perhaps he should just reach into her mind and suppress the memory of the murder story. He hadn't thralled her last night, but he'd done it the day before, and it was a little too soon for another thralling session. Still, given that he no longer needed to continue thralling her after every bite, it was probably fine to do it again.

Now that she knew he was immortal and that his venom bites came with several great benefits, like the possible gift of immortality, Sofia might be more inclined to forgive him his past sins.

Except, he didn't want her to be with him only because of what he could do for her. He wanted Sofia to love him for who he was, but maybe the first step toward that goal was learning to love himself.

Marcel had carried the guilt for long enough, and maybe it was time to confess his crime and submit to whatever punishment Edna deemed suitable.

Hopefully, it would be just a token whipping and some prison time.

Edna wouldn't sentence him to entombment three hundred years after the fact, right?

Enough time had passed that perhaps she wouldn't judge him as harshly.

Then again, he had nothing to say in his defense. Stupidity wasn't a mitigating circumstance, and neither was an emotional disturbance. Or was it?

He hadn't been thinking straight. He'd been in love, and Cordelia had played him like a skilled violinist, tugging on his heartstrings.

If only witchcraft were real, he could have claimed that he'd been bewitched. Three hundred years ago, that line of defense might have worked in a human court, but it wouldn't have worked in Edna's. Unless Cordelia was a powerful immortal who could manipulate his mind, she had no other power over him.

Except, she had.

She'd bewitched him with her smiles and her tears and her delicate touch, but he couldn't use that in his defense. It was entirely his fault that he had not only fallen for her deceit but had also committed a terrible crime to please her.

At the time, Marcel wouldn't have minded entombment. Hell, he would have welcomed it to escape the guilt. But now that he had Sofia, he didn't want to miss even one moment with her, and that meant keeping his crime a secret and living with the guilt because he couldn't guarantee that Edna would be lenient.

"Stop," Sofia murmured. "Your thoughts are so loud that they are waking me up." She opened her eyes and gave him a sleepy smile. "Last night was amazing. I thought I would be afraid of your fangs, but you look kind of cute with them."

"Cute?" Marcel arched a brow. "Those are deadly instruments."

Sofia stretched her long body, pressing her small breasts to his chest. "Instruments of pleasure. What a trip." She kissed the underside of his jaw. "If women knew what your venom can do, they would be beating down your door and offering you sex or lots of money just for a chance to experience that. It's like the best psychedelic on the market."

He cupped her round bottom. "How many psychedelics have you tried?"

"None, but I've heard people describe their experiences. I wanted to try it, but I was afraid. I don't like having no control over what's happening to me."

He gave her lush bottom a squeeze. "Last night, you didn't seem to mind giving up control to me."

Her expression turned serious. "That's because I trust you. I know that you will never do anything to hurt me, and you'll protect me with everything you have."

"I don't know how you can still think that after what I told you."

"Nothing has changed for me." Sofia put her hand on his chest. "What happened with that evil woman and her husband is ancient history, and you were a different man back then. If you were a human, you would have died and been reborn again at least four times by now, and the knowledge of what you had done would have been lost. The slate would have been wiped clean. It's only because you are immortal that you keep on suffering endlessly. If you ask me, you've been in hell for the past three hundred years, and you've paid for your crime. It's time for a new beginning." She smiled and rubbed herself against him. "With me. And since I'm going to transition and become a new person as well, we will have a new beginning together. Isn't that great?"

Marcel suspected that Sofia was still loopy from the residual effect of the venom. Otherwise, she wouldn't be so optimistic and cheerful.

Kian wouldn't be happy about them starting the process so soon. They were supposed to wait until after Sofia's death had been faked, but Marcel just couldn't tell her that last night. Her eagerness to start the process had infected him, and he'd thrown caution to the wind.

When her tummy rumbled, he asked, "Are you hungry? We can get breakfast at the lodge."

"I don't want to share you with anyone yet, and I don't want to dip my feet back into reality and face the day. Let's stay here and make love like there is no world outside of this bunker, and we are not planning to take down Igor."

Yep, Sofia was definitely loopy, but her happiness was contagious, and Marcel didn't mind following her advice and forgetting that anything existed outside of the two of them. They could stay in bed and make love until they passed out from exhaustion, and when they woke up, they could do it again.

Kian

"Your phone is ringing," Syssi said sleepily.

"I heard it." Kian tightened his arms around her. "I'm choosing to ignore it." He kissed the tip of her nose.

"What if it's an emergency?"

"It's always an emergency. I'm tired of all the emergencies I have to deal with."

"Just answer it, please."

He let out a breath and turned around to snatch the phone off the charger. It had stopped ringing, but seeing that the call had been from Eleanor, he decided to return it. She wouldn't have called if it wasn't important.

"What's up?"

"Did I wake you up?"

"No. I was already awake."

"I just wanted to give you an update on my talk with Sofia."

Alarm bells ringing in his head, Kian pushed up on the pillows. "Did she lie?"

"No, she believes that everything she told us is true, and she didn't hide any additional information except for the fact that her grandfather is Igor's second-in-command, but she's already told Marcel about that without any compulsion on my part."

This was indeed big news, and he was glad that Eleanor hadn't waited to call him.

"What does it mean for us?"

"Not much. I had a long talk with her while she was under my compulsion, so I know she was telling me the truth. Her relationship with Igor's second-in-command doesn't afford her any special status in the compound. She believes that it gives her only a slight advantage over other human Kra-ell offspring, allowing her to attend university for the past seven years and perhaps more leeway in choosing her bed partners. But that could be her take on it. The pureblooded Kra-ell don't believe in the concept of love, and having or showing emotions is considered a weakness. Her grandfather might care for her, but he doesn't show it. In any case, it makes me reassess our hypothesis about the tracker that was embedded in her. I don't think that he wanted his granddaughter to get caught just so he could follow the tracker to wherever she was taken. I suspect that they embed trackers in all the humans who are allowed to leave the compound. They want to keep tabs on them."

"That makes sense, but I still like the idea of driving the cat with the tracker around to see if we can catch something in the net."

"Poor cat," Syssi murmured. "She didn't sign up for getting Sofia's tracker."

"Neither did Sofia." Kian patted her arm. "The tracker is tiny, and Julian gave the cat an anesthetic."

"She didn't suffer," Eleanor said. "And she's getting more petting than ever. But back to the tracker. If it has a tail, catching it will be easier than traveling all the way to Karelia and capturing the Kra-ell guarding the entrance to their secret tunnel. And what's even more important, Toven won't have to go there either and drag Mia with him, which he will have to do because she enhances his powers, and he can't free the Kra-ell from Igor's compulsion without her help. Did you talk to him about it? He might refuse, and without him and Mia, we have no plan."

"Not yet." Kian turned the speaker on and put the phone on his lap. "I'll talk to him today, but the truth is that I don't want him to go there either. It's too dangerous. I'm waiting for Turner to come up with a plan before we make our next move, and I hope he can come up with something that doesn't involve Toven and Mia going to Karelia."

Eleanor snorted. "Good luck with that. Turner is smart, but he's not a miracle worker."

"Some say that he is, but we'll see. Did Marcel tell Sofia about her genetic potential?"

"He did, but he made a mess of it. The guy is not a smooth operator, and after Sofia told him about Valstar being so high up in Igor's organization, he started treating her like a suspect again, and she blew up. Given all the information she'd volunteered, it was uncalled for. I had to step in and calm things down. I took her on a long walk on the beach, explained that the clan is all about doing good things for humanity, about our efforts to free trafficking victims and rehabilitate them, and ended with explaining in more detail about immortals and Dormants. When I was done, she was all smiles and ready to get induced. I hope that Marcel didn't ruin all my good work with some other brain fart."

"Being suspicious is not a brain fart, but I know what you mean. Marcel is an engineer. Enough said."

She chuckled. "They are a special breed, aren't they? But as someone who is mated to the ultimate drama king, I sometimes long for the calm logic of the engineer types."

"Do I sense discontent?"

"Not at all. I love Emmett, and I'm very happy to have a man with flair. It's funny how atypical he is for a Kra-ell. Between the two of us, I'm more Kra-ell than he is."

"Hey, maybe you are Kra-ell," Syssi said. "You certainly have the look. You're tall, skinny, and your hair and eyes are dark. You are also a compeller."

Kian's brows took a deep dive. It hadn't occurred to him, but Syssi was onto something.

"Frankly, I don't care either way," Eleanor said. "But if I am descended from the Kra-ell, then the Kra-ell and the immortals must be really closely related for me to transition so quickly. I wasn't bonded to my inducer. I didn't even have any feelings for him. He was just a hookup." She chuckled. "Given my compulsion ability, I actually suspect that I came from Toven's line. Maybe my grandmother was a naughty girl."

"I hope that your theory is the correct one," Syssi said quietly. "The Kra-ell are only long-lived, not immortal."

Eleanor let out a breath. "Even if I'm their descendant, a thousand years is a very long time, and my mate will enjoy a similar lifespan. Besides, in a thousand years, we will most likely figure out how to turn everyone immortal."

Darlene

When Darlene woke up and opened her eyes, the sight that greeted her was not pleasant. The bedroom was in shambles. Eric was passed out on the bed and smelled as if he had showered in booze, yet she felt amazing.

As she remembered him tearing the bed apart, she sat up and gave the room a second look around. The bed frame was gone, but no evidence of splintered wood remained, and the mattress was somehow still supported and not on the floor. The pictures on the walls were hanging crookedly to some degree, the two bedside lamps were gone, and the dresser had been pushed aside, probably to vacuum the debris from under it.

It seemed that Eric had gotten much stronger during the days following his transition. When he was human, he couldn't have gotten free of the chains by demolishing the bed frame.

Was Max still around?

She lifted her hand to the spot on her neck where he'd bitten her and patted the skin. It wasn't tender, and there was no crusted blood or bumps where Max's fangs had penetrated her skin.

He'd bitten her through the nightgown, but Eric must have loosened the tie that had secured the high collar because the strings were hanging loose on both sides of the opening. Other than that, her nightgown was none the worse for wear, which was a miracle given what the bedroom looked like.

How had she survived it intact?

Darlene remembered the bed frame groaning as Eric had pulled on the chains, but then she'd found herself under him while the posts had toppled down.

"Oh, my God, Eric!" She tried to move him to his side so she could examine his back.

Those posts were massive. How was he sleeping on his back with fractured ribs?

"What?" he murmured sleepily.

"Wake up. You need Bridget to examine you."

"Why?" Eric cracked one eye open and then shielded it with his hand to protect it from the light streaming through the window.

"To check your back. The bedposts fell on you."

"I'm fine." He reached for her, pulling her against his body.

"Ugh, let go. You stink of booze."

"I do?" He cupped his hand over his mouth and exhaled. "Oh, I do. My bad. Max and I finished two bottles of whiskey last night." He lifted both hands with two fingers each. "Another perk of being immortal is incredible tolerance for alcohol. I can outdrink any human now."

Great. They had been celebrating while she'd been out of it.

"What happened?" She pulled away from him and fanned in front of her face to stave off the stench.

"Max was right. When he bit you, I lost my shit and wanted to attack him. Fortunately for him, my priority was to shield you from the toppling posts, so I pulled you under me, and he managed to escape." Eric lifted his arm and flexed. "I'm as strong as a gorilla now. I didn't expect that to happen so soon after my transition."

"Did Max see me naked?"

"He didn't see anything. I made sure of that. He returned to the bedroom to release me from the chains, but I was covering you."

She wasn't sure how that had worked while there had been wooden poles on top of him and he was naked, but it was healthier for both of them to pretend that Max hadn't seen anything.

"What about your back?"

"I'm immortal now, baby. Sticks and stones can't hurt me." He scratched at his side. "I'd better get up and wash the stink off. I want to kiss you and do other things to you."

Her lips curved in a smile, but the smile wilted as she imagined Eric and Max sitting in the living room and getting drunk while talking about her.

"What did you and Max talk about while you were imbibing all that whiskey?"

"This and that. Do you know that Dalhu made nude portraits of Amanda and that she had them hanging in their house? She only took them down after Evie was born."

"I didn't know that, but I wonder how you got to discuss Amanda's nudes. Were you talking about my nightgown?"

Eric's sheepish smile confirmed her suspicion. "Max said that immortals are not as prudish as humans and that nudity is not a big deal for them."

"I don't care." She tucked the hem under her knees. "Anyway, this thing's going into the trash because I'm never repeating this exercise. If I don't transition from Max's bite, we are waiting for you to grow fangs and venom."

The smile slid off his face. "I don't think I could go through that again either, but I need to know. Did you enjoy his bite?"

How to answer that? She enjoyed the effects of the venom. It had been an incredible trip, and the sense of physical well-being she felt now could most likely be attributed to the venom as well, but she hadn't enjoyed the bite itself.

"It hurt, but that wasn't the biggest issue. I wouldn't have minded if it were you. It felt wrong getting bitten by Max." She searched for better words, but every analogy she could think of didn't fit.

Max was a friend, and he was an attractive male, but she didn't want him.

"It just felt wrong. But then the venom hit me, and the effect was mind-blowing." She brushed a strand of hair off his forehead. "I have no doubt that it's going to be even better when it's you."

His smile was brilliant. "I'm positive that it will be the best you've ever had."

"Since Max's bite was the only other one, and it wasn't great, it's not such a big challenge to do better."

"Oh, yeah?"

"Yeah." Darlene slapped Eric's arm playfully. "Just go brush your teeth already, so you can come back to bed." She pulled the nightgown over her head and handed it to him. "Put this in the trash bin, will you?"

His eyes blazed with an inner light. "Yes, ma'am."

Sofia

Sofia yawned and stretched her arms over her head. "I think we have no choice. We need to get out of bed and get something to eat. I'm starving."

Smiling, Marcel caressed her bare back. "I can make a dash to the kitchen, raid the refrigerator, and bring the loot back here."

"Go for it." She cupped his cheek and pressed a kiss to his lips. "I'll take a shower while you're hunting for food to bring back to the cave."

Grunting like a gorilla, he punched his chest. "Me, Tarzan. You, Jane. I bring food. But first, shower." He kissed the tip of her nose and then jumped out of bed and sprinted for the bathroom.

She loved seeing Marcel smiling and joking around. He'd been so scared of her reaction to his confession, and the truth was that it had been a shocking revelation, but from a human's perspective of time, the crime had happened so long ago that the statute of limitations should have kicked in. Not that he could stand trial in a human court, but his clan laws were probably similar. Did premeditated murder even have a statute of limitations?

Had it been premeditated, though?

Yeah, it had been.

Marcel had followed Cordelia's husband home, not to have a chat with him or even to give him a warning. He'd planned to kill the man.

So why couldn't she bring herself to be repulsed by it or even judge Marcel harshly for it?

Perhaps her savage one-quarter Kra-ell was overriding the three-quarters human? Or maybe it was the influence of growing up with purebloods and hybrids and absorbing their attitudes? Or perhaps she was just blinded by love the way Marcel had been with that bitch.

Cordelia deserved to forever walk in the valley of the shamed.

Or did she?

Would the Mother of All Life fault her for plotting to get rid of her husband if he'd wronged her?

Probably not.

"Ugh, religion is so frustrating."

"Did you say something?" Marcel called from the bathroom.

"I was talking to myself."

With a sigh, Sofia tossed the blanket aside and slid out of bed. She needed to use the bathroom, but despite making love to Marcel in every possible position, she wasn't comfortable peeing in front of him yet.

Instead, she grabbed a fresh outfit and went to the bathroom in the next room over.

When she returned to the bedroom, she found Marcel sitting on the bed with his phone pressed against his ear.

"Perhaps I should start the coffee." She turned to go back out.

Marcel looked up. "It's Turner. He wants to speak with you."

"Now? Can't he wait for me to have some coffee?"

It surprised her that the strategist worked during the weekend. Not many humans were willing to give up their free days. Should she be glad or worried that he did?

Marcel had reassured her that his people were just collecting information and that they were not planning to attack the compound, but maybe they were going to help Jade and the others free themselves. Did that require working on a Sunday?

They must deem the matter urgent for some reason.

Perhaps Jade had contacted them with new information?

"Here." Marcel handed her the phone. "I'll make you coffee." He activated the speaker. "Sofia is here, Turner."

"Thank you," Turner said. "How are you this afternoon?"

Was it afternoon already? She hadn't checked the time.

"I'm very well, thank you. What can I help you with?"

"I need to know the wording Igor used to phrase his monthly compulsion sessions with you."

Sitting on the bed, she let out a breath. "It was more or less the same thing every month with only a few slight variations. I was to keep the existence of the Kra-ell a secret. I was to keep the location of the compound a secret. I was to do everything in my power to protect the compound and its inhabitants, and I was never to do anything that could endanger the compound and its inhabitants. I was to report to the security office any suspicious activity that might endanger the compound, and I was to follow the commands of my superiors in order of their hierarchy. Igor's command overruled commands given by Valstar, Valstar's commands overruled that of everyone under him, and so on. When I was away, I had to call once a week to report, and I had to come back in person once a month."

"Do you know if others received the same commands?"

"Igor held weekly assemblies which everyone in the compound had to attend, and he repeated the same instructions, except for the two last ones that were specific to me and the other students who got to leave the compound. Other humans got private one-on-one sessions with Igor only once in a while, if at all, and I don't know how often the hybrids and the purebloods got private sessions with him, but I think it was quite often."

Turner sighed. "That's what I thought. Igor is very thorough."

He sounded as if he admired the guy, which annoyed her, but she could understand how the strategist might be appreciative of another's talent.

"Does it make a difference?" She was afraid to hear Turner's answer.

"Regrettably, yes. Even if it was possible to deliver a message to your father, neither he nor your aunts could deliver it to Jade without reporting it to someone. The term Igor used was 'anything suspicious,' and delivering a secret message to Jade would definitely fall under that description."

Sofia's heart fell.

Turner was right. How come it hadn't occurred to her? She should have realized that her father and aunts would be bound by the compulsion. Now that she was free, it was so easy to forget the effect Igor's compulsion had on her life. She still had to contend with Tom's, but it didn't feel as oppressive and heavy-handed as Igor's.

"Here is your coffee." Marcel handed her a cup and sat down next to her on the bed.

"Thank you." She took a small sip. "So I guess the idea of helping a rebellion led by Jade is out."

"Don't worry. I will come up with a way to free your people. I have a couple more questions. Are Jade and Igor exclusive with one another?"

"Igor is not for sure, but I don't know about Jade. Maybe she's just more discreet than him. None of the pure-bloods are exclusive. It goes against the Mother's teachings and their tradition."

"That's what I thought, but I wanted to make sure. My last question is, how do the pureblood and hybrid females wear their hair?"

"Either loose, braided, or in a ponytail. Why?"

"If we find a way to supply a few main players with compulsion-blocking earpieces, they will need to hide them under their hair."

Hope surged in Sofia's chest once more. "The hybrid and pureblooded males wear their hair long too. Well, most do. I've seen two hybrids with modern haircuts. Maybe they were sent on an undercover mission."

"Excellent. That will make it easy for them to hide the earpieces."

"How are you going to get the devices to them? And wouldn't Igor's compulsion force them to report that?"

Turner chuckled. "Patience, Sofia. I'm still working on it."

Order Dark Gambit Reliance today!

JOIN THE VIP CLUB

To find out what's included in your free membership, flip to the last page.

The Children of the Gods Series

Reading Order

THE CHILDREN OF THE GODS ORIGINS

1: Goddess's Choice

When gods and immortals still ruled the ancient world, one young goddess risked everything for love.

2: Goddess's Hope

Hungry for power and infatuated with the beautiful Areana, Navuh plots his father's demise. After all, by getting rid of the insane god he would be doing the world a favor. Except, when gods and immortals conspire against each other, humanity pays the price.

But things are not what they seem, and prophecies should not to be trusted...

THE CHILDREN OF THE GODS

Dark Stranger

1: Dark Stranger The Dream

2: Dark Stranger Revealed

3: Dark Stranger Immortal

Dark Enemy

4: Dark Enemy Taken

5: Dark Enemy Captive

6: Dark Enemy Redeemed

Kri & Michael's Story

6.5: My Dark Amazon

Dark Warrior

7: Dark Warrior Mine

8: Dark Warrior's Promise

9: Dark Warrior's Destiny

10: Dark Warrior's Legacy

Dark Guardian

11: Dark Guardian Found

12: Dark Guardian Craved

13: Dark Guardian's Mate

Dark Angel

14: Dark Angel's Obsession

15: Dark Angel's Seduction

16: Dark Angel's Surrender

Dark Operative

17: Dark Operative: A Shadow of Death

18: Dark Operative: A Glimmer of Hope

19: Dark Operative: The Dawn of Love

Dark Survivor

20: Dark Survivor Awakened

21: Dark Survivor Echoes of Love

22: Dark Survivor Reunited

Dark Widow

23: Dark Widow's Secret

24: Dark Widow's Curse

25: Dark Widow's Blessing

Dark Dream

26: Dark Dream's Temptation

27: Dark Dream's Unraveling

28: Dark Dream's Trap

Dark Prince

29: Dark Prince's Enigma

30: Dark Prince's Dilemma

31: Dark Prince's Agenda

Dark Queen

32: Dark Queen's Quest

33: Dark Queen's Knight

34: Dark Queen's Army

Dark Spy

35: Dark Spy Conscripted

36: Dark Spy's Mission

37: Dark Spy's Resolution

Dark Overlord

38: Dark Overlord New Horizon

39: Dark Overlord's Wife

Dark God

Dark Whispers

Dark Gambit

Dark Alliance

A daring operation half a world away devolves into a full-scale crisis that escalates rapidly, requiring the clan's full might and technological wizardry to manage and survive.

Hardened by duty and tragedy, Jade is driven by a burning desire for revenge. When Phinas saves her second-in-command, Jade's gratitude quickly becomes something more.

When a dangerous foe turns the tables on the clan, complicating the Kra-ell rescue operation in unforeseeable ways, Kian and his crew bet all on a brilliant misdirection.

On board the Aurora, Phinas and Jade brace for battle while enjoying a few stolen moments of passion.

Drawn to the woman he sees behind the aloof leader, Phinas realizes that what has started as a calculated political move has evolved into a deepening sense of companionship.

Jade finds reprieve in Phinas's arms, but duty and tradition make it difficult for her to accept that what she feels for him is more than just gratitude and desire.

After all, the Kra-ell don't believe in love.

70: Dark Alliance Perfect Storm

After two decades in captivity, Jade is finally free, her quest for revenge within grasp, but danger still looms large. A storm is brewing on the horizon, gathering momentum and threatening to obliterate Jade's tenuous hold on hope for a better future.

Dark Healing

71: Dark Healing Blind Justice

The sanctuary is Vanessa's life project. The monumental task of rehabilitating the traumatized victims of trafficking doesn't leave much time for personal life, let alone dating or finding her one and only.

When Kian asks her to help the Kra-ell, she's torn between her duty to the sanctuary and a group of emotionally wounded aliens who no other psychologist can treat.

She's the only immortal with the necessary training to get it done.

The Kra-ell culture and the purebloods' nearly androgynous

alien looks shouldn't appeal to her, and yet, she finds one of them disturbingly attractive.

Is it the dangerous vibe he emits?

Does it speak to her on a subconscious level?

Or is it her need to put the broken pieces of him back together?

And why is he interested in her?

She cannot offer him a fight for dominance like a Kra-ell female would, but some strange and unfamiliar part of her wishes she could.

72: Dark Healing Blind Trust

Riddled with guilt over the crimes he was forced to commit, Mo-red is ready to stand trial and accept the death sentence he believes he deserves, but when the clan's alluring psychologist offers a new perspective on his past and hope for a better future, he resolves to fight for his life.

73: Dark healing Blind Curve

Kian is still reeling from the shocking revelations about the twins when a new threat manifests, eclipsing everything he's had to deal with up until now. In light of the new developments, Igor, the other Kra-ell prisoners, and the pending trial are no longer at the forefront of his mind, but the opposite is true for Vanessa. As her relationship with Mo-red solidifies, she is determined to save the male she loves, even if it means breaking him free and living on the run.

Dark Encounters

74: Dark Encounters of the Close Kind

Convinced that her family is hiding a terrible secret from her, Gabi decides to pay them a surprise visit.

Something is very fishy about the stories her brothers have been telling her lately. Her niece, a nineteen-year-old prodigy with a Ph.D. in bioinformatics, has gotten engaged to a much older guy she met while working on some top-secret project, and if Gabi's older, overprotective brother's approval of the engagement wasn't suspicious enough, he also uprooted his family and moved to be closer to the couple.

What Gabi discovers when she gets to L.A. is wilder than anything she could have imagined. Her entire family possesses godly genes, her brothers and her niece have already turned immortal, and she could transition as soon as she finds an immortal male to induce her. Finding a suitable candidate in a village full of handsome immortals shouldn't be a problem, but Gabi's thoughts keep wandering to the gorgeous guy she met on her flight over.

Could Uriel be a lost descendant of the gods?

He certainly looks like them, but that doesn't mean that he's a good guy or that he's even immortal. He could be a descendant of a different god—a member of an enemy faction of immortals who seek to eradicate her family's adoptive clan, or what is more likely, he's just an extraordinarily good-looking human.

75: Dark Encounters of the Unexpected Kind

Who is Uriel?

Is he a lost descendant of the gods or just a gorgeous and charming human who has rocked Gabi's world?

76: Dark Encounters of the Fated Kind

As Aru and his team embark on a perilous mission, their past and present converge in a meeting that holds the key to their fate.

As Annani and Syssi set out to unravel the mysteries of Syssi's visions about the gods' home world, the long-awaited wedding cruise sets sail with Aru, Gabi, and Aru's teammates on board.

While the gods find themselves surrounded by immortal clan ladies eager for their affections, they soon discover that destiny has a different plan for them.

Dark Voyage

77: Dark Voyage Matters of the Heart

As Annani and Syssi set out to unravel the mysteries of Syssi's visions about the gods' home world, the long-awaited wedding cruise sets sail with Aru, Gabi, and Aru's teammates on board.

While the gods find themselves surrounded by immortal clan ladies eager for their affections, they soon discover that destiny has a different plan for them.

The Children of the Gods Series Sets

Books 1-3: Dark Stranger trilogy—Includes a bonus short story: **The Fates take a Vacation**

Books 4-6: Dark Enemy Trilogy —Includes a bonus short story—**The Fates' Post-Wedding Celebration**

Books 7-10: Dark Warrior Tetralogy

Books 11-13: Dark Guardian Trilogy

Books 14-16: Dark Angel Trilogy

Books 17-19: Dark Operative Trilogy

Books 20-22: Dark Survivor Trilogy

Books 23-25: Dark Widow Trilogy

Books 26-28: Dark Dream Trilogy

Books 29-31: Dark Prince Trilogy

Books 32-34: Dark Queen Trilogy

Books 35-37: Dark Spy Trilogy

Books 38-40: Dark Overlord Trilogy

Books 41-43: Dark Choices Trilogy

Books 44-46: Dark Secrets Trilogy

Books 47-49: Dark Haven Trilogy

Books 50-52: Dark Power Trilogy

Books 53-55: Dark Memories Trilogy

Books 56-58: Dark Hunter Trilogy

Books 59-61: Dark God Trilogy

Books 62-64: Dark Whispers Trilogy

Books 65-67: Dark Gambit Trilogy

Books 68-70: Dark Alliance Trilogy

Books 71-73: Dark healing Trilogy

MEGA SETS

INCLUDE CHARACTER LISTS

The Children of the Gods: Books 1-6

The Children of the Gods: Books 6.5-10

TRY THE SERIES ON

AUDIBLE

PERFECT MATCH SERIES

Vampire's Consort

When Gabriel's company is ready to start beta testing, he invites his old crush to inspect its medical safety protocol.

Curious about the revolutionary technology of the *Perfect Match Virtual Fantasy-Fulfillment studios*, Brenna agrees.

Neither expects to end up partnering for its first fully immersive test run.

King's Chosen

When Lisa's nutty friends get her a gift certificate to *Perfect Match Virtual Fantasy Studios*, she has no intentions of using it. But since the only way to get a refund is if no partner can be found for her, she makes sure to request a fantasy so girly and over the top that no sane guy will pick it up.

Except, someone does.

> **Warning:** This fantasy contains a hot, domineering crown prince, sweet insta-love, steamy love scenes painted with light shades of gray, a wedding, and a HEA in both the virtual and real worlds.
>
> Intended for mature audience.

Captain's Conquest

Working as a Starbucks barista, Alicia fends off flirting all day long, but none of the guys are as charming and sexy as Gregg. His frequent visits are the highlight of her day, but since he's never asked her out, she assumes he's taken. Besides, between a day job and a budding music career, she has no time to start a new relationship.

That is until Gregg makes her an offer she can't refuse—a gift certificate to the virtual fantasy fulfillment service everyone is talking about. As a huge Star Trek fan, Alicia has a perfect match in mind—the captain of the Starship Enterprise.

The Thief Who Loved Me

When Marian splurges on a Perfect Match Virtual adventure as a world infamous jewel thief, she expects high-wire fun with a hot partner who she will never have to see again in real life.

A virtual encounter seems like the perfect answer to Marcus's string of dating disasters. No strings attached, no drama, and definitely no love. As a die-hard James Bond fan, he chooses as his avatar a dashing MI6 operative, and to complement his adventure, a dangerously seductive partner.

Neither expects to find their forever Perfect Match.

My Merman Prince

The beautiful architect working late on the twelfth floor of my building thinks that I'm just the maintenance guy. She's also under the impression that I'm not interested.

Nothing could be further from the truth.

I want her like I've never wanted a woman before, but I don't play where I work.

I don't need the complications.

When she tells me about living out her mermaid fantasy with a stranger in a Perfect Match virtual adventure, I decide to do everything possible to ensure that the stranger is me.

The Dragon King

To save his beloved kingdom from a devastating war, the Crown Prince of Trieste makes a deal with a witch that costs him half of his humanity and dooms him to an eternity of loneliness.

Now king, he's a fearsome cobalt-winged dragon by day and a short-tempered monarch by night. Not many are brave enough to serve in the palace of the brooding and volatile ruler, but Charlotte ignores the rumors and accepts a scribe position in court.

As the young scribe reawakens Bruce's frozen heart, all that stands in the way of their happiness is the witch's bargain. Outsmarting the evil hag will take cunning and courage, and Charlotte is just the right woman for the job.

My Werewolf Romeo

The father of my star student is a big-shot screenwriter and the patron of the drama department who thinks he can dictate what production I should put on. The principal makes it very clear that I need to cooperate with the opinionated asshat or walk away from my dream job at the exclusive private high school.

It doesn't help matters that the guy is single, hot, charming, creative, and seems to like me despite my thinly-veiled hostility.

When he invites me to a custom-tailored Perfect Match virtual adventure to prove that his screenplay is perfect for my production, I accept, intending to have fun while proving that messing with the classics is a foolish idea.

I don't expect to be wowed by his werewolf adaptation of Red Riding Hood mesh-up with Romeo and Juliet, and I certainly don't expect to fall in love with the virtual fantasy's leading man.

The Channeler's Companion

A treat for fans of *The Wheel of Time*.

When Erika hires Rand to assist in her pediatric clinic, she does so despite his good looks and irresistible charm, not because of them.

He's empathic, adores children, and has the patience of a saint.

He's also all she can think about, but he's off limits.

What's a doctor to do to scratch that irresistible itch without risking workplace complications?

A shared adventure in the Perfect Match Virtual Studios seems like the solution, but instead of letting the algorithm choose a partner for her, Erika can try to influence it to select the one she wants. Awarding Rand a gift certificate to the service will get him into their database, but unless Erika can tip the odds in her favor, getting paired with him is a long shot.

Hopefully, a virtual adventure based on her and Rand's favorite series will do the trick.

Note

Dear reader,

I hope my stories have added a little joy to your day. If you have a moment to add some to mine, you can help spread the word about the Children Of The Gods series by telling your friends and penning a review. Your recommendations are the most powerful way to inspire new readers to explore the series.

Thank you,

Isabell

FOR EXCLUSIVE PEEKS AT UPCOMING RELEASES & A FREE COMPANION BOOK

JOIN MY *VIP CLUB* AND GAIN ACCESS TO THE VIP PORTAL AT ITLUCAS.COM

TO JOIN, GO TO:

http://eepurl.com/blMTpD

INCLUDED IN YOUR FREE MEMBERSHIP:

YOUR VIP PORTAL

- **READ PREVIEW CHAPTERS OF UPCOMING RELEASES.**
- **LISTEN TO GODDESS'S CHOICE NARRATION BY CHARLES LAWRENCE**
- **EXCLUSIVE CONTENT OFFERED ONLY TO MY VIPS.**

FREE I.T. LUCAS COMPANION INCLUDES:

- **GODDESS'S CHOICE PART 1**
- **PERFECT MATCH: VAMPIRE'S CONSORT** (A STANDALONE NOVELLA)
- **INTERVIEW Q & A**
- **CHARACTER CHARTS**

IF YOU'RE ALREADY A SUBSCRIBER, AND YOU ARE NOT GETTING MY EMAILS, YOUR PROVIDER IS

SENDING THEM TO YOUR JUNK FOLDER, AND YOU ARE MISSING OUT ON **IMPORTANT UPDATES, SIDE CHARACTERS' PORTRAITS, ADDITIONAL CONTENT, AND OTHER GOODIES.** TO FIX THAT, ADD isabell@itlucas.com TO YOUR EMAIL CONTACTS OR YOUR EMAIL VIP LIST.

Check out the specials at https://www.itlucas.com/specials

Made in the USA
Coppell, TX
17 May 2025

49491000R00236